www.totallyr...

D0266823

CHRIS RYAN
SAS HERO

- Joined the **SAS** in **1984**, serving in military hot zones across the world.

- Expert in overt and covert operations in war zones, including Northern Ireland, Africa, the Middle East and other classified territories.

- Commander of the Sniper squad within the anti-terrorist team.

- Part of an 8-man patrol on the Bravo Two Zero Gulf War mission in Iraq.

- The mission was compromised. 3 fellow soldiers died, and 4 more were captured as POWs. Ryan was the only person to defy the enemy, evading capture and escaping to Syria on foot over a distance of 300 kilometres.

- His ordeal made history as the longest escape and evasion by an SAS trooper, for which he was awarded the Military Medal.

- His books are dedicated to the men and women who risk their lives fighting for the armed forces.

CHRIS RYAN

DEADFALL

RED FOX

DEADFALL

DEADFALL
A RED FOX BOOK 978 1 849 41010 6

First published in Great Britain by Red Fox,
an imprint of Random House Children's Publishers UK
A Random House Group Company

This edition published 2014

1 3 5 7 9 10 8 6 4 2

The Random House Group Limited supports the Forest Stewardship Council® (FSC®), the
leading international forest-certification organisation. Our books carrying the FSC label are
printed on FSC®-certified paper. FSC is the only forest-certification scheme supported by
the leading environmental organisations, including Greenpeace. Our paper procurement
policy can be found at www.randomhouse.co.uk/environment

MIX
Paper from
responsible sources
FSC® C016897

Set in Adobe Garamond

Red Fox Books are published by Random House Children's Publishers UK,
61–63 Uxbridge Road, London W5 5SA

www.randomhousechildrens.co.uk
www.totallyrandombooks.co.uk
www.randomhouse.co.uk

Addresses for companies within The Random House Group Limited
can be found at: www.randomhouse.co.uk/offices.htm

THE RANDOM HOUSE GROUP Limited Reg. No. 954009

A CIP catalogue record for this book is available from the British Library.

Printed and bound by CPI Group (UK) Ltd, Croydon, CR0 4YY

CONTENTS

AGENT 21

Real name: Zak Darke

Known pseudonyms: Harry Gold, Jason Cole

Age: 15

Date of birth: March 27

Parents: Al and Janet Darke [DECEASED]

Operational skills: Weapons handling, navigation, excellent facility with languages, excellent computer and technical skills. Trained in codebreaking.

Previous operations:

(1) Inserted under cover into the compound of Mexican drug magnate Cesar Martinez Toledo. Befriended target's son Cruz. Successfully supplied evidence of target's illegal activities. Successfully guided commando team in to compound. Target eliminated.

(2) Inserted into Angola to place explosive device on suspected terrorist ship, the *MV Mercantile*. Vessel destroyed, Agent 21 extracted.

(3) To extract skilled person from secure hospital site and work alongside

same; also inserted undercover alongside suspect. Mission to eliminate bomb threats to both civilians and major targets in the UK. Successful outcome.

AGENT 17

Real name: classified

Known pseudonyms: 'Gabriella', 'Gabs'

Age: 27

Operational skills: Advanced combat and self-defence, surveillance, tracking.

Currently charged with ongoing training of Agent 21 on remote Scottish island of St Peter's Crag.

AGENT 16

Real name: classified

Known pseudonyms: 'Raphael', 'Raf'

Age: 30

Operational skills: Advanced combat and self-defence, sub-aqua, land-vehicle control.

Currently charged with ongoing training

of Agent 21 on remote Scottish island of
St Peter's Crag.

'MICHAEL'

Real name: classified

Known pseudonyms: 'Mr Bartholomew'

Age: classified

Recruited Agent 21 after death of
his parents. Currently his handler.
Has links with MI5, but represents a
classified government agency.

CRUZ MARTINEZ (Presumed Dead)

Age: 17

Significant information: Succeeded Cesar
Martinez as head of largest Mexican drug
cartel. Thought to blame Agent 21 for
death of father. Highly intelligent.
Profile remained low since coming to
power. Thought to have drowned during
sinking of *MV Mercantile*.

MALCOLM MANN

Age: 14

Significant information: Borderline autistic computer hacker. Known to have cracked the security of a number of intelligence agencies. Has provided help to Agent 21 in the past. Currently living off the grid in Johannesburg, South Africa.

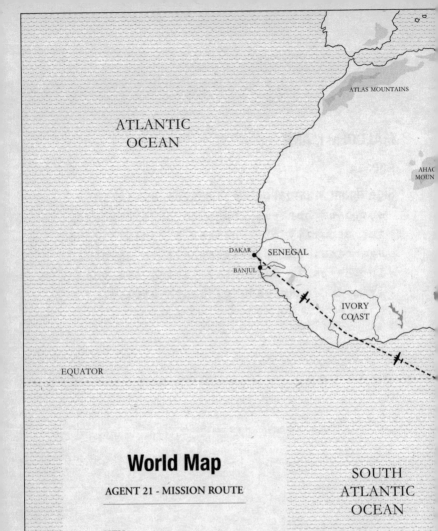

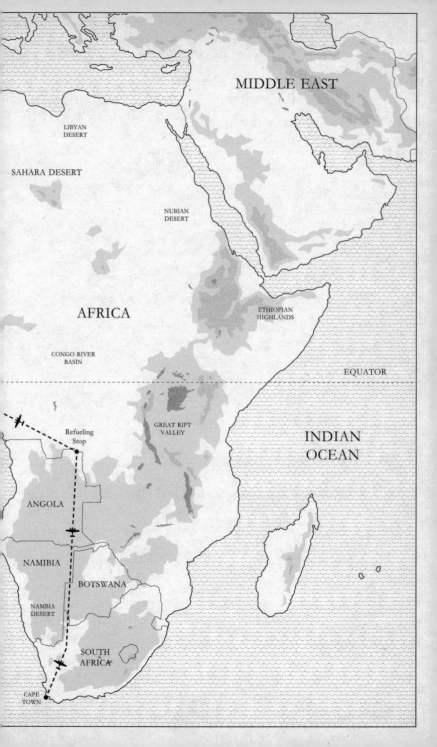

PART ONE

1

FUN WORLD

There had been a thin layer of frost on the ice-cold bottle of Coke. Beads of condensation ran down the glass.

Just like the bead of sweat that ran down the side of Zak's face.

This should be an easy op. Why, then, did he feel so on edge?

He hadn't touched his drink. He was too busy looking through the window of the café.

Zak could only half see his reflection, but it still surprised him. In another time and place, he might have thought he looked stupid. Not now. This new appearance had a purpose. His hair had been dyed blond and cut scruffily short. He had put in a set of

3

blue contact lenses. Fake tan had darkened his skin. With his bright red baseball cap on the table in front of him, he looked like a surfer dude. Not a teenage boy who spent all his time living on a windswept island off the coast of Scotland.

Amazing how easy it was to change the way you look.

He glanced across the table at Gabs. His Guardian Angel always managed to appear a little bit glamorous, even when she was in disguise. Today you could only see strands of her blonde hair tumbling down below the edge of a peaked beret. She wore a T-shirt with a sparkling Rolling Stones logo. In front of her was a half-drunk cappuccino.

'You should take a sip of your Coke, sweetie,' she murmured. 'If anyone's watching . . .'

'Nobody's watching.'

'*Zak!*'

Gabs's voice was suddenly severe. Zak flushed. He knew better than that. If Zak – or Raf, or Gabs, or anyone he'd met in the time his ordinary life had become extraordinary, and he'd gone from being Zak Darke to Agent 21 – was conducting surveillance on someone in this café, would *they* notice *him*?

Not a chance.

And it worked both ways.

A single sweep of the café told him that any one

of a number of people could have eyes-on. The waiter wiping down the coffee machine behind the bar. The tired mum with two kids eating ice cream at the next table. The waitress who had served them . . .

He gave Gabs an apologetic nod and took a pull on his Coke.

Then he stared out of the window again.

They were staking out a toy shop called Fun World. Four storeys high, and wide enough for six separate window displays. Each window was painted with a large picture of a clown's face. They were supposed to look happy, but they just freaked Zak out – he almost felt as if they were staring straight at him, and he had to suppress a shudder.

Once, when he was much younger, Zak's mum and dad had taken him to the huge London toy shop, Hamleys, to see Father Christmas. Fun World was similar in size, but nowhere near as busy.

Bottom line: this place gave him the creeps. It didn't look much fun at all.

Which kind of figured.

Because it wasn't like Agent 21 and his Guardian Angels had been sent to South Africa to go shopping for toys.

'You think he's in there?' Zak asked.

'Cruz?'

Zak nodded. Of *course* Cruz. Cruz Martinez, his former friend turned Mexican drug lord. Cruz Martinez, whose father had ordered the deaths of Zak's own parents, and had taken a round from Gabs's gun for his trouble. Cruz Martinez, who he'd last seen falling from a sinking ship into a stormy sea. Who everyone had insisted was dead, even though Zak knew in his heart he was still alive. Whose very name caused Zak's flesh to grow cold.

Whom intelligence operators had spotted three times in the past month visiting this very toy shop.

And nobody thought he was there to buy teddy bears.

'Yeah,' said Zak. 'Cruz.'

'I doubt it,' Gabs said. 'Saturday morning and everything. I don't think he'd rock up when it's busy.'

'It's not *that* busy,' Zak observed.

Gabs shrugged. 'Not a lot of money in this part of the world for buying toys.' She looked through the window of the café. 'There's Raf,' she breathed.

She was right. Raf had suddenly appeared. He was standing outside the main door of Fun World, and had removed his lightweight linen jacket and slung it over his shoulder. That was the signal. It meant he'd staked out the surrounding area and hadn't seen anything suspicious.

The op was a go.

Gabs drained her coffee cup and motioned at Zak to do the same. 'Remember,' she said to him. 'This is surveillance, nothing more. Understood?'

'This is surveillance, nothing more.'

Zak's handler Michael had used those exact words during their briefing session just two days ago on the bleak island of St Peter's Crag that was now his home.

'You're the only one who's been inside the Martinez inner circle. All you have to do is determine if anybody you saw during your time in Mexico is working at Fun World.'

'Surely they have security cameras in the store,' Zak had said. 'Can't you just hack in to those? I can look at the pictures, tell you if there's anyone I recognize. That would be safer, wouldn't it?'

'Much safer. Unfortunately, all the CCTV images are encrypted and uploaded to a server elsewhere. We've had our best people on it. They can't even locate the Fun World server, let alone decrypt the images. The only way we're going to do this is by putting you on the ground. Now listen, Zak: if you recognize anyone, do not – repeat do not *– try to apprehend them. Leave that to the experts. You just need to look like a kid in a toy shop. It's the only reason you're there.'*

*   *   *

'Understood,' Zak said.

Even though he'd just downed his Coke, his mouth felt dry. It was always like this in the moments before an op. A mixture of excitement and fear. You could get addicted to it. Zak already had.

He reached out to grab his phone. An important device. If he was in trouble, all he needed to do was type a code – 6482 – and Raf and Gabs would receive the distress call and be there in seconds.

As he picked up the phone, it vibrated. A single buzz. The screen lit up and Zak and Gabs exchanged a glance. Only four people knew this number: Zak himself, Gabs, Raf and Michael back in London.

He picked it up and swiped the screen.

His eyes widened. It was a picture message. The black and white image was grainy – it looked like a still from a CCTV image. But there was no doubt of what it showed: Zak, a bag slung over his shoulder, walking through customs at Johannesburg O.R. Tambo airport. That had been two hours ago.

Beneath the picture were the words: *Welcome to South Africa. Malcolm.*

Zak's eyes narrowed. He showed the screen to Gabs.

'*Malcolm?* How on earth did *he* know we were here?' she said.

The cogs in Zak's brain were already working

overtime. Malcolm was a highly intelligent computer hacker who had helped Zak during his last mission in London. A weird guy, but brilliant. The authorities wanted to keep him under lock and key, but Malcolm had escaped their clutches with Zak's help. Zak and his Guardian Angels were the only people who knew the hacker was living off the grid in South Africa, and they'd kept quiet about it. The guy deserved a break.

Zak was quite convinced that there wasn't a computer system Malcolm couldn't break into. That included airport security, and here was the proof.

'Stands to reason,' he muttered.

'What does?' Gabs said.

'If I know Malcolm, he'll have hacked into the airport's systems and will be running facial recognition software on anyone who comes through. A kind of early-warning system, in case anybody's coming to get him.'

Gabs thought about that for a moment. 'I don't like it,' she said.

'Me neither.'

'We should abort.' She raised one sleeve to her mouth, ready to speak into the hidden comms microphone wirelessly linked to Raf's hidden earpiece.

Like lightning, Zak grabbed Gabs's wrist and lowered it back to the table. He understood her panic. They were supposed to be off the radar and it looked like they'd been compromised. But Zak didn't see it that way. Malcolm was an odd-bod, no question. Not the kind of guy you'd want to be stuck in a lift with. But he was OK with Zak. This was just his strange way of saying hi.

'I trust Malcolm,' he said. 'It'll be fine. And anyway, maybe we could turn this to our advantage.'

'What do you mean?'

'If Malcolm can hack airport security, he can hack the CCTV in a toy shop. I know Michael said he'd put his best people on it, but I bet none of them are as good as Malcolm. We know where he lives.' Zak tapped his phone to bring up an address. 'Number sixty-seven Mandela Drive. It's nearby. Why don't we just ask him?' He looked over at Fun World. 'It's safer than walking straight into the lion's den.'

A moment's pause. Then Gabs shook her head. 'We have our orders,' she said. 'Let's get this over and done with.'

She left a bank note on the table – both Zak and Gabs had a pocketful of cash, just in case – then they both stood up and left the café.

The brutal African heat hit Zak like a hammer as he stepped out into the street. So did the noise of the busy road. Car engines, horns, people shouting at each other. They waited for a gap in the traffic, then

crossed. Neither of them spoke to or even acknow-
ledged Raf. And Zak didn't give Gabs any word of
farewell. He simply peeled off and entered Fun
World, leaving her to take up her position outside.

Time check: 11.13hrs.

The first thing Zak heard was the music being
piped round the shop. It was soft but frenetic – the
sort of thing you'd hear in a Tom and Jerry cartoon.
Music that begged you to have fun. He zoned it out
and concentrated on his surroundings.

He estimated that there were fifty customers on
the ground floor. Half of them adults, half children.
And there were ten shop assistants, each wearing a
smart red blazer. One of them was juggling with
four balls. Another was demonstrating a small,
remote-controlled helicopter.

One side of Fun World's ground floor was
devoted to teddy bears. Tiny ones, huge ones, and
every size in between. There was nothing menacing
about them, but like the clown pictures, they chilled
Zak. For a moment he stood statue-still, and
thought back to his briefing session . . .

'Watch this,' Michael had said, handing him an iPad.
Zak had tapped the screen and a video clip had started
playing. There was no sound, and the camerawork was
juddering. It appeared to have been taken in an area of

jungle – Zak could see thick, lush vegetation in the background. But the focus of the picture was a flight case on the ground, wide open, containing perhaps 200 cuddly elephants.

A hand appeared on screen. It held a scalpel, which it used to cut open one of these elephants, up to its breast, under the head and along its trunk. The hand folded the soft toy inside out, to reveal a plastic bag filled with a white powder.

'Cocaine,' Michael had said. 'Very high quality. Stashes of drugs like this have been popping up all over Asia, and a fair few in Europe too. It's not a bad hiding place, the guts of a soft toy . . .'

'Not a bad hiding place,' Zak muttered to himself. Then he shook his head. Surely none of the toys on display would be hiding any cocaine. He watched a little South African girl holding a Hello Kitty up to her mum, who shook her head and firmly put it back.

'May I help you, sir?'

Zak blinked. A shop assistant was standing in front of him. He was young, probably no older than sixteen, and had a name badge on his red jacket: 'Junior'. His skin was black, and his hair twisted into scalp-tight dreadlocks. Each of his cheeks had a thin, pale scar rising from the corner of his mouth to his ear.

Like a smile.

Zak didn't recognize the face. He relaxed slightly. 'Harry Potter wands,' he said. 'Do you sell them?'

'Of course, sir. Third floor. Shall I show you?'

'Don't worry, mate. I'll find them. Told my sister I'd get her a Hermione one.'

Zak cursed inwardly. *Keep a lie simple. The less information you give someone, the fewer holes they can pick in it* . . .

Junior looked puzzled. 'Who is Hermione?' he asked.

'She's . . . Never mind. Thanks for your help, mate.' Zak nodded at the shop assistant and headed towards the escalators at the centre of the shop. As the moving stairs carried him towards the first floor, he looked back down over the ground floor. The shop assistant with the weird scar was now nowhere to be seen.

He circled the first floor. There were fewer customers here, Zak realized, as he stepped past Xboxes and PlayStations and through a section of video-game cartridges. Every time he saw one of the shop assistants in their smart red blazers, he took a mental snapshot of their face. None of them rang any bells.

Second floor. Jigsaw puzzles and board games. He saw one kid drawing a house using an Etch A Sketch and felt a sudden pang as he remembered doing the same thing with his dad.

Keep your mind on the job, he told himself.

To his ten o'clock, in the far corner of the store, he saw a ceiling-mounted CCTV camera. A red light was flashing next to it. Was it Zak's imagination, or had he just noticed a tiny movement of the lens?

CCTV cameras move all the time, he told himself. Relax. You're nearly done. Another couple of hours, you'll be on a plane out of here.

Third floor. It was practically deserted. He walked past *Lord of the Rings* figurines, and models of characters he didn't even recognize.

'Harry Potter this way, sir!'

Zak flinched and turned suddenly. Junior had appeared from nowhere and was now standing right next to him. He grinned and nodded. 'This way, sir. This way.'

He pointed towards the far side of the toy store. There was a small replica of a castle, surrounded by wands and cloaks for sale. Zak shook his head. 'It's all right, mate. I'm—'

'This way, sir. You must come!' Junior lightly touched Zak's right arm and led him towards the miniature castle.

Zak's senses moved into high alert. Suddenly he wasn't in control. He yanked his elbow away from

Junior, but he was now aware of a second red jacket to his left-hand side.

Another young man. He had the same scars as Junior on his face.

Zak felt a chill in his guts and his eyes flicked around the toy store, looking for an exit, while his hands felt for the phone in his pockets. He needed to make the distress call.

Too late.

At exactly the same time, the boys grabbed an arm each. Their grip was strong enough to hurt as they dragged Zak towards Hogwarts, where he could just make out the sight of more red jackets lurking behind the castle entrance.

He gathered all his strength and suddenly released it in a frenzy of struggling. But the boys were powerful. They continued to drag him towards the far side of the store.

Through the entrance into the toy castle.

It was cramped in here. Maybe four metres by four. But three more boys in red jackets were waiting for him.

That made it five against one. Bad odds.

The walls were lined with shelves full of toys. Two of the boys were holding Harry Potter wands, the thin ends in their fists, the thick ends ready to strike.

Crack! One of the wands slammed against his

head. Then a second. Zak felt his knees wobble.

One of the guys punched him in the pit of the stomach. Air whooshed from his lungs and he bent double. A knee came up and cracked against the underside of his chin.

He was on the the floor, looking up. Five boys in red jackets were kicking him brutally, as hard as they could, in the stomach and the face. Blood spurted from his nose, hot and wet. He tried to cry out in pain, but without air in his lungs he couldn't.

Suddenly, one of the boys dropped to the floor. He was kneeling by Zak's side, and now his face was inches from Zak's. He too had scars on his cheeks. And he was holding something in his fist. It looked like a yellow golf ball, but was covered in black packaging. Zak saw the words *Golden Snitch* printed on the box.

The boy sneered and Zak saw yellow teeth like tombstones. He was bizarrely aware of the piped music still playing in the background.

The boy spoke. He had a whispering, rasping voice. 'Welcome to Fun World,' he said. Then with a grunt that suggested he was using all his strength, he whacked the snitch down on Zak's forehead.

A moment of blinding pain. A searing white light.

Then everything went dark.

2

THE WORM AND THE STONE

'You need to keep calm, Gabs,' Raf said. 'He's probably fine, and even if he isn't, we'll never find him if we're panicking. You know that.'

'*Don't* tell *me* to keep calm,' Gabs spat. 'Just *don't*, OK?'

And even Raf would have to admit that his voice had an edge of panic as he looked this way and that across the toy shop, desperately trying to spot their young protégé.

It was 11.45 a.m. Thirty-two minutes since Zak had entered Fun World. He should have exited the store by now.

Raf and Gabs had made the call to enter Fun World at 11.43hrs precisely. Now they were standing side by side on the escalator. Gabs had her phone in her right hand and was examining it carefully. A flashing green dot on the screen indicated how close they were to Zak's own handset.

They were getting closer.

'I had a bad feeling about all this from the beginning,' Gabs said. 'We should have aborted as soon as he got a message from that weirdo Malcolm. Nobody should know we're here. *Nobody*.'

Heads were turning in their direction. Gabs didn't care. A strange kind of numbness fell over her every time Zak was in trouble – which seemed to happen more and more recently. It was part of the job, of course, but that didn't mean Gabs had to like it. Sometimes it sent all her good sense and training out of the window. But she didn't care. Zak was like her kid brother, and she'd do anything to get him back.

And she knew that, beneath his wordless, grim exterior, Raf felt the same. Not to mention the fact that Zak had saved their lives several times now. They were soldiers, the three of them. OK, so they didn't wear camouflage gear or have a shouty sergeant major to deal with. They were a very special kind of soldier, and the wars they fought weren't reported on the six o'clock news. But what was true for every other soldier in the world was true for them: on the field of battle, you always look after your buddies.

Third floor. The green dot was flashing faster.

Faster.

They were walking to the far side of the store. Towards an area done up as a mock castle, full of Harry Potter toys.

Now they were inside the castle, and the green dot had stopped flashing.

Gabs looked around.

Then down.

She gasped. Then she bent down. On the floor was a smartphone, almost identical to Gabs's own. Just one difference: the screen was smashed. It looked like someone had dug a heel into it.

'It's his,' she breathed.

But Raf was already looking around. 'We need to access the CCTV,' he said. Then he swore. It was impossible. They'd already established that. All the camera images from the store were encrypted and beamed out to an unknown server. That was the whole reason they were here . . .

'What other exits are there?' Gabs said, pushing past Raf out onto the shop floor again. There were only five or six customers up here. With a sick feeling in her stomach, she realized Zak could have easily been abducted with nobody noticing.

Raf pointed to the right. There was a fire exit about fifteen metres away. They strode towards it and Gabs pressed down on the opening lever.

The door opened. But Gabs felt something as she touched the lever. Wetness. She looked at her fingertips.

'Blood,' she breathed.

They stepped through the fire exit and found themselves at the top of a metal staircase fitted to the back of the building. They looked down to the ground. They could see steel bins and a couple of parked cars. But no people. And certainly no Zak.

'Sir, madam, may I help you?'

A young African lad with tight dreadlocks and a red blazer had approached. Now he stood in the doorframe of the fire exit. His name tag said 'Junior' and he had a scar on each cheek.

'Did you see anybody leaving this way?' Raf demanded.

Junior smiled blandly. 'I must please ask you to step back inside the store. The fire exit is for emergencies only.'

'This *is* an emergency,' Gabs snapped.

'Madam, I *will* be forced to call security.'

Gabs felt Raf's hand on her wrist. 'It's OK, pal,' she said. 'Keep your hair on. We're coming back in.'

The two of them re-entered the store.

'You seen a kid about your age looking like he was

in trouble?' Gabs asked. She was struggling to keep her voice calm.

Junior gave an apologetic look. 'We see *many* young people in Fun World, madam. They come from all over Johannesburg.' He made a point of pulling the fire exit closed. Clearly feeling the wetness on the handle, he looked at his fingertips just as Gabs had done. His eyes showed no emotion. 'Paint,' he said under his breath.

'You might recognize this one,' Gabs insisted. 'Blond hair, baseball cap.'

Junior shook his head. 'I have seen nobody like that,' he said. 'I am sorry.' He inclined his head pleasantly, flashed them a smile, then walked away.

'*Wait!*' Gabs called. Junior stopped and looked back. 'Those scars . . .' she said.

Junior smiled. 'A tribal tradition,' he explained.

Gabs narrowed her eyes. Something about the scar worried her. She'd seen it before, but couldn't place it.

Junior walked away.

'I don't trust that guy,' Gabs said under her breath. 'I want to question him. Properly.'

But Raf's hand was still on her wrist. 'Look,' he said sharply.

She looked up. Junior had walked all the way to

the opposite side of the store. He was staring at them, his arms folded and a menacing glint in his eye. On either side were two other store assistants. They both had red jackets. And they both had scarred faces.

'There'll be others,' Raf said very calmly. 'We're unarmed and we've no backup. We need to get out of here. Even if we take them on ourselves, we'll waste time. And I've got a feeling time is something Zak doesn't have much of. Agreed?'

Gabs's jaw was clenched. But she nodded, and the two of them headed towards the escalator and descended back down to the ground floor in big strides.

'We still need to access the security-camera footage,' Gabs said as they stepped out onto the pavement. 'We *have* to know what happened.'

'It's impossible. Michael put his best people on it, remember?'

'Nothing's impossible. We just need to find the right guy.'

Raf pinched his forehead in exhaustion. 'What do you mean?'

'Exactly what I said. Somebody knows how to view the footage of these cameras. We just have to go find him.'

A silence.

'Sounds to me like you already have someone in mind,' Raf said.

'Yeah,' Gabs replied, striding north towards the underground car park where they'd left their vehicle. 'As a matter of fact I have.'

Pain.

Firstly in Zak's head. It throbbed where the toy had smashed against his skull. His whole head ached and he felt sick.

Secondly around his wrists. They were tightly tied together behind his back and they throbbed as much as his head. The blood flow was clearly restricted.

He was face down on a hard, concrete floor. The concrete had pulled all the warmth from him, and he was shivering. With a groan, he rolled onto his back, then squinted. Directly above him, in line with his body, was a strip light. It hurt his eyes.

What time was it? He didn't know. He still had his watch on, but couldn't see it. He didn't even know what day it was.

Zak forced himself into a sitting position and looked around. He was in a narrow aisle between two lines of metal shelving. They were about three metres high, and were filled with toys. This looked like a warehouse of some sort. He pushed himself up to his feet, his hands still tied behind his back, and took a deep breath as a wave of nausea and dizziness hit him.

The aisle was about forty metres long. He staggered to one end where he found an iron fire door with a metal bar across it. The metal around the base of the door had gone rusty. If moisture had got in through the bottom of the door to rust it like this, it probably meant it led outside. The sound of heavy traffic on the other side confirmed this.

Zak turned his back towards the door, then used his tied hands to push down on the bar. It didn't move. The door was locked.

He put his hand in his pocket. Nobody had stolen his cash – proof, if proof were needed, that this was not an ordinary abduction.

He prowled along the wall, counting the remaining aisles in this warehouse. Sixteen. All of them full of the same kinds of toys he'd seen at Fun World. Dolls. Colouring books. Even a stash of Harry Potter merchandise. Zak could do with a bit of wizardry now.

He felt panic rising in his chest, so he stopped to breathe deeply. He could see that his phone had been removed from his jeans pocket, so there was no hope of making a distress call. By twisting his head to look over his shoulder, he could see that his wrists had been bound with a plastic cable tie. Easy to apply. Impossible to remove without cutting through the plastic. And Zak had no knife.

He took a deep breath to steady his sickness, then ran to the end of the aisle he was in, keeping his feet light so they didn't echo round the warehouse. He had no way of knowing, after all, if he was alone in here. At the end of the aisle, he turned right and followed the wall again. There was another door here. Identical to the first.

He was about to try the bar again when he heard voices on the other side. He froze.

They were speaking French. *'Tu es sûr qu'il est au sécurisé?'*

Zak's fluent French kicked in; languages had been a big part of his training. *Are you sure he's safe?*

'Of course. The other door's locked. And if he tries to get past us, we'll deal with him. Anyway, he probably won't wake up. You hit him pretty hard.'

'Thought I'd killed him for a minute.'

'Good job you didn't. He told us to keep him alive, remember.'

'Who?'

'What do you mean, who? Señor Martinez, of course.'

Zak's blood turned to ice.

'That guy gives me the creeps,' said the first voice.

25

'Me too. I heard from one of the others that he's got big plans somewhere else in Africa. When he has big plans, it usually ends up being painful for someone. My guess is he wants to kill the prisoner himself. So, seriously, let's just leave him on the floor of the warehouse where he can't come to any harm. Martinez will be here in twenty minutes anyway. He was on his way to the airport, but he diverted when he found out we'd captured this kid. Don't know why he hates him so much, but he really does. If we're lucky, maybe he'll let us watch what he does to him . . .'

A short, ugly laugh.

Zak stepped away from the door.

His bones ached with fear.

He checked his watch. 12.20hrs.

He'd known Cruz, his archenemy, wasn't dead. And now he was on his way. By 12.40 he'd be here. Zak was trapped, unable to get out of this toy warehouse and unable to raise the alarm.

The panic grew stronger. Stronger than his fading dizziness and nausea.

He had twenty minutes.

Think, he told himself.

Think!

He was back on St Peter's Crag, walking with Raf along a rocky headland. Raf had stopped suddenly and bent down. When he stood up straight again, he was carrying a worm between his thumb and forefinger.

'Breakfast?' he offered, without even the hint of a smile on his serious face.

'Don't be gross,' Zak had said.

'I'm not. Seriously, Zak. Sometimes you have to make use of whatever you can find. There will be times when you'll think you're done for. Chances are you're not, if you can improvise with what's around you.' He bent down again to pick up a jagged piece of flint. He held it up with the worm. 'Most people would see a worm and a stone,' he said. 'You need to see a meal and a weapon. Humans have always improvised with what comes to hand, Zak. Most of them have forgotten how. You don't have that luxury.'

12.22HRS

Improvise.

Zak had to do it quickly. Two minutes had already passed. He had eighteen minutes before Cruz got here.

First things first: he needed to get these plasticuffs off. He couldn't do anything with his hands tied. But he was surrounded by toys. Surely nothing in here would contain a sharp blade. He headed back down one of the aisles, his eyes darting left and right, looking for something that might help him.

Cuddly toys.

Cheap, brightly coloured laptops.

Chemistry sets.

Painting kits.

A pile of children's night lights.

Jigsaw puzzles.

He stopped, turned round and stepped back to the night lights.

Improvise.

There were two types of night light – one covered with a crescent-moon shade, the other with a pale blue star. Zak awkwardly backed up towards the shelf and grabbed a crescent moon. He held it blindly behind his back and, after thirty seconds of fiddling, managed to unclip the shade.

Leaving a bare bulb connected to a piece of flex, with an electric plug at one end.

Zak felt a moment of excitement. He'd found his worm.

Now he needed a plug socket. He ran to the end of the aisle and looked along the length of the wall. He spotted a socket about three metres beyond the locked door and ran towards it, then crouched on the ground by its side.

The bulb of the night light was small – about the length of Zak's thumb and twice the thickness. Manoeuvring it carefully behind his back, he wrapped the hem of his T-shirt around the glass. Now that it was protected by the fabric, he cupped the bulb in his right hand and gently squeezed.

There was a muffled crack as the glass broke. Gingerly, so that he didn't damage the filament, Zak unfurled his fingers and let the shattered glass fall to the floor. He laid the broken bulb on the floor, then plugged the night light into the socket. It lit up. There was a glow behind him, and he could feel the warmth of the filament.

Carefully, he shuffled back towards the broken bulb. He shifted his wrist so the plastic cable tie was as close to the burning filament as he could make it. Not too close, though. An electric shock might knock him out again. He estimated that he was a couple of centimetres from the filament when he stopped and waited for the heat to do its work.

Flesh scorches quicker than plastic melts. So Zak knew the pain was coming. After only five seconds, his skin started burning. He gritted his teeth but didn't move his wrists away from the heat source.

Ten seconds passed.

Fifteen.

He pulled his wrists apart with all his strength. There was a little give in the warm plastic. But he reckoned it needed another ten seconds. His burning skin was agony. He thought perhaps he could smell it.

Twenty seconds.

Twenty-five.

He couldn't take it any more. With a gasp of pain he yanked himself away from the filament. But he couldn't give the plastic time to cool down again. Once more he strained against the cable tie, and this time he felt it stretch a little more.

And a little more. Like a piece of chewing gum being pulled from both sides.

A gap of five centimetres opened up between his wrists. He wriggled his hands out of the cuffs and immediately sucked at the burned flesh on his right wrist.

Ignore the pain, he told himself. *You're not out of here yet . . .*

3

EXOTHERMIC

12.24HRS

A white Range Rover pulled up outside a two-storey house in Mandela Drive, part of a well-off residential suburb to the south of Jo'burg. This was not the house Raf and Gabs actually wanted – they wanted number 67, which was fifty metres further down the street, but they would cover the final distance by foot.

First, though, Gabs needed something. She walked round to the back of the Range Rover and opened up the boot. Then she lifted the floor panel to reveal a spare tyre and a bag of tools. She helped herself to a black iron crowbar.

'Go easy on the kid,' Raf said. 'Remember, he

doesn't respond to adults. He's not quite all there in the head.'

Gabs ignored that. Her jaw was set and her eyes flashed. 'Ready?' she asked Raf.

'Ready.'

Number 67 was at the corner of two streets. There were two entrances to the house – the main one facing onto Mandela Drive, and a side entrance facing onto Cape Road. As soon as they hit the junction, Gabs and Raf peeled away from each other. Raf took the main entrance while Gabs headed for the side.

The wooden door had a spy hole in it and Gabs wondered if she should step away and hide round the side of the porch. But she decided not to. She reckoned that, when the occupant of this house saw someone he didn't recognize at the front door, he'd be in a hurry to leave by the side entrance. He wouldn't be stopping to check if there was somebody else here.

Gabs gripped the crowbar firmly and listened carefully. A few seconds later, she heard the doorbell ringing.

Footsteps inside, heading to the front door.

Then faster footsteps, heading back into the house.

Towards the side door.

She heard someone fumbling at the latch – and she raised the crowbar slightly.

The door opened.

A figure appeared.

He was a slight boy. Skinny, even. His brown hair was tousled and looked as if it could do with a wash. He wore square glasses with thick rims which made his eyes look a bit bigger than they really were.

And he looked scared.

'Hi, Malcolm. I'm Gabs.'

Malcolm looked panicked. His eyes flickered to the crowbar and he stepped back to slam the door shut. But Gabs was too fast for him. She thrust the crowbar into the gap between the door and the frame to stop it closing, then barged through.

Gabs was a lot stronger than she looked. As the door swung inwards, it knocked Malcolm to the floor; his glasses fell down his face at an angle and he stared up at her, like a shocked rabbit.

'Don't kill me,' he whimpered.

Gabs ignored that and paused a moment to take in her surroundings. This side entrance led directly into the kitchen-diner. It was spotlessly clean. Boxes of cereal were lined up on the worktop – seven of them, in a precise row. Next to them were seven apples and seven bananas. All neatly arranged.

The kitchen table was piled high with unopened

iMac boxes. Maybe twenty of them. At one end of the table, a computer terminal was plugged in. A long power cable led to the nearest wall, and the screen was filled with code that Gabs couldn't decipher.

She sensed Raf entering the room behind her as she looked back down to Malcolm.

'Nice place you've got here, Malcolm,' she said briskly. 'Wonder how many bank accounts you've hacked to be able to pay for it.'

Malcolm shook his head to deny it. 'My name isn't Malcolm,' he gabbled.

'Relax, sweetie,' Gabs said. 'If we were going to turn you in, we'd have done it ages ago. And if I was going to kill you, you'd already be dead. If you want to know the truth, our organization has been helping you hide all this time. Now *we* need *your* help.'

Malcolm blinked.

'It's Zak. He's gone missing. You're going to find him. Get up.' She bent down, grabbed Malcolm's arm and pulled him to his feet.

'Zak?' Malcolm said. 'I don't know who you're talking about.'

He was a *very* bad liar.

'How did you hack in to the airport's security cameras?' Gabs demanded. 'Don't try to deny it,

Malcolm, I saw the picture you texted Zak just a couple of hours ago. How did you do it?'

Malcolm didn't reply and so, as quick as lightning, she wrapped her free hand around his neck.

'Here's the problem, sweetie. Nobody else knew Zak was in South Africa. If I decide that you're behind this, things are going to get *very* unpleasant for you. Now tell me: *how . . . did . . . you . . . do . . . it?*'

Malcolm stuttered as he answered. 'Th-there's a police database. It lists all current CCTV installations in South Africa. It's just a matter of breaking into the relevant servers and decrypting . . .'

'Spare me the details, brainiac. There's a toy shop called Fun World. Can you hack its systems?'

'I can hack any system,' the boy replied. He didn't sound like he was boasting. Just telling the truth.

'Then do it. Now. Before I get angry.'

Malcolm didn't move, so Gabs moved her lips up to his ear. 'You *really* wouldn't like me when I'm angry, Malcolm.'

The terrified kid started nodding furiously, so Gabs let go of his neck and he hurried to the computer terminal. His fingers flew over the keyboard even before he was fully sitting down. Now his face was bathed in the light of the screen.

Raf and Gabs stood behind him.

'A bit over the top?' Raf murmured.

Gabs didn't reply.

12.26HRS

Estimated time till Cruz's arrival: fourteen minutes.

And counting.

Were the guards he'd heard on the opposite side of the other door armed? Most likely. Even if they weren't, there were at least two of them. Zak couldn't risk taking them on. He needed to break through the fire exit that he hoped led out onto a main road. But he couldn't use brute force. If he banged something heavy against the door, it would alert the guards. Besides, he doubted he was strong enough.

He needed to do something cleverer than that.

Improvise.

An idea came to him.

The science sets were in the same aisle in which he'd woken up. 'Build your own alarm clock' kits, 'My First Electronics Kit', chemistry sets . . .

Zak ripped open one of the chemistry-set boxes and examined the contents. He saw a neat row of sealed test tubes, each marked with its contents.

Bright blue copper sulphate. Useless.

Deep purple potassium permanganate. Useless.

Dull grey iron filings. Strips of magnesium. They'd burn brightly, but they were no good for what he had in mind. He put the chemistry set to one side, took a deep breath and tried to remember his school chemistry lessons . . .

Exothermic reactions: chemical reactions that give off loads of heat. He'd learned about them in class one day, then gone home to learn more on YouTube. He'd seen exothermic reactions capable of melting metal. 'Don't try this at home, kids,' the guy on the video had said as he put his safety goggles on. How had he done it? What had he used?

It came to him in a flash.

Etch A Sketches.

He'd seen piles of them. He ran to the next aisle, nursing his burned wrist as he went and found the Etch A Sketches, eight of them, stacked in boxes, one on top of the other. Gathering them up in his arms, he carried them over to the fire exit and quickly began unboxing them. He stood over one of the units and, with a sharp jab, brought his heel down on the face. The face cracked immediately. Zak wormed his fingers into the crack and pulled the face of the Etch A Sketch away. He had a grey, powdery residue on his fingers.

Powdered aluminium.

He dumped it out of the body of the Etch A Sketch, then broke open the remaining units. Two minutes later, all the powdered aluminium was piled by the fire exit. He pressed it up against the rusting base of the door.

Powdered aluminium and iron oxide. The mixture would produce a high-temperature thermite reaction. Hot enough to burn through the door.

All he needed now was a way to ignite it.

And he didn't have one.

12.31HRS

Estimated time till Cruz's arrival: nine minutes.

Eight minutes.

Bile rose in Zak's throat. He either had eight minutes to escape, or eight minutes before he would die.

Matches would be no good, even if he had any on him. Nor would a cigarette lighter. The thermite mixture needed a sudden blast of intense energy to get it going. He considered the strips of magnesium ribbon from the chemistry set. They might do it, but he had nothing to ignite them with.

And it wasn't like he could stroll out and ask the guards for a light.

Think.

Improvise.

Zak ran back along the aisles until he came to the science kits again. He ripped open the box of 'My First Electronics Kit' and rummaged through the contents. He found them almost immediately: a small soldering iron with a red handle, and a small coil of solder.

He grabbed them, then ran along the aisle to collect the other two items he needed: a kids' hand-held torch, and one of the brightly coloured laptops.

Back at the exit, he got to work.

There was no time to dismantle the laptop carefully. Zak simply unboxed it and smashed it down on the ground, hoping the noise wouldn't travel to the far side of the warehouse where the guards were waiting. The outer shell came apart immediately and Zak hurriedly dismantled the machine.

Inside was the optical drive. A sticky label on the casing told him it was a DVD burner. That was all he needed to know. He smashed the drive down against the ground until its casing started to disintegrate. Seconds later, he was inside, and he immediately found what he was looking for: the small laser diode that was the core component of the burner.

Moving quickly, he unscrewed the end of the torch and removed the bulb. Then he took the soldering iron over to the power socket and plugged it in.

Estimated time: five minutes. Sweat trickled down the nape of Zak's neck. He was cutting this very fine.

It took thirty seconds for the soldering iron to get up to temperature. The time passed horribly slowly. Zak's hands trembled as he touched the end of the solder to the wire. It immediately formed a little ball of molten metal, which fell to the concrete floor because of Zak's shaking hands.

He took a deep breath, steadied himself, then continued soldering. He needed to fit the laser diode into the bulb socket. Fiddly work at the best of times. Almost impossible when you're working against the clock, your skin is sweaty and your hands are trembling.

And you know you'll be dead in four minutes if you don't get this right.

12.38HRS

Two minutes and counting.

Zak was done. He pointed the torch away from him and switched it on. A pale pink, pencil-thin beam shot from the torch into the plaster wall of the warehouse. Almost immediately, the plaster started smoking. His makeshift laser was working.

Zak ran back to the door. He stood about three metres away from the aluminium and iron oxide mixture. Then he shone his laser at the powder.

Ten seconds.

Nothing happened.

'*Come on*,' Zak whispered to himself.

His hand was shaking again. He slowed his breathing down, then adjusted the focus of the beam so it was a little closer to the door.

Still nothing.

A sound from the opposite side of the warehouse. Voices. Speaking English this time.

'He's lying in the third aisle, Señor Martinez.' Zak recognized the voice of one of his guards.

And he recognized the next voice that spoke too. 'Show me.'

Cruz. He was here.

'Come on,' Zak breathed again. 'Come *on*!'

It happened suddenly. The thermite mixture ignited like a massive Roman candle firework. Blinding light. And it was hot. *Very* hot. Zak had to step back three paces and shield his eyes from the intense heat and light. Clouds of acrid smoke billowed up and caught in the back of his throat.

But it was working. The fire-exit door was buckling as the bottom part melted in the intense heat.

'*Il a disparu!*' a voice shouted out, with more than a hint of panic. *He's disappeared!*

'Find him,' Zak heard Cruz shriek. '*FIND HIM!*'

He had only seconds. Zak heard footsteps running down a nearby aisle. He couldn't wait any longer.

The burning of the thermite mixture was beginning to subside.

Zak ran towards it and gave the door a solid kick about halfway up.

Movement. But the door remained shut.

Another kick.

To his left, Zak could see an African boy running towards him, his eyes fierce and the scars on his cheek plainly visible.

He was ten metres away, and closing in.

Zak knew he only had one more chance.

He ran at the door again and kicked it with all his strength.

It sprang open.

The boy was five metres away as Zak jumped over what remained of the thermite mixture.

In less than a second he was outside.

As he had suspected, the fire door led out directly onto a busy main road. In either direction, there were two lines of traffic – a weird mixture of rickety old trucks with farm animals in the back, and spanking new BMWs. Zak barely stopped to check his path was clear. He ran across the first two lanes to the concrete central reservation. Several horns sounded, and one truck swerved to miss him. But he made the centre of the road safely, where he turned left and started to spring.

He looked over his shoulder. The boy with the scarred face was standing there, breathless, staring after him.

Zak continued to run. About fifteen metres away, he saw a white minibus pulled up on the far side of the road, facing towards him, with a line of three people waiting to board.

Bush taxi.

He sprinted across the remaining two lanes of traffic, his lungs burning with exertion. The driver was just about to close the door as he reached it, and he gave Zak a strange look as the boy jumped on board and handed over a fistful of South African rands. He shrugged, accepted the money, then pulled out into the traffic.

Zak was still standing up as the bush taxi drove back past the warehouse he'd just escaped. But the African boy with the scarred face was no longer there. Someone else had taken his place.

Cruz looked older than when Zak had last seen him. His dark hair had been cropped short and he had filled out a little so he looked less gangly. But his eyes had lost none of their deadness. They were narrow and expressionless as he watched the bush taxi zoom past.

Then Zak noticed something else. Cruz's right hand was hanging by his side. It was holding a handgun.

And the African boy with the scarred face hadn't disappeared after all. He was lying at Cruz's feet.

Was he dead? Had he been shot?

Zak couldn't tell. The bush taxi had moved on and his enemy was out of sight.

He collapsed into a seat, sweat draining from his body, and ignored the strange looks of the other passengers in the vehicle as he tucked his laser torch into his jacket and allowed the taxi to transport him – if not to safety, then away from the immediate threat.

13.00HRS

'How long will this take?' Raf said.

No answer. Malcolm just continued to type what looked like gobbledegook into the computer.

'Seriously, Gabs,' Raf said. 'We're wasting our time. If none of Michael's people could do this, there's no way this kid can even—'

He stopped.

The screen had suddenly divided into sixteen segments. Each segment showed a different black-and-white image.

And each image showed, quite clearly, a different area of the Fun World shop floor.

'How did you—?' Raf breathed.

Gabs interrupted him: 'We need to see footage from 11.10 a.m. this morning. Can you do that?'

Again, Malcolm started tapping the keyboard, his hands a blur. The images flickered, to be replaced by almost identical pictures, only with customers in different positions. Every two seconds, the images changed as the footage moved forwards in time.

Gabs found she was holding her breath.

'There!' she said suddenly, pointing to the bottom left segment of the screen. 'That's him.'

Malcolm enlarged the small image. There was no mistaking Zak, with his newly bleached hair.

'Third floor,' Malcolm said.

Almost in response to his words, the black and white Zak looked directly into the camera. Then the picture jumped to a moment a few seconds later. One of the shop assistants was leading him across the room. The scars on his cheeks were perfectly visible.

'Junior,' Gabs hissed.

'Let's get back to the shop,' Raf said, his voice

urgent, his face grim. 'I think I would like a word with our friend with the funny face after all.'

'Wait,' said Gabs. She kept her eyes on the screen as the camera footage showed a second boy approaching Zak and grabbing his other arm. They disappeared into the mock castle where Raf and Gabs had been just a little while before. 'I want to see him come out,' she said.

She held her breath as they waited for someone to emerge from the castle. Nobody did. Not for a good twenty seconds.

She almost wished she hadn't waited. When Zak emerged, he had an arm slung over each of two scar-faced shop assistants. His face was beaten and bloodied and Gabs wasn't sure whether he was even alive. Her knees buckled. Thankfully Raf was there to hold her up.

'Watch,' he instructed.

They kept their eyes on the footage. The boys dragged Zak over to the fire exit. One of them put his hand to the back of Zak's head and yanked it down brutally. Zak's legs fell from underneath him and his face slammed on the metal lever. Zak had his back to the camera, so they couldn't see any blood flow out of his nose. But looking at her fingertips, which were still stained red, Gabs knew that was what had happened.

'They're going to kill him,' she whispered.

'Actually, they're not,' said a new voice in the room.

Gabs, Raf and Malcolm spun round.

There, standing in the doorway of the side entrance, was Zak. His face was covered in blood and bruises. His clothes were ripped. But he was alive and he was here.

Gabs couldn't help herself. With a low moan of relief, she ran towards Zak and wrapped her arms around him. 'What happened, sweetie?' she said. 'What *happened*?'

There was a pause.

'I'd *like* to tell you, Gabs,' Zak said, his voice slightly strangled. 'I really would. But it's a bit difficult to speak when you're crushing my ribs like that.'

Even Raf had a big smile on his face. He strode over to where Gabs was still hugging Zak and put one strong hand on his shoulder.

Which left Malcolm, still sitting at the computer, a look of total bewilderment on his face.

'Does anybody feel like telling me what's going on?' he asked.

4

HACK ATTACK

'How did you know where to find us?' Raf demanded.

Zak shrugged. 'Worked it out. If I was in your shoes, I'd have come to Malcolm for help too. Unless you know someone else in South Africa you haven't told me about.'

They had pulled the chairs out from under the kitchen table and were sitting in a circle. Malcolm's face was twitching slightly. He wouldn't catch anybody's eye. Made sense. He'd thought he was completely off the grid – must have been quite a shock to learn that he wasn't. Zak continued to explain what he'd just been through.

'So, how did you escape from the warehouse?' Gabs asked.

'I improvised,' Zak said. He felt impatient to tell

them the real news. 'Listen, I heard the guys who abducted me chatting. They were talking about Cruz. He's up to something somewhere else in Africa. He was on his way to the airport when he diverted to come and . . . well, you know . . . *deal* with me.'

He saw Gabs close her eyes for a moment.

'Whatever it is, I got the impression it's something big,' Zak continued. 'Something *violent*. He's going to hurt a lot of people.' He paused. 'I think we need to find out what he's doing. And stop him.'

Gabs and Raf exchanged a look.

'It's not a lot to go on, sweetie. And Africa's a big place. He could be headed anywhere.'

'But we know he's leaving South Africa by air.' He looked directly at their reluctant host. 'And we also know somebody who can identify passengers coming in and out of the airport. Right, Malcolm?'

Malcolm stared at his feet. His eyes flickered up to Gabs and he looked momentarily terrified.

What did you say to him? Zak mouthed the words in Gabs's direction.

Gabs managed to look a little bit sheepish. She turned to Raf. 'Why don't we take a walk,' she suggested.

'Good idea,' Raf said.

They stood up and left the house by the side

door. Zak knew perfectly well that they wouldn't be walking anywhere, but would have eyes on both entrances to the house.

'It's good to see you, Malcolm,' he said, not quite sure if he meant what he said.

No answer.

'What's with all these computers?' He pointed at the pile of pristine iMacs on the table. Next to them was a pile of boxed iPhones.

'Security,' Malcolm mumbled.

'Huh?'

'I never use one computer for more than a week. Or one phone.'

'Right. Makes sense, I suppose.' He looked at the phones. 'Can I take one? I lost mine.'

Malcolm shrugged. 'Sure. The number's on the bottom of the box.'

'I suppose you've memorized them all.'

'Of course.'

Zak smiled and started unboxing the phone. 'You know, we saved a lot of lives in London, you and me.'

Malcolm looked up briefly. 'That woman tried to hurt me.'

'What, Gabs? She was probably just worried. Her bark's worse than her bite.' Zak paused for a moment. 'Actually, that's not true. Her bite's worse than her bark. But only if you're a bad guy, and she knows you're not that.'

Malcolm creased his forehead, but he didn't say anything.

'This guy we're after,' Zak pressed. 'If you can get into the airport security systems, maybe we can find out where he's flying to.'

'Why should I?' Malcolm jutted his chin out aggressively.

Zak narrowed his eyes. How should he play this? He could threaten to turn Malcolm in, of course, but he knew this boy well enough to realize that it would probably backfire. Maybe he should appeal to his better nature. No, Malcolm didn't think like the way most people do.

Instead he stood up. 'You're right,' Zak said. 'Maybe it's too difficult, even for you.'

'What?'

'Too difficult. Don't worry about it, mate. We'll find someone else who *can* do it . . .' Zak started towards the door.

'*Wait.*'

Zak had his back to Malcolm, which meant his peculiar friend couldn't see him smile.

'Which airport? There are three in Johannesburg. But it doesn't matter if you don't know which one. I've got access to all of them.'

Zak turned to see that Malcolm was blinking furiously and dragging his chair back to the computer screen.

'He'll have his own aircraft. I'd say Rand Airport was the most likely, wouldn't you?'

Malcolm nodded. Already his fingers were a blur over the keyboard. Zak took a seat next to him.

'What's the name of the passenger?' Malcolm asked.

'Cruz Martinez. But he won't be travelling under that name. We need to find a jet that was due to take off sometime after midday, but which was then delayed.'

Malcolm nodded and continued to type.

'Why do you like doing dangerous things?' Malcolm asked suddenly.

Zak frowned. 'I don't know if I like it exactly. It's just what I do.'

'But *why*?'

It wasn't a question Zak could easily answer. But he didn't have to. Malcolm was tapping on his computer screen. 'There!' He was unable to hide the excitement in his voice. '*There!* A Cessna due for take-off twelve-fifteen p.m. Re-scheduled for thirteen forty-five.'

Zak looked at his watch. 13.40. 'Can you get a passenger list?' he asked.

'I can do better than that,' said Malcolm. With a click of his mouse he brought up a new window. Four photographs appeared, with names and other information to the right.

They were all male. Two belonged to the captain and first officer. Their names were Paco and Joaquin and they both looked South American. The third was an African man. He was lean, with pronounced cheekbones and very dark eyes. According to the screen his name was Sudiq.

But all Zak's attention was on the fourth face.

A face he'd seen less than an hour ago. Dark hair. Dead eyes. The name next to the picture suggested his name was Rodrigo, but Zak knew that to be a lie. It was Cruz Martinez.

'Where's the aircraft headed?' he asked.

Malcolm tapped at the keyboard again. Instantly a map of Africa appeared. A red dotted line led from South Africa, across Botswana and Namibia, then up to the northern border of Angola. Here there was a little red dot. 'Refuelling stop,' Zak murmured to himself. 'The aircraft must have a very long-range tank to get that far.'

From Angola, the red line passed over the South Atlantic before hitting the Ivory Coast, then continuing north-west to Senegal. Another red dot indicated its final destination: Dakar, the capital city of Senegal.

'What does a Mexican drug dealer want to do in north-west Africa?' Zak mused. Malcolm didn't answer. He just stared at Zak with rapidly blinking eyes. 'Wait there,' Zak said. He stood up and hurried out of the house.

Sure enough, Raf and Gabs had taken up surveillance positions – Raf at the edge of the property, Gabs at the corner where the two streets met. Two children were playing football in the road and Zak noticed that they kept throwing glances at these strangers. He gave a low whistle. Raf and Gabs immediately looked round and, when he nodded his head at them, followed Zak back into the house.

Malcolm was still at his computer. As soon as he saw Gabs, he looked at his shoes again.

'Well?' Raf said.

'Cruz is on a Cessna heading north-west to Dakar in Senegal. Taking off about now.'

Gabs smiled. 'You two boys should do this for a living,' she said. Malcolm blushed.

'I say we follow him,' Zak added. 'There must be plenty of flights, right? Malcolm, can you find out if . . .'

'Forget it,' said Raf.

Zak blinked. 'We have to find out what he's doing, Raf. We know what Cruz is capable of.'

'I *mean*, forget the commercial flights. Cruz hates you, Zak. And you've just wound him up even more. He's also subtle, and he has influence. Trust me, it's not so difficult to sabotage a plane if you know how. If we're going to follow him, I want to be behind the wheel. I'll make a call. We can have our own aircraft waiting for us.'

'Whoa, hang on a minute,' said Gabs, holding her palms out flat. 'When did we all decide to zoom off all over Africa? Any of you ever heard of a little thing called orders?'

'Zak's right, Gabs. We know what Cruz is capable of,' Raf replied. 'We need to keep tabs on him. If we don't follow him now, he could go to ground for months. Years, even.'

'But . . .' Gabs shook her head in frustration. 'Zak's just *escaped* from that psycho. It's *madness* for us to go chasing after him again. Seriously, guys, this isn't a joke. Cruz is a killer, and Zak's top of his list. Have you forgotten what he tried to do last time he caught up with Zak?'

'It'll be different this time,' Zak said with a slight smile.

Gabs raised one eyebrow. 'Oh? How?'

'I'll have you with me.' Zak gave Gabs his most

charming smile. 'You *are* intending to join us, aren't you?'

Gabs blinked, then looked at Raf. 'I thought *we* were meant to be in charge here,' she said.

Raf gave a very serious nod, but his eyes were sparkling.

'*Boys!*' Gabs said in total exasperation. 'You're impossible sometimes.' She turned to Zak. 'Yes, of *course* I'm intending to join you.'

'Me too,' said Malcolm.

All three of them fell silent.

In a single movement, they all turned to look at the gangly boy with his thick glasses and greasy hair.

'What?' Malcolm asked. 'I just found this guy, didn't I? If it wasn't for me you wouldn't have got anywhere.'

Gabs spoke carefully. 'Thanks for the offer, Malcolm. It's kind of you. But this is dangerous and we really work better on our own . . .'

'If you work better on your own,' Malcolm retorted, his skin suddenly flushed, 'what are you doing here?'

Silence.

'He's got a point,' Zak said quietly.

Raf said nothing, but Gabs had the air of a woman who thought things were slipping out of her control. 'Guys,' she hissed. 'Seriously, look at him . . .'

It was true. With his thick-lensed glasses and his greasy hair, Malcolm didn't have the bearing of someone suited to field work. But to Zak he'd more than proved his use in the past, and something told him that Malcolm might do so again.

Persuading Gabs, however, wasn't going to be easy.

'Dakar's a major city,' he said slowly, thinking out loud. 'It's not like we'll just be able to walk round the streets and hope to see Cruz. Malcolm knows how to find people. He found me this morning, and he's just found out where Cruz is going. I say he comes.'

'Agreed,' said Raf.

Gabs looked from one to the other. 'This,' she said firmly, 'is a very bad idea. Remember I said that when everything goes wrong.'

Without another word, she stormed out of Malcolm's house.

Raf watched her go, then turned to Zak. 'She'll be OK when she calms down,' he said mildly. 'But we'd better hurry before she changes her mind.' He turned to Malcolm. 'You don't need any more clothes,' he said. 'Chances are we'll be changing into something that blends in a bit better when we get to Senegal.'

Malcolm was already marching into another room just off the kitchen. He said nothing.

'I hope this is a good idea,' Raf murmured.

'Trust me,' said Zak. 'It just feels right.'

'We'll see. Give him two minutes to get his stuff together. I'll meet you outside.'

Malcolm's stuff, which he brought back into the kitchen thirty seconds later, comprised a cellphone, a laptop and a circuit board that sprouted a mess of wires like coloured spaghetti.

'School project?' Zak asked, one eyebrow raised.

Malcolm didn't speak, or even look at Zak as he stuffed these items into a beaten-up khaki shoulder bag.

'You sure about this, buddy?' Zak said.

Malcolm blinked at him, and for a moment Zak wondered if he'd heard what he said. But then he nodded vigorously. Not for the first time, Zak noticed something very childlike about him.

'I'm bored here anyway,' Malcolm said. 'And it's time to move on.' He slung the bag over his shoulder and started towards the door. Halfway there, he stopped by a bookcase. There was a small framed photograph here: a picture of a middle-aged woman, rather plump, with a short bob of dark brown hair flecked with grey. Malcolm picked it up and looked at it.

'Who's that?' Zak asked.

Malcolm returned the photo to its shelf where it slipped onto its back. 'Nobody,' he said with a note of finality. 'Are we going or not?'

And without looking at Zak he strode out of the side entrance to the house.

Zak followed. As he walked past the bookcase, he glanced at the photograph. Who was it? Malcolm had no immediate family and he didn't seem like the type to get sentimental over anyone. Why then did he have a photograph on display in this supposedly secret house of his?

And if it was that special to him, why didn't he slip it into his rucksack?

Zak stashed that question in a corner of his mind. Then he turned his attention to the job in hand. Absentmindedly rubbing the patch of skin he had burned when freeing himself from the plasticuffs, he hurried towards the side entrance of Malcolm's house and stepped out once more into the thick wall of the South African heat.

Raf was standing twenty-five metres away talking into his mobile phone. Malcolm loitered by the door. He had a sturdy key in his hand and looked like he was deciding whether or not to lock the door. He shrugged for a moment, then dropped the key in his pocket without bothering to lock up. Zak sensed

Malcolm didn't intend to return to this house, ever.

Gabs was walking briskly along Mandela Drive, disapproval about their plan of action oozing from her even at a distance. An uncomfortable thought touched Zak's mind. For the first time ever, they somehow didn't quite feel like a team.

But he dismissed that idea. It would pass. For now, they had work to do.

5

THE DARK CONTINENT

Zak didn't know who Raf had called, or what he'd said. He didn't need to. All he knew, as they pulled alongside the runway of a private airfield in a remote area to the west of Jo'burg, was that a fixed-wing aircraft was waiting for them. It was about thirty feet in length, painted in red and white. A refuelling lorry was just driving away from the plane and two guys in blue overalls stood by it, wilting in the heat.

'Cessna 172,' Raf said as the Range Rover came to a halt about thirty metres from the aircraft. He shook his head. 'Seriously, is that the best they can do?'

'What's wrong with it?'

'Nothing, if you don't want to travel further than a thousand miles or so – *and* that's assuming excellent flying conditions and hoping we've got an auxiliary long-range tank fitted. We'll need to refuel three times, maybe more.'

'Four thousand miles,' Malcolm said suddenly.

'What is?' Raf asked.

No reply.

'What is it?' Zak repeated.

'Estimated distance from Johannesburg to Dakar.'

'Did you just work that out?'

Malcolm nodded. 'There's a margin of error,' he admitted. 'But only about a hundred miles either way.'

Raf inclined his head. 'Well, there you go.'

'Cessna 172,' Malcolm added. 'Decent safety record, but not perfect. August 1969, Rocky Marciano killed in one. September 1978, two crashed over San Diego, 144 dead. May 1987 . . .'

'Yeah, all right Malcolm, thanks.'

Zak smiled. Malcolm was weird, but you had to hand it to him: his brain was something else.

A pause.

'I don't like flying,' said Malcolm.

'You can always go home, sweetie,' Gabs murmured.

'No thank you. I don't want to go home. I want to stay with you.'

Zak turned back to Raf. 'You *do* know how to fly this thing safely?'

'What? Yeah, of course. Gabs is pretty good too. We haven't given you any flying lessons yet, have we? You can have a go if you want.'

'I think I'll leave it to the experts, if it's all the same to you.'

'Chicken.' Raf's eyes gleamed suddenly. 'She *is* pretty, though, isn't she?'

'If I didn't know better,' Gabs said, 'I'd think you only wanted to go after Cruz because you fancy racking up a few more flying hours.'

'What a ridiculous notion,' Raf said. Then he winked at Zak.

'So how *are* we going to refuel?' Zak asked.

'We'll do what we normally do, Zak. Wing it.'

Zak and Raf grinned at each other. Gabs rolled her eyes.

Zak grabbed an empty rucksack from the back of the Range Rover. Then they left the vehicle where it was, and jogged towards the aircraft, where he caught sight of his face in a side window. It was still bruised from his encounter in the toy shop, but he'd grown used to the dull ache of his skin. Moments later, they had climbed the staircase and were inside.

Zak had always expected private planes to be glamorous affairs. Not this one. There were only four seats and they were very cramped. The whole aircraft stank of petrol. Raf pointed out a long-range tank at the back of the cabin with a certain amount of relief. 'Much bigger tank than usual,' he said. 'Someone's made some modifications. We might get away with only refuelling once.'

'Whose aircraft *is* this?' Zak asked as they strapped themselves in.

'British government,' Raf said. 'At least, as good as. It's kind of off the books. They'll be paying some locals to maintain it for them so people like us can make use of it when we need to. Officially, we're not here, remember?'

Right, Zak thought. *We're not here.* Only of course they *were* there, and Zak had to quash a moment of panic. This had all happened so quickly. Maybe Gabs was right. Maybe they *shouldn't* be going after Cruz alone.

But if *they* didn't, who would?

'Let's get strapped in for takeoff,' Raf said, flicking switches on the instrument panel in front of him. A GPS positioning screen lit up, but Raf seemed to pay more attention to the small mechanical compass stuck on the dashboard, and Zak remembered something Raf had told him a long time ago: *We might have all sorts of modern technology to help us, but that doesn't mean you should forget the old ways.* Now that he'd been on the job for a while, Zak knew what he meant. There was something reassuring about that compass. As Raf continued to prepare the aircraft for flight, Zak noticed that Malcolm's hand was shaking.

'Make sure you pay attention to the safety announcement,' Zak said.

'What?' Malcolm looked puzzled.

'It's a joke, Malcolm.' But he clearly didn't get it. 'Nervous?' Zak asked.

'No,' Malcolm shot back aggressively, his skin reddening again. 'I'm not scared.'

Zak sniffed as the aircraft's engines kicked into life. 'You should be,' he said quietly. 'Very nervous. Fear isn't a weakness, you know. It's just our mind's way of telling us to be careful.'

Like a child, Malcolm repeated himself stubbornly. 'I'm *not* scared.'

'Fine,' Zak shrugged as the aircraft suddenly juddered into motion.

The Cessna turned a sharp corner then suddenly gained speed, pushing the passengers back into their seats. Zak didn't feel like arguing. There was a long flight ahead, and something told him Malcolm would have plenty of opportunities to be scared in the days to come.

15.30HRS

Cruising altitude 8,500 feet. It was a cloudless sky and the flight was smooth. Zak felt a sense of fierce exhilaration at being up here in the air, so far from the normal life he'd left behind. At times he missed it, but right now he felt like he was more free than he'd ever been.

He patted down his pockets and drew out a pair of aviator shades to protect his eyes from the sun. Malcolm had none, and Zak saw him shield his eyes with one hand and stare at his lap.

The sight of the continent below was awesome. The earth was parched, but there were several shades of brown and gold that made it look strangely colourful. To the north-west, a river with all its tributaries glinted a deep, intense blue. Zak had heard people call Africa the dark continent, but from the air it didn't look dark at all. A far cry from anything else he was used to, maybe. Different to everywhere else he knew. But not dark.

'Where are we?' Zak asked after an hour.

'We've just crossed the border into Botswana, sweetie,' Gabs said. Her peevishness seemed to have disappeared, but Zak decided it wouldn't be a good idea to take that for granted. He was about to ask where they would be setting down to refuel when the aircraft's radio burst into life.

Zak fully expected to hear a barrage of air-traffic control babble. He didn't. Instead he heard the voice of their handler Michael.

And he didn't sound pleased.

'*Who am I talking to?*' Michael demanded.

'Just the three of us, Michael,' Gabs said calmly. She turned to Zak and put one finger to her lips.

'*I'd have thought* you, *at least, would have better sense, Gabriella,*' Michael said. '*And as for you, Raphael, I'd appreciate it if next time you wanted to play games, you didn't go over my head.*'

Raf said nothing. He just kept his fists on the yoke as he kept the plane flying steady.

'*I've a report from the airfield in Jo'burg that four of you boarded the plane. Who is the fourth person?*'

Another pause as Raf and Gabs glanced at each other. Malcolm looked up, suddenly alarmed. Zak shook his head at his companion in warning, and mouthed the word: 'Quiet.'

'Your intel is incorrect, Michael,' Gabs said. 'There's only myself, Raf and Zak.'

'*That's not what I've been told.*'

'Then you've been told wrong.'

Another pause.

'*Don't think you've heard the end of this, you three. But while you're on the trail of Cruz Martinez, you might as well know that we're tracking his aircraft. He's just touched down in Gabon presumably to refuel. I'll keep you updated of his progress.*'

'Why, *thank* you, Michael,' Gabs said in her best little-girl voice. Zak noticed, however, that her face remained intense and serious.

'*Don't try that on me, Gabriella,*' Michael snapped. '*Something's not right about all this. We go for months without a sighting of Cruz, then all of a sudden we're playing catch with him over the skies of Africa. Be very, very careful when you're on the ground. Do you understand that, Agent 17? And you, Agents 16 and 21?*'

'Understood,' Gabs stated.

'*Zak, are you there?*'

'Yes, Michael.'

There was a pause. '*How much do you know about Spitfire pilots during the Second World War?*'

Zak groaned inwardly. Michael always had some history lesson he wanted to impart. He saw Raf rotate one finger in the air, as if to say: keep him sweet.

'Er, not that much, actually,' he said.

'*If a Spitfire pilot got hit by an enemy plane – a Messerschmitt or similar – his best bet was always to fly directly at the oncoming aircraft. That way, the enemy*' *craft would be too busy trying to avoid a collision to spend time aiming accurately at the Spitfire.'*

Another pause.

'You three are the Spitfire,' Michael continued. *'Cruz is the Messerschmitt. But there's a difference, Zak. I think Cruz will risk a collision just to get a good shot at you. You need to be very, very careful.'*

'There's another difference,' Zak said. 'We're not flying directly at him. We're creeping up behind.'

Silence.

'No heroics, Zak. Cruz Martinez wants you dead. Make sure he doesn't get what he wants. On this occasion, I want you to leave the fancy stuff to Raphael and Gabriella.'

'Roger that,' Zak mumbled, but he didn't know if his words reached Michael's ears. The radio had cut out. There was just the hum of the aircraft and the chilly silence of its four passengers.

15.45HRS

Malcolm looked green. He clearly hadn't been joking about not liking flying, so Zak tried to chat with him to take his mind off things. And, also, to clear something up in his own mind.

'Feel like telling me who that photograph was of?' he asked. He sounded blunt, he knew, but there was no point tiptoeing around Malcolm.

'Not really.'

'You know,' said Zak, 'you've really got a way with words sometimes.' He shrugged and looked out of the window.

A pause.

'My cousin,' Malcolm said. Zak turned to see that his companion was looking a little bit sheepish. He reminded himself that Malcolm didn't really *mean* to be rude. It was just the way his brain worked. And there was something else. Zak was the closest thing this kid had to a friend. He owed Malcolm a bit of patience.

'She looked older than you.'

Malcolm nodded. 'Twenty-four years, six months and three days older,' he said. His forehead creased. 'Her name is Matilda. I miss her. She looked after me before . . .' He waved one arm vigorously in the air. 'Before all *this*.'

'Where does she think you are now?' Zak asked.

Malcolm shrugged. 'Dead, I suppose.'

Zak felt a pang. He also had a cousin who he'd been close to, before 'all this'. Her name was Ellie, and she too thought Zak was dead. It struck him that he and Malcolm were more alike than he'd previously thought.

'I'm sorry,' he said, and the two boys fell silent.

21.00HRS

The African continent slipped away beneath them. Zak slept a while. He needed it. When he awoke, a quick time check told him he'd been in the air for five hours. They had flown right over Angola, where he had faced Cruz once before, and he had missed it. Malcolm still had his eyes closed. There was a vast expanse of shimmering sea to the west, and the setting sun had stained the sky a streaky salmon pink. And they were losing height.

'Where are we now?' Zak asked.

'Cameroon,' answered Raf.

'Shouldn't we be refuelling soon?'

A flicker of a smile crossed Raf's lips. 'Funny you should mention that,' he said. As he spoke, Zak felt his stomach go as the plane lost more height. It was clear that Raf was planning to bring the aircraft in to land.

Zak peered at the terrain ahead, squinting through his shades. 'I don't see a runway,' he said.

'Who said anything about a runway?' Raf asked.

'I thought . . .'

'There's every chance,' Gabs said, 'that official landing strips will be policed. We've violated the airspace of about five countries so far, and we don't have any kind of documentation. A bribe would probably get us out of any sticky situation, but let's not risk a run-in with the Cameroonian authorities. After all, we're just passing through, right?'

'I still don't understand. If we're not going to get petrol at an airfield, where are we going to get some?'

'Same place you normally go,' Raf said. 'A petrol station. We just need to find one.'

They couldn't be higher than a thousand feet now. The terrain below was dry, withered brush. About 500 metres to the north there was a road of sorts, heading from east to west, but Zak couldn't see any vehicles. Raf suddenly banked steeply and the Cessna swerved to the east.

They continued to lose height until they were no more than 100 feet from the ground.

'I saw a village along here,' Raf said. 'And where there's a village, chances are there'll be a . . .' He paused and squinted. 'Bingo,' he said.

At first, Zak couldn't see what Raf was referring to. The plane was fifty feet from the ground when he spotted it: something up ahead – a low concrete building set back a few metres from the side of the road.

'Hold on,' Raf said. 'This could be bumpy.'

The Cessna hit the ground ten seconds later, then bounced back up into the air before hitting the earth again. Malcolm was awake now and Zak could sense him tensing up as the aircraft juddered and rumbled to a halt outside the concrete building.

There was a tree at the front of the building. Three African men had been sitting underneath it, sheltering from the evening sun. They wore no shoes or tops, their trousers were rolled up above their ankles, and one of them wore a floppy-brimmed hat. Now they were standing, staring at each other in astonishment. Ten metres from their position, between the tree and the building, was a very old petrol pump.

Raf killed the engine.

'There's a rifle leaning up against the tree,' Gabs observed quietly.

'Got it,' said Raf.

Two of the men were venturing towards them, their faces creased with astonishment at this new arrival. One of them – the guy with the hat – hung back by the tree.

'Zak, stay with Malcolm. Gabs and I can deal with this.'

Zak didn't argue, but he did find his eye lingering on the guy under the tree. He knew Raf and Gabs would have their eye on him, though.

His two Guardian Angels stepped out of the plane, one from either side, leaving the doors open. Raf put one hand into the back pocket of his jeans and held up a wad of American dollars. That got the men's attention. Their faces broke out into broad grins and one of them pointed at the petrol pump, then at the Cessna. He understood what they wanted.

Raf spoke with them for maybe thirty seconds, then he and Gabs returned to the plane.

'We need to move it closer to the pump,' Raf said. He started the Cessna's engine and the aircraft trundled off the road towards the pump, where one of the two attendants started filling it with fuel.

Raf stepped out again and started handing money to the second attendant. All Zak's attention was on the guy with the hat, however. He had stepped casually up to the tree, and was now slinging the rifle over his neck. Zak felt he knew what the man was thinking: that with a few squeezes of the trigger he could earn himself not only the money Raf had offered, but an entire aircraft.

'Gabs,' Zak warned.

'I know, sweetie. I'm on it.'

'He's got a gun,' Malcolm breathed.

Gabs bent down slightly and felt underneath her seat. She pulled something out and laid it on her lap.

'So have I,' she said.

It was a flare gun, about twice the size of a regular handgun, and half as deadly as the AK-47 assault rifle that the man was now brandishing as he shouted at them. His two companions looked over their shoulders and identical expressions crossed their faces – they were torn between selling Raf their petrol and going all in with their mate.

Neither of them seemed to notice Gabs slip out of the plane, clutching the flare gun out of view behind her back.

Bang! The gunman fired a shot into the air. A flock of birds rose up out of the trees and Malcolm started violently. Zak grabbed his arm to reassure him, but Malcolm pulled it away.

Having not got the reaction he wanted, the gunman sneered at Raf, aiming his rifle at him. But he paid no attention to Gabs. He clearly thought he had nothing to fear from a woman.

That was his big mistake.

As Raf held up his hands, Gabs skirted round the little group. The gunman's eyes flickered towards her as though she was a mild irritation, but he kept his focus – and his gun – on Raf.

Until Gabs was five metres away.

With a sudden, lightning-fast movement, she aimed the flare gun – not at the gunman's head or chest, but at his feet. There was a massive whooshing sound as she fired the flare into the hard ground, and a burst of light and smoke that made Zak clench his eyes shut.

It was only ten seconds later, when the smoke had cleared, that he was able to take stock of the situation again. The gunman was face down on the ground. He didn't seem to be hurt, but Gabs had relieved him of his weapon and was now holding *him* at gunpoint.

Raf was talking urgently to the other two attendants. They nodded vigorously, clearly eager to do what he said, and continued to fill the plane with fuel, while casting occasional terrified glances at the grim-faced Gabs.

'Does she do that sort of thing a lot?' Malcolm asked in a slightly awed voice.

'Yeah,' Zak nodded. He was sweating profusely with the tension. 'Quite a lot.'

'Why didn't she just kill him?'

Zak turned to look at his companion. 'Why kill someone,' he asked, 'when you don't have to?'

Malcolm looked confused, and Zak had to remind himself once more that he wasn't like other people.

Five minutes later, the refuelling was complete. Zak and Malcolm watched as Gabs forced the gunman to walk away from the plane with his hands on his head. Ten metres. Twenty metres. Thirty. He was clearly happy to keep walking, and he kept on going of his own accord as Gabs returned to the plane, the rifle still in her hands. Raf paid the attendants the remainder of the money, then climbed back into the pilot's seat.

Malcolm looked even more confused. 'Why did he still pay them the money?' he asked Zak. 'We've got a gun.'

A dark look crossed Raf's face. 'We're not thieves,' he said. 'And these people have next to nothing.' He started up the engine. 'You're a clever guy, Malcolm, but you've got a lot to learn about the world. Maybe this is a good place to start.'

As the Cessna reversed, Zak saw Malcolm's forehead crease. He looked confused. Maybe a bit embarrassed. Like a kid who had been told off at school.

The Cessna turned in a wide circle, then started to gather speed, bumping and jolting along the dry, stony road. After twenty seconds, Raf pulled back gently on the yoke and the plane lifted into the air, then banked again towards the north.

Twilight was falling over Africa. The harsh ground seemed softer, somehow. As they continued to climb, Zak stared out with a kind of wonder. In a patch of ground dotted with trees perhaps 750 metres to the west, he saw a herd of some kind of animal thundering across the plain. They looked strangely human. Baboons, perhaps? He couldn't quite tell, and was about to ask Gabs what she thought when his daydream was broken by the crackling of the radio bursting into life again.

A few seconds of interference. Then Zak instantly recognized Michael's voice.

'*Raf, do you copy?*'

'Go ahead,' Raf said calmly.

'*Have you refuelled?*'

'Roger that.'

'*Any problems?*'

'Nothing we couldn't deal with.'

'*Good. Listen carefully. The Martinez aircraft has changed direction.*'

'What do you mean? He's not heading for Senegal any more?'

'*Oh, he's heading for Senegal all right. Just not Dakar. Can Zak hear me?*'

'Loud and clear,' said Zak.

'*Cruz's father had drugs processing plants in the Mexican jungle, right?*'

Zak remembered very well a day he'd spent at such a place. He had only known Cruz for a couple of days at the time, and they had been friends back then.

'Right.'

'*Well, guess what. If our intel is correct, Cruz has just landed in a remote area of tropical rainforest in the south of Senegal, about fifty miles from the Gambian border. I rather doubt he's heading there on holiday. You need to follow him.*'

Zak, Raf and Gabs all smiled at Michael's sudden change of tune.

'*It's going to be a tight landing, Raphael. They've set down in a small deforested stretch about a hundred metres long. It's the only place to land for about fifty miles around, and it'll be dark by the time you get there. Are you up to the job?*'

Raf thought for a moment. Then he turned to Gabs. 'We've got parachutes, right?'

'Right.'

'Can you tandem in with Zak?'

She looked over her shoulder. 'What do you say, Zak? Fancy a night jump? I promise not to get you caught in the jungle canopy.'

Zak couldn't help feeling a twist of anxiety. He'd never parachuted before, and this was hardly the time and place for a beginner.

'What about . . .' He almost said the word 'Malcolm' but stopped himself just in time. He nodded, but the decision was already made.

'Send me the coordinates,' Raf spoke into the radio. 'We're on our way now.'

6

HOP AND POP

Night had fallen. The moon was full – a huge milky disc to the south – but it didn't give them much light to see by. Zak could only make out the geography of the continent below from occasional clusters of twinkling lights. Tiny villages, larger cities, roads and, occasionally, rivers passed beneath them. Many of the smaller settlements did not even register on Raf's GPS screen, which glowed dimly in the darkness.

At Gabs's instruction, both Zak and Malcolm had felt underneath their seats. Under Zak's seat was a freefall parachute, and also a small emergency survival tin. Zak checked its contents: a new cigarette lighter, waterproof matches, a couple of pieces of magnesium strip, two candle stubs cut down to an inch, sticking plasters and antiseptic wipes, a roll of gaffer tape, a long reel of fishing twine – all in a watertight metal tin about 5cm by 10cm. The items under Malcolm's seat were bulkier: a long coil of thin, tough rope; a six-inch knife with a broad blade; a Leica spotting scope for observing things in the distance; a notebook and pencil. Zak scooped it all up and loaded it into his rucksack.

'We're about ninety minutes away,' Raf said quietly.

Gabs looked over her shoulder at Zak. 'OK, sweetie,' she said. 'Listen carefully. The reason we need to parachute in is that Raf can't possibly land this plane during the hours of darkness without any visual on this tiny landing strip. We'll need to light some fires to indicate where he has to set the aircraft down.'

'And you'll need to do it quickly,' Raf added. 'We've barely got enough fuel as it is. I won't be able to circle for long.'

'I'll be wearing the chute,' Gabs continued. 'You'll be strapped to my front, facing forward. Raf's going to get us to about two thousand feet above the canopy, then we're going to hop and pop.'

'What's that?'

'Hop out of the plane and pop the chute

immediately. We'll be too low to allow ourselves any freefall. Raf, what's the wind state?'

'We've got a stiff south-westerly. It'll probably change as we lose height. I'll keep you posted.'

'We'll need to take that into account as we jump. But otherwise, Raf will try and get us directly over the coordinates of the landing zone. You OK with all that?'

'I guess so,' said Zak.

In truth, there was an urgent question in his mind. Why didn't Gabs parachute in by herself? Was it just because they needed to build these signalling fires quickly? Or was there something more to it than that? Raf was clearly about to attempt a very dangerous landing – at night time, and into an area not designed for landing planes. Nobody had said as much, but there was a high risk of injury, even death. Were his Guardian Angels planning for that eventuality? It wasn't just that they'd never get Malcolm to jump out of a plane. Had they silently made the decision that in the event of an accident, Zak's strange friend was the least important member of their group?

He glanced sideways at his companion. Malcolm looked nervous. But then, he'd looked nervous since the moment he'd set eyes on the plane. Perhaps he hadn't had the same thoughts as Zak.

Ninety minutes passed very quickly. In what seemed like no time at all, Zak felt the Cessna losing height and Gabs started strapping on her chute, then turned back to look at Zak again. 'OK, sweetie,' she said. 'It's cramped in here, but you'll have to sit on my lap while I strap you to me.'

In other circumstances, the way in which Zak and Gabs struggled to strap themselves together might have been comical. In truth it was deadly serious. There was no margin for error. When Raf banked the plane, Zak knew that he was positioning the aircraft over the drop zone and he felt a burning nervousness in his guts. He'd always known that para-chuting was a skill he'd have to master, but he never reckoned he'd have on-the-job training like this.

Talk about being thrown in at the deep end. Like, 2,000 feet deep, and nothing to break his fall if any-thing went wrong.

'We've got a weak northerly,' Raf announced. 'I'll fly just south of the landing strip. Sixty seconds till target.'

'Ready, sweetie?' Gabs breathed.

'As I'll ever be,' replied Zak.

'Then let's step outside, shall we?'

Zak stretched out his palm to shake Malcolm's hand. Malcolm didn't take it, but looked nervously out of the window.

'*Go!*' Raf hissed urgently.

From their awkward sitting position, Gabs stretched out her arm and slid open the side door of the Cessna. The sudden roar of the air outside was deafening, and Zak felt his hair blowing all over the place with the rush of wind. He felt his stomach lurch with sudden anxiety. This had only been meant to be a simple surveillance operation. How had it come to this?

'Move carefully!' Gabs shouted. 'We need to stand on the landing wheel and grab hold of the diagonal crossbar that leads to the wing.'

'OK!' Zak yelled back. 'Let's get this over with.'

Walking gingerly in tandem, Zak and Gabs eased themselves out of the plane. The rush of air was even fiercer here as they positioned themselves over the landing wheel. Gabs reached out to grab the diagonal crossbar while Zak took deep breaths to steady his nerves. He tried to look down. Now that they were closer to the earth, the moonlight gave them a bit more to go on, and Zak could just make out the canopy of the rainforest, though he couldn't really tell how high or how thick it was. To the north-west, maybe a kilometre away, he could see a faint, silvery reflection of moonlight in a narrow river that snaked lazily away from them. Other than that, the terrain appeared featureless from up here. There was certainly no sign of a landing strip.

He just had to hope Raf was navigating properly.

'Thirty seconds!' Raf's voice was just audible above the noise.

Twenty seconds.

Ten.

'Go! Go! Go!'

Without hesitation, Gabs hurled them both from the edge of the aircraft.

For the first couple of seconds, Zak felt like he'd left his guts behind. He was hurtling blindly through the darkness, and struggled with a weird mixture of fear and exhilaration.

But almost immediately, he felt as if he was being yanked from above. He and Gabs had suddenly stopped accelerating and now were drifting more leisurely towards the ground. A sudden sense of peace almost took Zak's breath away. The only noise was the distant grind of the Cessna's engine some-where far behind and above him, and the thumping of his heart.

He scanned the rainforest canopy below as they drifted downwards. Sure enough, about thirty metres to the north, there was a deforested strip – a band of darkness among the trees. It was difficult to see where its edges began, and from up here, Zak could tell that it was no more than three hundred metres, probably less.

As they fell, he felt Gabs shifting her weight behind him. Their angle of descent altered slightly. Now they were directly above the landing strip with no more than 300 feet to go.

Two hundred feet.

A hundred.

The sound of the Cessna circling was even more distant. A different sound hit Zak's ears – an animal's piercing shriek rising out of the thick rainforest below. He didn't know what it was, but it chilled him anyway . . .

'Start walking!' Gabs shouted. 'Like coming off an escalator.'

They were almost on the ground. Zak moved his feet and immediately felt earth beneath them. Only when he found himself running to keep up with himself did he realize how fast they had been moving through the air. They ran together for maybe ten metres before coming to a halt, while the chute wafted down onto the ground behind them. He felt Gabs's arms around his waist, unbuckling the straps that held them together. When they were undone, she turned and quickly started gathering the billowing mass of material into her arms.

'Nice landing,' she said. 'A great first jump, sweetie. Now let's get to work.'

The landing strip was narrow – no more than forty metres, which was, Zak estimated, only a few metres wider than the wingspan of the Cessna. Raf was going to have his work cut out. He looked up. He could hear the aircraft, just, but couldn't see it. The trees of the rainforest, which were a good fifteen metres high in places, must have been blocking his line of sight . . .

'Find dry twigs,' Gabs ordered Zak. 'Leaves, anything that will burn. Stay out from under the jungle canopy, though. The vegetation will be wet there. Hurry, Zak, we don't have much time.'

He bent over and started feeling the ground. Bone dry. By the faint light of the moon, he looked around. The split branch of a tree lay about three metres away. He gathered it up, then continued to hunt.

It took three or four minutes before he had a small pile of combustible material. It was brittle twigs, mostly, and large, parched palm leaves that crumbled to fine powder if he wasn't careful with them. He stopped for a moment when he heard the noise of the Cessna get louder. Suddenly it roared overhead. Its lights made Zak wince, but he had noticed a slight change in the sound of the engine. It sounded lower, as though it was gurgling.

'He's almost out of fuel!' Gabs shouted. 'We can't wait any longer. Bring what you have over here.'

Zak gathered his kindling and fuel up in his arms, then ran the fifteen metres to where Gabs was standing. They were about thirty metres from the eastern end of the landing strip.

'We need four fires,' Gabs instructed briskly, 'two sets, both opposite each other. They need to be at the edge of the landing strip so that Raf can see where the rainforest starts. Two need to be at the very end so he knows how much distance he has, two more about halfway along so he has line of sight when he comes down at an angle. Do you have the survival kit from the plane?'

Zak nodded and pulled it out of his pocket.

'Leave me a candle stub and some waterproof matches. You take the rest.' She pointed east. 'You do the two fires at the end. That way. *Go!*'

Zak ran. He felt a cold twinge of nervousness prickle down his spine. The Cessna hadn't sounded good at all. Raf needed to land. Soon.

The landing strip didn't stop suddenly. The vegetation simply grew gradually thicker. Zak stopped about ten metres in front of an area where the brush was beginning to grow back. Beyond that point he was vaguely aware of another large, immobile shape. Somewhere at the back of his mind he knew this must be Cruz's aircraft, and a voice told him to be on high alert. But his priority was getting Raf and Malcolm down safely. He divided his fuel into two piles, one at either edge of the landing strip. Then he removed the survival kit that he'd taken from the Cessna, and used the lighter to light a candle stub, then set this to the dried leaves. They immediately crackled and smouldered.

Zak resisted the temptation simply to pile all the rest of his fuel on top of this kindling. *Patience*, he told himself. *You'll only smother it.* He gradually fed the smallest twigs into the burning leaves. When they started to take, he laid slightly larger ones in a wigwam formation over the tiny blaze. Only when the flames were licking thirty centimetres into the air did he add the final, larger branches. Then he sprinted to the opposite edge of the landing strip and did the same thing all over again.

He looked back. Gabs's fires were already burning. They were small, but the bright orange light was intense in the thick darkness. Their four fires were burning.

And not a moment too soon.

Zak saw the Cessna banking in the air, then turning so that it was facing directly towards him, along the length of the landing strip. It was difficult to tell, because its lights were very bright, but it looked as if the plane was skimming only metres above the tops of the canopy, and its wings were wobbling turbulently.

The engine coughed and spluttered and the Cessna lost a couple of metres of height. Zak felt his skin prickle with anxiety. The engine started turning over again, but Zak could tell just by the sound of it that the fuel tank was almost empty. He backed away from the landing strip, up against the edge of the rainforest. The Cessna was over the landing strip now, perhaps 250 metres from his position. It was below the level of the trees.

But something was very wrong.

The nose of the Cessna was pointing downwards. If the aircraft didn't straighten up, the nose was going to hit the ground before the landing wheels.

'Straighten up!' Zak barked in terror, even though he knew nobody could hear him. '*Straighten up!*'

The engine coughed again – and the Cessna plummeted. There was a horrific grinding noise as the propeller hit the ground.

The aircraft lights died. Suddenly, Zak was watching everything silhouetted only by the light of their tiny fires. The grinding noise doubled in intensity and Zak's ears went numb as he saw the dark outline of the Cessna flip over in the air. It moved incredibly quickly, as though time had suddenly doubled in speed, then came crashing upside down onto the ground.

It still had momentum, and scraped along the landing strip with horrific speed. Sparks flew up from where the top of the aircraft touched the ground. Zak heard himself shouting – '*NO!*'

Half of him wanted to run towards the Cessna. The other half wanted to cringe backwards into the safety of the rainforest. In the end he did nothing. There was nothing he *could* do, except stand and stare as the crash-landed plane ground to a sudden halt.

Almost silence.

The engine was dead. There was just the crackle of the signalling fires.

And the sudden patter of Gabs's feet as she sprinted towards the crash site from the other end of the landing strip.

'Get them out!' she yelled. '*Quickly!*'

As if suddenly brought to life, Zak thundered towards the plane. He could smell burning. By the time he reached the plane, Gabs was already on the other side, pulling open the door next to Raf's pilot seat. Zak yanked open a door on his side and peered into the interior of the aircraft.

Malcolm was still strapped into his seat – upside

down, of course. In the darkness, Zak couldn't even see if he was conscious. He grabbed Malcolm's shoulder and shook it. 'Are you OK?'

Malcolm groaned.

Relief flooded over Zak. He fumbled in the dark to unbuckle Malcolm. His companion tumbled from the seat, but Zak was ready to catch him, even though the sudden weight made the muscles in his arms burn. '*Get him away from the aircraft!*' Gabs shouted. '*There's still oil in the engine, petrol in the fuel lines. It could blow at any second.*'

'Can you walk?' Zak hissed.

'I think so,' said Malcolm.

Zak put him down onto his feet, then wrapped Malcolm's right arm over his shoulder. Together, they hurried away from the Cessna.

They were only ten metres away when it exploded.

The force of the blast threw them several metres forward. They landed on the ground with a solid, painful thump. Zak immediately scrambled round to look back at the Cessna. It was a huge, orange blaze, and the heat pumping out of it was ferocious. Zak squinted. He could see neither Raf nor Gabs, and a knot of panic twisted in his stomach.

'Gabs . . .' he breathed. 'Raf . . .' And then he screamed at the top of his voice. '*Gabs! Raf!*'

'They might be dead,' said Malcolm, his voice weak and croaky, but his words typically blunt.

'*Shut up, Malcolm!*'

Zak edged nearer to the flames. He winced at the heat, but couldn't quite bring himself to edge round to the other side. He was afraid of what he would find.

And then he saw them. Two figures, silhouette black, emerging around either end of the burning plane. Gabs to his left. Raf to his right. As they grew nearer, he saw that their faces were covered in soot and dirt. Raf had a swollen bruise on his left cheek.

Their faces were serious, yet calm.

But they looked like they meant business.

Gabs used the light of the burning Cessna to tend to any wounds Raf and Malcolm had sustained. They were surprisingly few. Raf's face was only bruised; while Malcolm had a more serious cut on his elbow, where his clothes had torn and something had sliced a gash about five centimetres in length. It was bleeding badly. Gabs tore a strip from his shirt and used that to bind the wound tightly. The blood flow stopped after a couple of minutes of pressure, but it would clearly need constant attention.

The Cessna had burned down to a smouldering

skeleton of metal and the small signalling fires were just a memory. It was very dark.

In one way, Zak thought, that was a good thing. The noise of the air crash had been bad enough, but nothing was more likely to announce their presence here than a blazing aircraft. But it also made him feel vulnerable. There were sounds nearby in the jungle that he hated. Slithers and squawks, all of them magnified by the darkness. None of his training on St Peter's Crag had prepared him for jungle wildlife.

He patted down his jacket. The torch he had modified back in the warehouse was there, but it wouldn't give them any light now.

Fortunately, Raf had it covered. He drew a thin Maglite out of one of his pockets. Its beam cut cleanly through the darkness. 'Have you still got that gaffer tape?' he asked Zak.

Zak nodded and reached inside the survival pack for the roll of tape. He handed it over to Raf, then watched as he placed the Maglite on top of Gabs's assault rifle and fixed it there with several loops of tape around the body of the weapon. He raised the rifle and embedded the butt into his shoulder. Then he shone it in the direction of the second aircraft that Zak had almost forgotten about, hidden at the end of the landing strip and half covered by the encroaching rainforest.

Cruz's plane? It had to be.

'Gabs,' Raf said. 'Keep an eye on Malcolm. Zak, come with me.'

They walked silently towards the aircraft. 'What are we looking for?' Zak asked.

'I don't know,' Raf replied. 'I'll tell you when we find it.'

This aircraft was in a much better state than the Cessna. Zak reminded himself that it had probably landed before nightfall. The pilot hadn't been flying blind. And yet there was something about it. An aura. Zak felt nervous just approaching.

'The doors are still open,' Raf breathed, pointing his torch at them. They were ten metres away and, with a sudden, sick feeling in his gut, Zak thought he could see, through a cabin window just behind the open door on the right, a figure still sitting at the instrument panel.

He grabbed Raf's arm. 'I see it.'

They approached carefully, with Raf keeping the assault rifle and Maglite firmly pointed straight ahead.

They reached the open door.

Zak looked in.

He caught his breath.

The pilot and co-pilot – Zak vaguely remem-bered their faces from the images Malcolm had accessed on his computer screen – were dead, but he'd half been expecting that.

He wasn't, though, prepared for how gruesome they would look.

They'd both been shot in the back of the head. Each had a chunk of skull missing, and a hideous exit wound on their foreheads. Zak was aware of a buzzing sound, and realized that, even in the darkness, there were insects buzzing around the sticky, open wounds. He recoiled from that noise as much as from the sight.

But it was not the head wounds that made his blood turn to ice. It was the cuts on the corpses' faces. Each man had a fresh slash reaching from the edge of their lips, across their cheeks and up to their ears.

Just like the boys who had abducted Zak that morning.

'Looks like someone's left a calling card,' Raf breathed, before switching off the torch so they didn't have to look at that gruesome sight a second longer.

PART TWO

7

SMILER

Dawn is noisy in the jungle.

Eighty kilometres, as the crow flies, from the landing strip, a group of twenty boys – none of them older than fifteen, some as young as nine – sat in a circle listening to the sound of the rainforest waking up. They were a strangely dressed bunch. Some wore black vests and baggy red trousers. Others had plain khaki shirts, or camouflage jackets, or sleeveless jackets with pouches along the front. Four or five wore long links of bullets around their necks, like scarves. One or two had green metal helmets. Rather more had red, black or blue bandanas wrapped round their foreheads.

All of them carried guns.

Every second, the screech of a different bird echoed from a different direction. The trees surrounding them shook as those birds, animals and reptiles that had taken shelter in their branches started to move. Behind it all was a white noise of buzzing as insects rose in great clouds to meet the morning.

And a young boy screamed so loudly that it almost drowned out all these other sounds.

He was kneeling by the fire in the centre of the circle, with his hands tied firmly behind his back. The fire itself was covered with green leaves and grasses. It was there not for heat or light, but to emit massive clouds of smoke to repel mosquitoes. It was only half successful. A pall of smoke certainly hung thickly around this small clearing, and all the boys blinked heavily to keep their smarting eyes moist and smoke-free. But the mosquitoes swarmed anyway – over their hands and feet. Also over their faces, though they seemed to avoid the scar tissue that led from the corner of each boy's mouth, up across the cheek and to the earlobe.

Nobody seemed bothered by the mosquitoes, though. The boy in the centre was already too busy screaming and whimpering to pay them any mind. And those sitting in the circle were watching him closely with enjoyment.

There was an older man too, standing in front of the young boy. He had a viciously sharp, broad-bladed knife in his right hand.

'Shush,' he said loudly.

The boy stopped shouting, but he could not stop a series of sobs escaping his lips.

'Shush, shush, shush,' the man repeated, this time in a much quieter voice. 'You should not be shouting. You should be thanking us. After all, you *begged* us for this opportunity.'

It was true. The young boy *had* begged these people to let him join them.

His name was Kofi, but for as long as he could remember, everyone had called him Smiler. When he was five years old, a young English woman had come to live in their village for two months. She had also taught Kofi English, and he knew he now spoke it far better than most of the other villagers; his parents had hoped speaking English well would lead to chances in life for him. And it was the English woman who had given him the name Smiler because he always seemed to have a grin on his face. She was now long forgotten, but the name had stuck, even though most of the villagers didn't know what it meant.

Smiler had continued smiling until the day before his ninth birthday. That was the day he, his mother and father had woken to find a mamba in the small wooden hut they called home. It was coiled lazily by the entrance and Smiler's father had tried to shoo it away with a long stick he used when walking through the jungle.

But the mamba didn't want to be shooed away.

Smiler could still remember the moment it bit his dad. It had sunk its teeth into his calf muscle and hadn't let go for a full five seconds. Then, roused and angry, it had turned its attention to Smiler himself. The mamba had been only a metre away from him when his mother grabbed it, one hand by its throat, the other by its tail. She had run with it out of the hut, screaming for help. But the snake was strong, and as it flailed its lithe body, it had managed to work itself free of her grasp. It bit her three times on the face in quick succession before more men arrived to kill it.

But by then it was too late.

Smiler's mother was dead by sunset. His father was dead by dawn.

He celebrated his birthday as an orphan.

That had been two years ago. The villagers had done their best to look after him, but he was nobody's child and their own families had to come first. Little by little, Smiler began to starve.

When two boys with scarred faces turned up at the village, everyone had kept their distance. Whispered rumours found their way to Smiler. They were from a bad crowd. They were what remained of the West Side Boys.

Over the next few days, from overheard snatches of conversation, Smiler learned just who the West Side Boys were.

They came from Sierra Leone, 500 miles south of Smiler's native Senegal. It had been a war-torn country, filled with different groups of armed fighters. The West Side Boys were one of these groups. Many of them were just children, some of whom had been forced to torture and kill their own parents. This had turned them into brutal, desperate, cruel killers. They made it their job to murder foreign peacekeepers in their country.

But then, in the year 2000, some British soldiers had arrived to deal with them. The soldiers had been members of something called the SAS. Smiler had never heard of that – but he understood from the way everyone spoke that they were the best soldiers in the world. They had wiped out the West Side Boys. Killed them all.

Or so everybody thought.

From the conversations Smiler overheard, he learned that a few had survived. They had given themselves a new name – the East Side Boys. They had given themselves a distinctive marking on their faces. It showed who they were. And it showed they were tough.

And they had started recruiting, not just in Sierra

Leone, but all over West Africa. Now there were hundreds of them.

When the two East Side Boys knocked on Smiler's door, Smiler's blood had run cold. He thought of running away, but for some reason that idea made him even more scared. And so, timidly, he'd opened his doors to them.

The boys were friendly. They'd brought food with them, and let Smiler eat as much as he wanted. They'd even let him have a few mouthfuls of palm wine. He had pretended to like it so that he could feel like part of their gang.

They came back the next day. And the next. All the time, they were nothing but friendly. Smiler had to admit that the scars on their faces were strange, but he decided that the rumours he'd heard about the wickedness of the East Side Boys were all wrong.

On the fourth day, they'd asked if he wanted to join them. It would mean leaving the village, of course. But their life was exciting, and he'd always have enough to eat.

Smiler had said yes.

In fact he'd done more than that. He'd *begged* them.

And even when he learned about this initiation rite, where the scars of the East Side Boys would be carved into his cheek with a sharp knife, he still wanted to join them.

Having lost one family, he was being offered a new one. It was not the sort of opportunity his parents would have wanted for him. But it was an opportunity he now desperately needed.

The head of this new family was the man now holding the glinting blade in front of Smiler's face. Smiler didn't know his real name. Everyone called him Boss. He was much older – older even than Smiler's dad had been when he died. His dark hair, flecked with grey, was tied back in dreadlocks. Although he didn't share the East Side Boys' scars, his cheeks were deeply pitted and pockmarked. He had a bad smell about him.

Smiler tried to concentrate on Boss's dirty fingernails – the colour of yellow wax – and not on the knife he was holding. He was beginning to have second thoughts about joining this new family.

One of the East Side Boys sitting in a circle around him had a portable CD player. He pressed PLAY and held it above his head. The speaker spat out a barrage of frenzied drum rhythms and somebody launched into aggressive-sounding rap over the top. Smiler spoke a little English, but he couldn't understand the words at all. His new friends had told him it was somebody called Tupac Shakur, and that they would teach him the words after his initiation. But not before.

Initiation.

It was time.

There was no point screaming any more.

They'd tied his hands behind his back for his own good, they'd said. If he tried to stop Boss mid-slice, he could damage his face even more.

Now the man was grabbing Smiler's hair with his left hand.

The boy trembled and sweated. His eyes were very wide as he watched the blade approach his right cheek.

It felt as cold as ice on his skin. Then it sliced very slowly down his cheek. His breath came in short, sharp gasps.

At first it didn't hurt. All Smiler felt was blood oozing down the side of his face. The rap music grew louder as the man swiftly moved to his left cheek.

Slice.

Blood.

And then . . . *pain.*

Someone approached from behind and cut the rope binding his wrists. His hands flew to his cheeks, and blood oozed through the gaps between his fingers. He shrieked in agony.

Then he was flat out on the ground. Two boys were pinning his arms down, while a third placed two pieces of cloth against the bleeding wounds to stem the blood flow. He wriggled and kicked, but the boys were too strong. He wasn't going anywhere.

'Relax, my friend,' said a voice. He didn't know who it belonged to. 'You're one of us now.'

He screamed again.

'Yes,' said the voice. 'You're one of us. Smiler's an East Side Boy.'

The scream turned to a pathetic whimper.

'And when you're an East Side Boy, you're an East Side Boy until you *die*.'

He said the word 'die' with a rasp so unpleasant that for a moment it even made Smiler forget about the pain in his face.

They gave him palm wine to drink. It made his head woozy, but helped a little bit with the pain. One of the East Side Boys had given him bandages, and shown him how to wrap them round each of his fists so he could press them against his bleeding cheeks, and stop the blood.

He sat on the log and listened to the man talking.

'You, you, you and you,' he said, pointing to four of the East Side Boys in turn. 'You have a job to do. It means going up the river to Banjul.'

Smiler blinked. Banjul was the capital of The Gambia, the small, thin country that Senegal surrounded completely. It was a small port town on the west coast of Africa. It must be at least a hundred miles away. Why would the man want to send his East Side Boys there?

'There is a customs official,' the man continued. 'We have offered him a lot of money to let certain boxes pass into The Gambia unopened. He has refused our very generous offer.' The man gave an unpleasant smile. 'So I want you to kill him.'

If the East Side Boys were surprised by this offer, they didn't look it. Smiler, though, felt sick.

'The rest of us, we travel into the rainforest to meet with some of the others,' the man announced.

'Where are they, Boss?' one of the East Side Boys asked.

Boss smiled. It wasn't a nice look. 'You'll find out,' he said. 'We're going to meet someone important. Someone *very* important.' He raised his knife up to his eyes and examined the blade. It glinted in the sunlight and Smiler thought he could still see a smear of his own blood on it. 'I've known his family for a very long time, and I want you to be on your best behaviour. Do you understand?'

He gave the East Side Boys an unpleasant leer. They leered back. Smiler didn't know what Boss meant by 'best behaviour'.

And he wasn't sure he wanted to. He was beginning to realize he'd made a big mistake.

8

TINY TEARS

Zak didn't know what it was that woke him: the screeching sound from the rainforest, or the mosquitoes having breakfast on his skin.

But then, it wasn't like he'd had a refreshing night's sleep.

At Raf's insistence, they'd pulled the corpses of Cruz's flight team out of their aircraft, and dragged them a good thirty metres away to the edge of the rainforest. 'It's fresh meat,' Raf had said bluntly. 'We don't want to stay too close to it.'

The four of them had then spent the remaining couple of hours of darkness in the protection of the aircraft's cabin. Zak found himself in the pilot's seat, and his skin recoiled from a patch of sticky wetness by the headrest. His few moments of sleep were haunted by images of overturning aircraft and African boys with scarred faces chasing him down jungle pathways. He woke feeling like he hadn't slept at all.

Malcolm was still sleeping in the seat behind him. He was nursing his wounded elbow as he slept. The rag that bound the wound was soaked in blood and a couple of flies buzzed around it. Zak tried to shoo them away, but the flies ignored him.

Raf and Gabs were already up and about, so he slipped out of the cabin to join them in the clearing. He immediately noticed the hooded shapes of two vultures in the tree under which the corpses were lying. Cruz's pilots weren't rotten enough to be carrion yet, but in this heat they soon would be.

Zak shuddered, then hurried towards his Guardian Angels. They were standing at the edge of the runway, about halfway along the landing strip, looking into the rainforest. Their faces were thoughtful.

Gabs nodded at Zak as he approached. 'Look at this, sweetie,' she said.

Zak saw that there was a rough track leading into the jungle. A vehicle of some sort had made it – the tyres had formed two narrow strips on either side of the path.

'Looks like someone was waiting for Cruz,' Gabs continued.

'And they left us a trail,' said Zak. 'It could lead us right to him.' He peered along the path into the jungle. Something had caught his eye. He stepped five metres along the track, and bent down. From a patch of lush, damp, high grass he lifted out a child's doll. It was in the shape of a naked baby, quite bald, and was made out of sturdy plastic. Its lips were puckered, waiting for a child to insert the teat of a toy milk bottle. The limbs were twisted and one of the eyes was missing.

He remembered an advert he'd seen on TV back in the days when he was just an ordinary kid. It was for a baby doll that cried by itself. 'Tiny Tears,' he muttered to himself.

'What did you say?' Raf called.

Zak didn't reply. He weighed the doll in one hand – it was heavier than it looked. Stepping back towards the clearing, he handed the doll to Raf.

Raf took a knife from his pocket and plunged it deep into the doll's plastic chest. He used the sharp blade to saw down the abdomen, then ripped the doll's chest apart.

Zak was not surprised to see it filled with a fine white powder.

'Cocaine?' he asked.

Raf laid the doll on the ground, then pulled a lighter from his pocket. He held the flame to the inside of the doll for a few seconds and the powder spat and crackled, then suddenly ignited. Raf stepped back as smoke billowed from the doll's chest, and nodded grimly. 'Cocaine,' he confirmed. 'Nothing else burns quite like that. Looks like someone got careless, leaving it lying around like that.'

'Either that,' said Gabs, 'or they're doing a Hansel and Gretel on us.'

'What do you mean?' Zak asked.

'You know, leaving a trail for us to follow.'

Raf shook his head. 'I doubt it, Gabs. Cruz has no way of knowing we're on to him.'

'Maybe,' Gabs said. She didn't sound massively convinced. 'I still don't think it's a good idea to follow that trail precisely. There could be any number of traps set along its way. If we're going into the jungle, I say we keep to one side of it. Just in case.'

Raf and Zak nodded. 'Agreed,' they both said. Zak looked over at the aircraft where they'd spent the night, and where Malcolm was still sleeping. 'If I thought we'd end up in the jungle, I'd never have suggested bringing him,' he muttered. 'I'm sorry.'

'We can't change it,' Gabs said briskly. 'He's our responsibility now. Anyway, you never know. He might still prove useful. Go wake him. This is difficult terrain. Neither of you have any jungle survival experience. There are a few things you need to know before we set off.'

Zak nodded, then ran back towards the aircraft.

Malcolm was just waking up. As he opened his eyes, he looked around suddenly, obviously unsure where he was. An expression of horror crossed his face, but he mastered it when he saw Zak standing by the plane.

'Come on, mate,' Zak said, gently but urgently. 'We've got to get moving.'

'Where to?' Malcolm demanded.

'You'll see.'

He led Malcolm back to where Raf and Gabs were sitting cross-legged on the ground. When Malcolm saw the trail leading into the jungle, he couldn't help fear writing itself all over his face. They sat down too, then Zak looked expectantly at Gabs. Malcolm, as usual, avoided all eye contact with the grown-ups.

Gabs gathered her thoughts for a moment, then cleared her throat. 'We're heading into the jungle,' she said. 'We don't know how long we'll be in there, and we don't know what we'll find. But the jungle is very unforgiving, and we can't afford to let our guard drop for a moment. There's an abundance of life in the rainforest. Most of it knows what its regular food is, and doesn't like to change diet. But there are creatures in there which, if they're surprised or frightened, will attack. You need to think before you do anything. Be careful where you're putting your feet. If you're thinking of sitting down on the floor, or on a log, or by a tree, check it first. And remember to look up as well as down.'

'Snakes?' Malcolm asked in a small, frightened voice, directing his questions to Zak even though it was Gabs speaking.

'Possibly. But deadfall is a much bigger danger.'

'What's that?'

'Dead wood falling from the treetops. It can kill you in a second, so watch out for it. We'll walk in single file: Raf first, then Malcolm, then Zak, then me. It's important never to let the person ahead out of your sight. On your own, you've got next to no chance of making it out alive – Raf and I will be able to find water for us all, and we know which plants are safe to eat, so you need to stick with us. Don't eat anything unless we've told you it's safe.'

She paused for a moment, and allowed that to sink in, before continuing her lecture.

'We're going to keep several metres to the left of this path,' she said. 'My guess is that whatever vehicle made it will be following a ridge line, like an upside-down "V" through the jungle.'

'Why?' Zak asked.

Gabs shrugged. 'Otherwise they'd have to keep crossing ridge lines up and down, which would be almost impossible. Animals use these ridge lines too, but they'll probably keep their distance from us.'

'Probably?' Malcolm asked, slapping at his face to kill a mosquito that was chewing his cheek.

'Yes. Probably.'

'I'm scared,' he said.

'Good. A little bit of fear keeps you sharp. But just do what Raf and I tell you and you'll be OK.'

'Anyway,' said Raf, standing up, 'I *like* the jungle.'

Malcolm looked at him as if he was insane.

'Pitch black at night, nice and quiet. Best place in the world to get a decent night's sleep.' He winked at Malcolm as he stood up. 'I think Gabs has just about covered everything,' he said. 'Shall we go?'

Malcolm turned to Zak. 'Was that a *joke*?' he asked.

Zak shook his head. 'No, mate,' he said. 'I don't think it was.'

There were few preparations to make. They had very little gear – just Zak's rucksack and Malcolm's. No spare clothes. Nothing. But before they set out, Raf quietly took Zak over to Cruz's aircraft. 'We'll need to keep a careful eye on Malcolm,' he said. 'He's not really jungle material, if you know what I mean.'

Zak wasn't sure *he* was jungle material either, but he kept quiet.

'I'm worried about that cut on his arm too. Wounds can get infected very quickly in the jungle. All that warmth and moisture. You'll need to keep an eye on it. He responds better to you than to us.'

'Right.'

'Go search the corpses,' Raf said. 'I need some sort of water bottle. See what you can find.'

Zak was about to say, 'Why me?' But he knew what kind of response he'd get. So, with one eye on the vultures in the trees, he ran towards the corpses.

They were already beginning to smell, and clouds of flies buzzed around them. Thick clusters of mosquitoes had congregated along the bloody knife marks on the dead men's faces. Zak shook the insects away from his own face as he bent down at the first corpse, doing his best not to look too closely at the catastrophic gunshot wound in the man's head. He patted the body down, but found nothing but a wallet which he quickly discarded. He swallowed another mouthful of air, trying not to breathe through his nose, then moved on to the second body.

Here, he had more luck. This man had a small hip-flask in his side pocket. Zak grabbed it and ran away from the stench of the rotting flesh before twisting the top open. Inside, the flask smelled of alcohol, but it was empty. Zak ran with it back towards Raf's position.

'Will this do?' he asked.

Raf nodded, and took the flask from Zak. 'You got that big knife?' he asked. Zak felt in his rucksack and handed it over. With a sudden yank, Raf jammed the knife into the body of Cruz's aircraft, just below the wing. Zak was surprised by how easily the metal ruptured. A thin trickle of pale liquid started dribbling out of the hole.

'Fuel,' Raf said. 'Easiest way to light a fire, and we'll need one in the jungle.' He carefully filled the flask up to the brim, then twisted the cap back on and slipped the whole thing in his pocket. 'Let's go,' he said.

Zak was sweating badly and the perspiration was soaking into his clothes, making them damp. When they joined the others – they were still standing between the track and the charred, smouldering remains of the plastic doll – he saw trickles of sweat pouring down Malcolm's face and damp patches in Gabs's hair. 'We're going to need water,' he said.

'We'll find some as soon as we can, sweetie,' Gabs said. 'Let's start walking.'

The dawn chorus of insects had gone quiet. It was strangely silent all around. Zak, though, had the uncomfortable sensation of eyes peering out of the jungle towards them. It was as if they were always on the edge of his vision, and whenever he turned to see them, they receded back into the bush. *It's just your imagination*, he told himself. But he noticed that Malcolm was looking around nervously in the same way.

This was a creepy place. No question.

They set off at a slow march in the order Gabs had instructed. Within ten paces, the jungle canopy was above them. It protected them from the rising sun, but the air was thickly humid – Zak couldn't tell whether his skin was wet from sweat or from water vapour.

For the first forty metres, the vegetation was only up to their waists. Zak took care to step in the path trampled down by Raf and then Malcolm, but he still laid each foot carefully on the ground – he wasn't good with snakes either. And although he knew that the footsteps of this little group of humans would be like thunder to a jungle reptile, and would send them slithering out of their way, he still didn't want to risk inadvertently treading on a thickly coiled body. The very thought made him shiver.

They'd been going for less than five minutes before Raf had to get his knife out again and start cutting through the vegetation that blocked their way. Thick, knotted vines and tree branches grew out at crazy angles, covered with moss and lichen. Every forty paces or so, Raf would hold up one hand to tell them all to stop. Then he would head to his right to check they were still following the path made by Cruz's vehicle.

Those were the worst moments. Standing still, peering into the dense jungle, wondering what was out there, watching and waiting . . .

Zak's senses were on high alert, and he felt almost at one with the rainforest. He noticed everything. The shaking of individual leaves. The dripping of moist condensation from a branch up above. The way Malcolm was nursing his bad arm, and wincing occasionally in pain.

Then they would move on again, treading carefully, looking up for deadfall, always keeping one eye on the person in front, and trying to ignore the moisture that now poured out of them.

They'd been going for an hour when Zak suddenly noticed a change in the air. The temperature had dropped suddenly and he found himself shivering. He stopped in his tracks and looked around. There was a new sound: the leaves in the canopy above were rustling together. It sounded ominous, but not as ominous as it looked. Zak gazed up: the whole canopy appeared to be moving, swaying back and forth with the wind that was picking up.

He noticed that the others had stopped. Raf was looking up too.

'We're going to have rain,' he said.

'Are you sure?'

'Trust me. If we get up above the canopy we'll see a weather front rolling in. We need to stop.'

Zak gave him a confused look. 'We can manage a bit of rain, can't we?'

Raf smiled grimly. 'Not jungle rain,' he said. 'I think we can risk stepping up to Cruz's trail for a moment. The ground's a little higher there. Come on.'

He cut a way at right angles through the thick bush. The others followed and within a couple of minutes they had reached the narrow path cut into the jungle just hours previously. A thought struck Zak: the jungle was so thick and knotted that who-ever had driven this vehicle must surely have known where they were going in order to avoid tree roots and other obstacles. There was no doubt that they were now heading to an actual *place*, even if they didn't know what it was.

Zak was about to make that comment when the rains came.

There was no warning. No tiny pitter-patter of rain spots. It was as if someone had simply turned on the tap. He had never known anything like it. Even under the canopy of the jungle it felt like a million showers were blasting down on top of him. The water steamed and sizzled all around him and he almost found it difficult to breathe without sucking in raindrops.

He felt Gabs grab his hand. Raf had done the same to Malcolm, and now they were all moving towards a massive tree trunk where the canopy overhead was a little thicker. They huddled here where the rain was fractionally less intense. Rivers of rainwater gushed downhill – enough to knock them from their feet – and Zak understood why Raf had made them move to higher ground.

'*How long's this going to last?*' he yelled. But his voice went unheard above the noise of the rainstorm. Instead, following his Guardian Angel's lead, he opened his mouth up to the sky and drank what rainwater he could. That, at least, was refreshing. He could tell that he'd lost a good deal of water in the hour they'd been trekking.

The rain lasted for ten minutes. Then it stopped as suddenly as it had started, as if the tap had been switched off again. All four of them were saturated and covered in splashes of mud.

'We'll dry off sooner than you think in this heat,' Gabs said. 'Let's get off the path and keep on walking.'

But Zak wasn't going anywhere. He'd just seen something.

'What is it, Zak?' Raf asked quietly.

Zak pointed at a tree trunk ten metres from their position. Something was pinned to it at head height. He found that he was holding his breath as he stepped towards it.

He was a metre away when he understood what he was looking at.

In some ways, it reminded him of a miniature scarecrow. The stuffed figure was twenty centimetres high and dressed in a straw-coloured dress. But it was not the dress that captured Zak's attention. Nor was it the gruesome way in which a sturdy six-inch nail pinned the figure to the tree through its abdomen. It was the head: the tiny skull of a small animal, its intricate bones on display and its jaw fixed in a hideous grin.

Zak shivered. Raf and Gabs were suddenly next to him.

'There's another one over there,' Gabs said quietly. She was right. A second figure was nailed to a tree about ten metres away.

'I've seen something like these before,' Zak breathed. 'In Mexico, at Cruz's house. They called them *La Catrina* – statues of women with skulls for faces. A kind of Mexican tradition.' He grimaced. 'As traditions go, I think I prefer Morris dancing.'

'I don't know,' Gabs said. 'I think it's a good sign.'

Zak blinked in confusion. 'Why? Surely it's there just to scare people away.'

'Exactly,' she said. 'And that means we're on the right track.'

'I suppose that's one way of looking at it.' Zak continued to eye the figure with distaste.

Gabs reached out one hand, ripped the figure from the tree and dropped it on the ground.

'Let's take the nails,' Raf said.

'What for?'

'You never know.' He wiggled the end of the nail and eased it out of the tree trunk. Then he walked over to the second doll, ripped it from the tree and removed the other nail.

Zak found himself staring at the stuffed toys. The jaws of their gruesome skeleton heads had fallen open and they were staring up towards the jungle canopy.

'They're just dolls, sweetie,' Gabs said quietly from behind him.

Zak gave her a look. He wanted to say that the cocaine-stuffed baby they'd found at the landing strip was also just a doll. That didn't mean it wasn't dangerous.

But he kept quiet, and they continued their trek through the jungle.

9

ALL CREATURES GREAT AND SMALL

'What's that?'

They stopped still, and listened hard. There was a babbling noise, almost like a human laughing. It sounded like it came from the treetops, though not too close.

'Chimpanzees, probably,' said Gabs a moment later. 'That's what it sounds like. Hope we don't bump into any. They can be a real nuisance.'

'A nuisance how?'

But Gabs didn't answer.

Morning had turned to afternoon. It was now three o'clock. Gabs had been right. The rainwater had soon evaporated from their clothes, but Zak still wasn't dry as the sweat continued to pour from his body. He felt dirty. Greasy. And *very* thirsty.

Every forty-five minutes or so, Raf would stop, having found a particular kind of vine in his path. 'Fresh water vine,' he explained to Zak the first time he located one. 'In some parts of Africa they call it "tourist skin" because its skin peels away like tourists' in the sun.' Sure enough, the outer layer of the vine was coming away in sections, like damp wallpaper. Raf would cut strips of vine from the plant and hand them round. Zak soon learned the trick of throwing his head back and holding a cut end of the vine above his mouth, then letting the water trickle in. It didn't totally relieve the burning thirst at the back of his parched throat, but it was better than nothing.

At 16.00hrs, Raf raised his hand again. All four of them stopped. Raf inclined his head slightly. 'I think I can hear water,' he said.

Zak listened very carefully. Sure enough, he could hear a distant trickle somewhere off to their left.

They changed direction, but moved more slowly now. Each time he passed a tree, Raf carved a notch into the bark. Zak didn't have to ask why. Each patch of rainforest looked identical to the next. If they didn't mark their path carefully, they'd never find their way back.

After ten minutes of careful trekking, the water source came into sight. It was a stream about two metres wide, but fast flowing. A gap in the canopy above let beams of sunlight in, which reflected off the water like twinkling diamonds. It was beautiful and Zak couldn't stop looking at it. The others were right by him, all three of them equally stunned.

Then Zak heard a roar.

It was a terrifying sound. Low, throaty and snarling. It shattered the stillness of the jungle and made him start violently. His brain screamed at him to run, but it was as if his muscles had turned to ice. His stomach was in his throat. He looked desperately around, trying to find out what animal had made that ferocious, angry sound. It had come from the opposite side of the stream, but at first Zak couldn't see anything. Whatever beast had just snarled its warning at them, it was too well camouflaged . . .

'*Don't move a muscle . . .*' Gabs hissed.

Malcolm was either not listening or had decided to ignore her. He turned away from the stream and was obviously about to run.

Gabs grabbed him and held him fast. '*Do what I say.*'

And while this was going on, Zak's eyes finally picked out the creature. He had only ever seen leopards in pictures. But he immediately recognized the shape of the head and the distinctive spots. It was crouching low, mostly covered by foliage, so that only its head and its lean, muscular shoulders were really visible about five metres from the far bank of the stream.

Zak felt his eyes lock with the cat's, and in that exact moment the leopard roared again, revealing a full set of adult teeth, like white daggers set in the pink hilt of its jaw. And again, Zak's brain screamed at him to run.

But Gabs was speaking again, her voice little more than a breath. She sounded like she was trying not to move her lips any more than necessary.

'If we run,' she whispered, 'it *will* chase us. It's a hunter. That's what hunters do. Stay *absolutely* still. Don't frighten it, or startle it. And don't maintain eye contact – it will take that as a challenge.'

Instantly, Zak ripped his gaze away from the leopard. He could still see it from the corner of his eye, though – a yellow and black blur nestled in the dark green foliage.

Seconds passed. They felt like hours. Zak forced himself to breathe, slowly and steadily, but he could feel the tremors as he inhaled.

The leopard stayed perfectly still. So did the humans.

The only noise was the rushing of the stream.

Movement.

Zak couldn't help his eyes flickering towards the leopard. He saw the lithe, sinewy body turning 180 degrees as the big cat slunk away into the forest.

Nobody moved or even spoke for a good thirty seconds.

It was Raf who finally broke the silence. 'We need to drink and wash, then get away from the water,' he said very quietly. 'It's obviously a watering hole, and that leopard won't be the only animal that uses it.'

'What if it comes back?' Malcolm had an edge of panic in his voice. His glasses were wonky on his face, and had steamed up slightly.

'I don't think it will. It doesn't want a fight any more than we do. Don't drink the water till I've checked a few metres upstream for dead animals.'

Raf started walking carefully towards the stream. Zak was reluctant to follow – the roar of the leopard was still echoing in his ears and he could still see those sharp teeth in his mind – but his throat was parched; he needed water. A minute later, when Raf had announced it safe, he was kneeling by the river bank, filling his cupped hands with cool water and glugging it back.

He had just swallowed his third mouthful of water when he felt a sharp pain in the side of his abdomen. '*Ouch!*' he hissed. His fingers felt towards the location of the pain. There was a bulge beneath his shirt, the size of a golf ball.

Gingerly, he lifted the shirt up.

It looked like a slug, only bigger. And it was clamped fast to his skin! As Zak lifted his shirt a bit higher, he realized that although it was the biggest, it wasn't the only one. There were eight more of these slug-like creatures, each the size of his thumbnail, suckered onto his skin.

'Er, Gabs,' he said quietly. The other three were all bending down and drinking. '*Gabs!*'

She looked over her shoulder, her eyes narrowed and she stood up. 'OK, sweetie,' she said. 'Try not to panic. They're leeches. They probably attached themselves to you when you brushed past them in the bush.'

Malcolm was looking at Zak's abdomen with wide eyes. He scrambled to raise his own shirt and a look of relief passed his face when he saw nothing, but then he frowned. Bending down, he rolled up his right trouser leg. Sure enough, four or five of the revolting little beasts had stuck themselves to his skin. He whimpered and tried to pull one of them off. It wouldn't shift. 'Get off!' he shouted. '*Get them off me!*'

'Leave it,' Gabs said sharply. 'They'll fall off by themselves when they've drunk enough blood.'

Malcolm turned white.

'She's right, mate,' Raf added. 'They're not as bad as they look. I saw one in Borneo once, had eight big teeth and feeds off the mucus up your nose . . .'

'*Raf!*' Gabs said. 'That's *not* helpful. Seriously, Malcolm, we've probably all got them. They'll have fallen off by nightfall.' She pointed at the especially large leech on Zak's side. 'But that's a bull leech. It'll get three times bigger than that if we let it, and could hurt a lot. We need to deal with it.'

Zak felt a bit faint as he nodded and lowered his shirt over the bull leech. 'How?' he asked.

'We'll burn it off. But let's find somewhere to make camp first. It'll be dark in a couple of hours and it'll take us that long to make a shelter.' She turned to Raf. 'We should get away from the water before feeding time.'

Raf nodded and, wordlessly, led them back up the way they'd come.

Zak felt as though his whole body was crawling with creatures as they navigated from tree notch to tree notch, and he could see that Malcolm, up ahead, was trembling. The patch of skin where the bull leech was sucking his blood throbbed painfully. He resisted touching it through his shirt to see how fat it was getting.

Keep your mind on the jungle, he told himself as

they continued to trek. *Don't let your concentration lapse*.

Twenty minutes passed before Raf stopped again. They found themselves in a small clearing, about five metres by five. The canopy overhead was still thick, but the ground was fairly clear. The trees all around were covered with large palm leaves. 'Wait here,' Raf said, before disappearing into the jungle again. He returned a couple of minutes later. 'Cruz's path is about thirty metres away,' he said. 'We're still on the ridge line, so water can't run down towards us.' He bent over, scraped some leaves away from a patch of ground and touched the earth. 'Dry,' he said. 'We'll be OK here if there's another rainstorm.'

Zak looked up. There were no dangerous-looking branches, no trees that seemed likely to come tumbling down on them. 'No deadfall,' he said.

Raf nodded his agreement. 'How's that leech?' he asked.

Zak carefully lifted his shirt. He saw, to his horror, that the bull leech had almost doubled in size. So too had the smaller leeches. He couldn't help wondering if he had any blood left.

'Let's get a fire going,' Raf said. 'Zak, Gabs, we need dry wood. Malcolm, stay with me. We'll cut down some palm leaves to make a shelter.'

After the rainstorm they'd had, Zak didn't much

fancy their chances of finding dry wood. But in fact, in this elevated position, it was plentiful. That didn't make collecting it easy. 'Just stick to the edge of the clearing, keeping us in view, and careful what you pick up,' Gabs told him. 'Snakes like to hide in the shade of log piles. Don't pick up a puff adder by mistake.'

Zak gave her a sick look, then went about his business very cautiously.

Fifteen minutes later, each had collected an armful of wood and Raf had constructed the frame of a shelter. It was the shape of an A-frame tent, made from long, straight branches lashed together with natural cordage that he had stripped from a tree, and only just big enough for the four of them to lie under it. Raf and Malcolm had collected a pile of massive palm leaves, each of them almost Zak's height. They were splitting them down the middle then laying them, fronds down, across the shelter, like tiles on a roof.

'It's not much,' Raf said, 'but it'll keep the rain off us. Let's get that fire going.'

Zak was glad of the hip-flask full of petrol. By dribbling some of it over a nest of twigs he was able to get their fire kindled in next to no time. 'Keep it small,' Gabs told him. 'It'll be easier to control. We don't need much.' Zak nodded his agreement and started laying slightly larger bits of wood over the little blaze in a wigwam formation. Minutes later, the fire was flickering thirty centimetres high.

'Let's have a look at that leech now, sweetie,' Gabs said.

Zak raised his shirt again. The disgusting, slug-like creature was larger than a tennis ball now and its black-grey skin glistened unpleasantly. While Zak was looking at it, one of the smaller leeches suddenly fell off his skin, leaving an ugly red welt with a small pinprick in the centre where it had sucked at his blood.

Gabs took a thin twig and stabbed one end into the heart of the fire. Thirty seconds later she pulled it out. The tip was glowing red hot. 'Stay still, sweetie,' she murmured. Then she pressed the burning tip into the flesh of the bull leech. It squirmed suddenly. Zak winced as the pain suddenly grew worse, but Gabs kept the burning stick firmly against the leech. In a matter of seconds, it popped off Zak's flesh and flopped to the ground. Instantly, Zak stamped his heel on it. The leech exploded in a squelch of innards and Zak's own blood. Then Gabs removed the remaining leeches, which fell off at the slightest touch of the hot twig.

Malcolm had rolled up his trouser leg and was looking in disgust at his own leeches. They too had doubled in size. Gabs walked over to him and, still using the same burning twig, popped them all off.

'Better?' Gabs asked him.

Malcolm nodded so fast that he had to stop his glasses falling off his face.

'Do you want me to do you?' Zak asked.

Gabs shook her head. 'I think I got away with it,' she said.

'Where's Raf?'

They looked around. There was no sign of him, but Gabs didn't look worried. 'He's probably gone off to find some food for us all. Come here, Malcolm, I want to look at that wound of yours.'

Malcolm sat by the fire. He looked in a bad way; all the colour had drained from his already pale face, and he seemed to be trembling. He refused to look Gabs in the eye as she carefully undid the makeshift dressing to examine his wounded elbow.

The sight of it turned Zak's stomach. The gash itself looked fairly clean, but the flesh was raw and glistening. Worst of all, it seemed to be moving. He took a closer look. He could see four – no, five – tiny maggots wriggling around in the gore.

'Oh my . . .'

'What is it?' Malcolm demanded. '*What is it? What is it?*' He wriggled his arm free of Gabs's grip and held the elbow up at an awkward angle so he could see it. His eyes bulged. 'Get them off me,' he screeched, looking at Zak in desperation. '*Get them off me!*'

'No,' Gabs said sharply. She grabbed Malcolm's wrist again, holding it firm. 'Listen carefully, Malcolm. I know it's not very nice, but at the moment those maggots are your best friends. They only eat dead and decaying flesh. They're keeping the wound nice and clean for you. I'm not saying it won't get infected. It's very likely, in this temperature and humidity. But removing the maggots will only make it worse.'

Malcolm stared at her like she was insane.

'She's right, mate,' Zak said quietly. 'We'll clean it properly when we have medical supplies. But for now . . .'

Malcolm's chin drooped to his chest in defeat. Looking sick, he said nothing, but allowed Gabs to bind the wound again.

She was just finishing up when Raf reappeared. He was carrying what looked like a big lump of tree bark. 'Anyone hungry?' he asked brightly.

Zak watched him suspiciously as he sauntered over, and joined them sitting round the fire. He rested the lump of bark on his crossed legs.

Zak peered in. He wished he hadn't. It was a seething cauldron of bloated white grubs, not unlike the maggots in Malcolm's elbow, only ten times fatter.

'Palm grubs,' Raf said. 'Fantastic source of protein. Actually, they're a delicacy in some parts of the world. I was pretty lucky to find them.'

There was a stunned silence round the camp fire. Then Malcolm shot to his feet and stormed over to the edge of the clearing.

'You don't have to eat them raw,' Raf shouted. 'I'll cook them if you like!'

Malcolm folded his arms and stared out into the jungle with his back to them.

Raf looked at Zak and Gabs, his eyes wide with innocence. Gabs's expression was flinty. 'Was it something I said?' he asked.

When night falls in the jungle, it falls quickly. You need to be ready.

Zak was surprised by how suddenly the darkness surrounded them. One moment the sound of the insects was deafening as they struck up their evening chorus. The four of them huddled around their little fire, which Raf kept going with lumps of moss to create smoke. 'It'll keep some of the mosquitoes away,' he'd said. Maybe, but Zak still felt like he was being eaten alive.

The next moment it was dark. The insects had

risen to the top of the jungle canopy. Everything was silent.

They fed the small fire from the pile of wood they'd collected. It was more welcome for its light than for its heat. Zak looked at the tired faces of his companions, and realized they all needed to sleep. Especially Malcolm, who nursed his wounded arm and was looking paler by the minute.

'We'll keep watch in two-hour sessions,' Raf said when Zak suggested sleep to him. 'I'll go first, then Gabs, then you. I think we'll have a good twelve hours of darkness, so that means two watches each.' Nobody questioned why he hadn't included Malcolm in the rota. He was staring into the heart of the fire, and didn't look like he'd even heard them.

An animal screeched nearby. Zak started, then drew a deep breath. 'How much further do you think we have to go?' he asked.

'Hard to say, without knowing our destination. But wherever Cruz was headed, it can't be far. Nobody takes a vehicle a very long way off-road through primary jungle. It's just too difficult. My guess is we'll catch up with him tomorrow.' Raf's eyes narrowed. 'I'm looking forward to asking our young drug lord a few questions.'

Zak said nothing. The thought of seeing Cruz again knotted his stomach more than anything the jungle could throw at him. And he didn't share Raf's calm eagerness. Cruz was clever. *Very* clever. Whatever the next day held, it was unlikely to be straightforward.

And very likely to be dangerous.

He felt Gabs's hand on his shoulder. 'Get some sleep, sweetie,' she said. 'You too, Malcolm. We'll wake you when the time comes.'

Zak nodded. He pushed himself to his feet and walked over to the A-frame shelter, where he stretched himself out on the ground, his head at the fire end. Malcolm did the same, lying right next to him, uncomfortably close. Within minutes, Zak's companion was asleep.

Zak, though, found it harder to nod off on this uncomfortable ground, with so many thoughts and worries whizzing through his head. He rolled onto his front. Beyond the fire, at the edge of the clearing, he saw Raf and Gabs standing apart, talking quietly. He wondered what was so secret that they had to say it out of earshot, and for a moment he resented them.

But then a wave of tiredness crashed un-expectedly over him. In seconds, he was asleep.

He woke with a start. Gabs was shaking him gently.

He sat up, half expecting to be back on St Peter's

Crag, and not understanding where he really was. Then it all came flooding back, and his stomach knotted itself again.

'What time is it?' he breathed. The inside of his mouth was dry, and he felt caked in dried sweat.

'Midnight,' Gabs said.

Zak crawled out of the shelter. He noticed that Raf was sleeping soundly on the other side of Malcolm. He brushed himself down, then nodded at Gabs who took his place in the shelter. Then he stepped over to the fire and sat by it, cross-legged, glad of the warmth now, even though it was still humid in the jungle.

He couldn't see the edges of the clearing, which freaked him out. Sitting by the glow of the flickering fire, he felt that a million eyes could be watching him, while he would never see anyone – or anything. He let the flickering blaze die down a little, and sat for twenty minutes by the glowing embers, lost in thought, trying to drive images of snarling leopards and gruesome warning dolls from his mind.

Then he shook himself back to reality. The fire was very low and he needed to feed it. He pushed himself back up to his feet and stepped five paces towards the pile of wood he and Gabs had collected. He bent down in the darkness to grab a piece.

He knew, as soon as his fingers came in contact with it, that he hadn't touched a log. It was dry and smooth, and had a little give to it, like a piece of hard rubber.

And it hissed.

Zak snapped his hand away, just in time to hear a sudden slithering sound. He could just make out the shadow of a snake's head rearing up.

He froze.

Time stood still.

The snake hissed again and Zak's blood thumped harder through his veins.

Should he run? Get to the other side of the fire. No. He would startle the snake, make it more likely to strike. And he knew he couldn't outrun it.

He was holding his breath, unwilling to make even the slightest sound or movement.

His pumping blood was ice cold. It was going to strike any second. Surely . . .

Movement. The snake was lowering its body.

Zak heard the soft shimmer of scales rubbing together. The dark, reptilian shadow moved like oozing treacle. It slid away from the log pile, towards Zak himself. With a sound like a knife being sharpened on a steel, it slid between Zak's feet. He felt it brush his shoe. Very slowly, he looked over his shoulder. The snake was a good metre and a half long and no thicker than a Smarties tube. Now it was edging round the remains of the fire and off out into the clearing.

Zak exhaled very slowly. Every limb was trembling. He stood there for a full minute before he even dared to move. Now he could hardly bring himself to take another log from the woodpile. Not without knowing *exactly* what he was touching.

What was it Gabs had said before they set out from the landing strip? *You need to think before you do anything.*

Good advice for life. But excellent advice, he now realized, in the jungle.

He looked around. The AK-47 with the Maglite taped to the body was lying a couple of metres from the fire. He picked it up, then shone the torch's beam in the direction of the wood pile. By the bright light he satisfied himself that there were no more unwanted guests. Then he grabbed a couple more bits of wood and set them back on the fire.

He settled down again, still shaking. Morning couldn't come quickly enough.

10

PRUSIK

The mosquitoes, hovering above the canopy, announced the arrival of dawn minutes before the sunlight reached the forest floor. But Zak was still awake, his head filled with thoughts of long, thin snakes and short, fat leeches.

Raf was stoking more moss on the fire to make smoke.

Zak decided not to mention the snake. Both Raf and Gabs seemed edgy, and he didn't see the sense in giving them anything more to worry about.

'At least we made it till morning without any more rain,' he said.

Raf grunted.

'Does that *really* keep insects away?' Zak asked, pointing at the moss. He showed Raf his arm, which was covered with angry, purple welts. 'They've had a pretty good go at me.'

'It would be worse without the smoke,' Raf said quietly as the fire began to billow. 'Probably.' He looked over to where Gabs and Malcolm were still asleep in the shelter. 'I meant what I said last night,' Raf continued. 'I think there's a good chance we'll catch up with Cruz today. If we do, make sure you don't act without thinking. I know you two have a history, but just keep your wits about you, OK?'

Zak nodded.

'And I'm still worried about Malcolm. If that wound gets infected, he'll go downhill fast.' He swore under his breath. 'I don't know how we ended up babysitting him in the jungle. Something's not right about him.'

Zak gave him a half smile. It was true that Malcolm was rude. True that he was hardly the kind of kid you wanted hanging around when the going got tough. But Raf and Gabs had taken a dislike to him from the get-go. Malcolm was OK when you got to know him. Kind of. Back in London, he'd shown that he had guts. And he was no doubt cursing his bad luck at being here just as much as Raf and Gabs were cursing their bad luck at having him along.

'I'll look out for him—' Zak said, but he was

interrupted by another sound. An excited babbling. He had heard the same sound yesterday, and Gabs had said it was chimpanzees. Now it was much closer. Zak looked up. In the half light of the dawn, he could just make out dark shapes in the treetops above. Four of them? Maybe five? It was difficult to tell.

He heard Raf curse under his breath. 'Wake the others,' he instructed. 'We need to get moving.'

As he spoke, something came crashing out of the trees. It landed directly on the smouldering fire, kicking up a cloud of ash and sparks and forcing Zak to jump away. He just had time to see that it was an old branch, about the length of a man's forearm, before a second branch – twice as long as the first – came hurtling through the air. It whacked Zak on his right shoulder.

'*Ow!*' he shouted. 'What the . . .?'

Suddenly the noise of the chimpanzees was twice as loud. It was like mad, hysterical laughter. Sticks and branches were raining from the canopy, thudding down on the forest floor.

Zak ran to the shelter, where Gabs and Malcolm were already waking up to the noise.

'What is it?' Gabs asked, her eyes keen.

'Chimps,' said Zak in disgust.

Gabs's lips thinned. She looked like she wanted to

tell somebody off. But then a branch flew straight into the shelter, missing her head by inches. She grabbed Malcolm and pulled him towards one edge of the clearing, just as some kind of fruit, the size of a small melon, splatted onto the ground half a metre from where Zak was standing.

'Thanks a bunch!' Zak shouted. Then he jumped out of the way as two more fruits pelted towards him. He looked over at Raf, who was hurriedly stamping out the fire and sprinkling dirt over it. Zak ran over to help him. It took another twenty seconds to extinguish the fire to Raf's satisfaction. Then they sprinted to where Gabs and Malcolm were standing, ignoring the chimps' missiles all the while.

They plunged back into the thick forest, settling easily into their marching order of the previous day. For a moment, Zak thought the chimps were following them across the treetops. But after a few minutes, the sound of their babbling faded. Once more, Zak and his companions were on their own.

He was very hungry. They hadn't eaten properly for two days, after all. It was a great relief when, after about an hour of trekking, Raf stopped next to a tree with a familiar fruit. 'Mango,' he said.

'Bit strange to find it growing here, isn't it?'

'Not really.' Raf looked around, as though he was searching for something. After a few seconds he saw it: a dilapidated old shack, only just visible about twenty metres into the forest. It had clearly been deserted for decades. 'An old hunter's house, probably. Someone ate a mango here years ago and left the seeds. You don't have to *make* things grow in the jungle, you just have to *let* them. Anyway, we're lucky nothing else got to it first.' They picked the fruit, and even Malcolm ate greedily, allowing the juice to dribble down his chin and smear his fingers. Then they moved on, relentlessly, through the jungle.

It was about midday when Raf suddenly lifted up one hand. They stopped immediately. Raf pointed to a tree about seven metres from his position and, with a shudder, Zak saw another straw man with a tiny animal skull pinned to the bark. And five metres beyond it, another tree, with another warning sign.

They huddled together. 'I think we're close,' Raf breathed. 'Have you noticed how the vegetation has been getting a little thinner?'

Now he mentioned it, Zak saw he was right. Over the last hour or so, Raf hadn't needed to use his knife so much to cut a path through the forest. Now they had a good ten or fifteen metres of visibility.

'Zak, Malcolm, I think you two should wait here

while Gabs and I scout ahead. Gabs, give Zak your weapon.'

Gabs handed over the AK-47 she'd confiscated from the guy at their pit stop. 'Locked and loaded, sweetie,' she murmured in warning. 'Don't use it unless it's an emergency. It'll be heard for miles around.'

Zak accepted the weapon – he'd learned how to handle it safely back at St Peter's Crag – then bent down and examined the ground beneath the tree that played host to the first straw man. It was dry, and there were no insects that he could see. He settled down with his back against the trunk, the assault rifle laid over his crossed legs. Malcolm joined him.

Raf and Gabs slipped off into the jungle. Within seconds, Zak could neither see nor hear them. It was as if they had melted away.

Malcolm was trembling slightly. He kept glancing across his shoulder at the maggoty wound on his elbow. Zak thought it best to take his mind off it.

'Bet you're wishing you never came,' he said quietly as they sat with their backs against the tree.

Malcolm took off his glasses and started cleaning them with his dirty T-shirt. He said nothing.

'When all this is finished, I can try to get in touch with your cousin . . .'

'I don't want to talk about it, OK?' Malcolm said sharply.

A pause.

'I know what it's like to be on your own, Malcolm,' Zak said in a very quiet voice. 'I know what it's like to miss people. Seriously, if you can't talk to me about these things, who *can* you talk to?'

'Which bit of "I don't want to talk about it" don't you understand?' Malcolm snapped.

Zak fell silent.

They sat quietly for ten minutes, the bad feeling between them festering.

Then, from behind, Zak felt a hand over his mouth. His body went rigid. A quick glance told him that Malcolm's mouth had been covered too. He tried to shout out, but his voice was muffled.

'It's me, sweetie,' said Gabs's voice behind him in little more than a whisper.

Relief flooded over him. His body relaxed and Gabs's hand dropped from his mouth. She and Raf walked round to face them, then crouched down to their level.

'We're closer than we thought,' Gabs breathed. 'Fifty metres, max.'

'What have you found?' Zak asked.

'Come and see. Tread very softly. You too, Malcolm.'

Zak's heart was pumping hard again as they continued carefully through the jungle. Each time a twig snapped underfoot, he winced, as though it could be heard for miles around. In truth they were very quiet, and after ten minutes Raf signalled at them to stop again. He pointed. 'There,' he whispered.

Zak peered through the forest. Twenty metres away he could make out a wall.

It had two layers. On the outside was a thick, wire mesh with diamond-shaped holes which were big enough to see through, but too small to get your fingertips into – the sort of thing that a sturdy fence might be made from. Only this was much higher than your average fence – twelve metres at least. Inside the mesh, but touching it, was a secondary wall made from long, straight wooden logs. These were not so high – maybe only seven or eight metres – but they completely obscured his view through the mesh.

'What's going on in there?' Zak whispered.

Raf shrugged. 'The walls are too high. We can't see over. And I don't fancy trying to climb any of these trees, do you?'

Zak looked around. Raf had a point. All the trees in the vicinity were very tall and straight with thick trunks. Their branches only started spreading from the trunk about ten metres above the ground. They were impossible to climb.

Malcolm had slumped, dejected, at the foot of one of these trees. 'Look after him,' Gabs said quietly. 'I'm going to try and get a closer look.'

'Wait,' Zak said sharply. 'It would be much better to get into the treetops, wouldn't it?'

'Didn't you hear Raf?' Gabs said, with a hint of impatience. 'They're too high.'

But Zak shook his head. 'No they're not,' he said. 'I've got an idea.'

Zak needed a stick first of all. It only took a minute to find a suitable one; it was about fifty centimetres long, perfectly straight and no thicker than his forefinger. He peeled off the rough bark, then asked Raf for his knife. While his Guardian Angels watched with expressions of deep suspicion, he carefully cut a perfect cross into one flat end of the stick, taking each of the two incisions about five centimetres into the wood.

From his rucksack he took the small notebook they'd found in the plane. He'd had no idea what good this would be in a survival situation, but he was glad to have it now. He tore out two pages, then carefully folded each one in half then positioned them at right angles. Then he slid them, corner to corner, into the incisions at the end of his stick. He nodded with satisfaction. It was starting to look like an arrow, and this makeshift feathering would help it fly straight.

He took the coil of fishing twine from the survival pack and started winding one end of it around the end of the arrow, just above the point where his feathering ended. This would keep the paper in place, and would also fix the twine to the arrow. He took the rope from his pack and tied the other end of the twine to it. Then he turned his attention back to the arrow itself.

Zak carved a groove around the circumference of the stick, just below the feathering. Next, he removed the lace from his right trainer and tied a knot in one end. He threaded the knotted end of the lace around the groove, stretched the remainder along the length of the arrow, and wrapped the other end around his hand. The knot kept the lace in place, but it would unravel as soon as he catapulted it up into the treetops.

He turned to his Guardian Angels. 'Get the idea?'

'Very good, sweetie,' Gabs murmured admiringly. Even Malcolm looked quite impressed, though he looked away quickly when Zak caught his eye.

Zak looked up and raised the arrow above his

head. He positioned it at an incline of about sixty degrees, his eyes fixed on the lowest branch of a tree about ten metres away.

He squinted slightly, then flicked his wrist.

Kept steady by the paper feathering and catapulted by the boot lace, the arrow shot from his hand. There was a faint whistle as it lifted the fishing twine into the air behind it, before arching over the branch Zak had been aiming at. As the twine hit the tree, the arrow fell, hanging limply over the branch.

Zak picked up the coil of rope along with what remained of the twine, then carried both over to the tree. Standing directly underneath the suspended arrow, he gently eased more twine upwards, so the arrow gradually lowered back down to earth. When it was within reach, he started tugging that instead.

The twine tightened. Now, as Zak pulled, the twine yanked the rope to which it was attached up and over the branch, then back down to earth. In a minute or so, Zak was holding two ends of the rope, which was looped snugly over the branch ten metres in the air.

There was now no need to explain to Raf and Gabs what to do. They each took one end of the rope. Raf tied his end round the base of the tree trunk to secure it while Gabs tied hers to a thick tree root that was emerging from the jungle floor just a few metres away.

Raf looked up. 'Nice work, Zak.' He squinted a little. 'It's not the thickest branch in the world, though. I'm not sure it'll take my weight, or Gabs's. I think you'll need to be the one to climb the rope. When you get up there, you can loop it over something sturdier.'

Zak nodded. He was happy with that. He'd climbed ropes in the school gymnasium back in the day. How different could this be? He stretched out one hand to grab the rope.

'Hold on, buddy,' Raf said. 'Have you ever heard of a prusik knot?'

'A what?'

There were still three or four metres of slack rope where Gabs had tied her end to the root. Raf took the knife and cut it off, then cut it again into two. Wordlessly, he walked over to Zak. 'Let me see your belt,' he said.

Zak lifted his T-shirt, and allowed Raf to tie the rope around his belt in a configuration Zak hadn't ever seen before.

Raf then tied the other end to the climbing rope. 'I'd kill for a carabiner,' he said.

'A what?' Zak asked.

'It's a metal loop. Makes this stuff much easier.

Remind me to take you climbing when we get back home.' He indicated the knot where the two ropes were tied. 'This is the prusik,' he said. 'You can slide it up the climbing rope when there's no weight on it, but it'll hold tight when there is.' He tied a loop at the end of the second piece of rope, then tied the other end to the climbing rope with another prusik knot. 'Put your foot in here,' he said, indicating the loop.

Zak did as he was told.

'Now,' Raf instructed. 'Push your foot down and move the top knot up the rope. Then take your weight off the foot knot and move that up. Keep doing it and you'll get up to the branch in no time.'

Zak slung his rucksack – now only containing the spotting scope – over his shoulder, then did as Raf had told him. Little by little, he worked his way up the rope. In less than a minute he had left the ground far behind and was grabbing hold of the branch supporting his climbing rope.

He looked towards the fencing. Even at ten metres up, there was still too much tree foliage to see through the mesh clearly. He'd need to get higher. No problem. The branches were more numerous here. He would be able to clamber quickly and silently up into the treetop.

He looked down. Raf and Gabs were untying the

rope from its supports and Zak pulled it up so he could loop it round a thicker branch, then started climbing higher.

After only thirty seconds, his head emerged above the canopy of the jungle. The sight was awe-inspiring: deep blue sky, but with threatening rainclouds boiling somewhere in the distance. Green jungle as far as his eye could see, interrupted only by a lazy azure river about a mile away, snaking into the distance. Brightly coloured birds chirped and flittered above the trees.

But Zak quickly pulled his attention from all that, and looked towards the compound they'd stumbled over.

He could tell at once that something strange was happening there.

11

LATIFAH

It was some sort of camp.

Zak realized immediately, without fully knowing how, that the high walls and barbed wire were not there to keep people *out*. They were there to keep people *in*.

The log-and-mesh fencing formed a rough circle. The distance from one edge of the circle to the other was about 300 metres. Inside was a series of huts with corrugated iron roofs. There were eight or nine, arranged in no particular order that Zak could make out. On the far side, almost exactly opposite Zak's observation tree, was a large gate. It was the only way in or out of the camp and was guarded by two armed figures, one on either side. They had headsets that covered one ear, and a boom mike by the side of their mouths. This was clearly how they were communicating across the camp.

Zak checked the position of the sun. It was behind him. Good. He could use the scope without the sun reflecting in the lens and giving away his position. He put it to his eye and focused in on two other guards towards the centre of the camp.

They were no older than Zak himself. Each carried an assault rifle and wore the same sort of headset as the guards at the gate. They wore mismatched clothing – camouflage vests, black T-shirts, khaki trousers, bandanas. And they both had scars on their cheeks. Just like the kids who had abducted him back in Jo'burg.

Kids.

The camp was full of them, and not just the guards. They sat in rows between the huts, cross-legged. To their left, Zak could just make out piles of soft toys. Dolls, bears, elephants. There were also packets of white powder. Zak found he was holding his breath as he homed in on one child. He couldn't see the kid's face, but guessed from the long, matted hair that she was a girl. She took a cuddly bear in one hand, and a packet of white powder in the other, stuffed the powder inside the bear, then rested it on her crossed legs. Zak couldn't see her hands, but could tell from the movement of her elbows that she was sewing.

A minute passed. The girl placed her handiwork

to her right, then started all over again, stuffing another toy and sewing it up.

Zak counted thirty-two children doing exactly the same work. The piles on their left grew smaller. The piles on their right grew larger. And all the while, the guards walked among them, carrying assault rifles and wearing insolent, aggressive looks on their scarred faces.

One of the workers put up his hand. Instantly, two of the armed guards stalked towards him. They spoke for a moment, then one of the guards whacked the worker hard against the side of his head with the butt of his rifle. The other guard shouted something, his voice curt and aggressive, the sound reaching Zak above the treetops. The kid sat up again, head bowed, and carried on working. The two guards laughed and continued their rounds.

Zak had to fight back an urge not to yell out at these two bullies from where he was. But he reminded himself why he was here. He'd be doing nobody any favours by getting captured now.

Then came a commotion on the far side of the camp, just outside the gates where there was a rough jungle path leading up to them. It was clear for about twenty metres, then it disappeared into the rainforest. Approaching the camp along this road, Zak saw a group of people. He trained his scope on them.

There were eleven of them, all young boys with the exception of the man at the front. He had dark skin and grey hair tied back in dreadlocks, and Zak could make out a sour, arrogant expression on the man's face. And although he had never seen him before, he felt a strange sensation as he watched him. Almost like recognition. It made his spine tingle unpleasantly.

The sound of more shouting drifted up into the treetops. The guards inside the camp gate conferred with each other for a moment, then one of them opened the gate while the other knelt down in the firing position, his gun aimed squarely at whoever was about to walk in. When he saw the man with dread-locks, however, he lowered his gun. The newcomers filed inside and the guards fastened the gate again.

Zak continued to scan the camp. He hadn't yet seen what he was looking for. He zeroed in on as many faces as he could find, but not one of them belonged to Cruz. There was no sign of his nemesis, no sign that they had successfully closed in on him.

Birdsong. It came from the forest floor. It repeated three times before Zak tore his eyes away from the camp, realizing that it wasn't a real bird, but one of his companions down below. Almost regretfully, he lowered his scope.

Then, quickly, he raised it to his eyes again.

He had seen a glimpse of someone different. A woman. She had white skin and her hair was in a bob. She had stepped out from one of the buildings with one of the young guards at her side. But now that Zak looked again, she was gone.

He felt himself frowning. Had he recognized that woman's face? He thought so. He racked his brain, trying to place her, but he couldn't. Not for the life of him.

More fake birdsong from the forest floor. Zak stowed his scope, then arranged the rope over a thicker branch and lowered the ends down to the ground. He gave it a minute for Raf and Gabs to secure the ends, then prusiked back down from the treetops.

'Well?' Gabs whispered.

Zak explained what he'd seen.

'But no sign of Cruz?' Raf asked.

Zak shook his head. 'None.'

'We *need* to know if he's there,' Gabs said. She gave Raf a serious kind of look. 'I'm going in.'

'No way,' said Raf. Gabs raised a dangerous eyebrow. 'The camp is full of kids, Gabs. If anyone sees you, you'll stick out like a . . . well, like an adult in a camp full of kids.'

Gabs's face grew stony. 'Before you even *suggest* it,' she said, 'we're *not* sending Zak in there.'

'It's our only option,' Raf said. 'Unless you think we should send Malcolm in.'

They looked over at Malcolm, who was slumped against the base of a tree, sweat pouring off him, glasses slipping down his nose. He looked like he was talking to himself.

'Of *course* not,' Gabs hissed. 'But if you think I'm going to sit around out here while Zak risks—'

'Er, excuse me,' Zak interrupted, raising one finger. 'Do I get a say in this?'

Gabs glowered at him.

'It makes sense for me to go,' he said. 'If I wait for nightfall, I'll have a chance of getting over the walls unseen.'

'They've got personal comms,' Gabs objected. 'You saw it with your own eyes. It'll only take one of them to see you and the whole camp will know you're there.'

'I can help with that,' Malcolm said in a small voice.

Gabs's face grew even darker as the three of them turned round to look at him. '*How?*' she almost growled.

Malcolm reached inside his rucksack. He pulled out the tangled mess of circuit board and wires that Zak had seen him pack when they left Jo'burg. 'I made this myself,' he said. His voice trembled slightly, and Zak noticed that his hand was shaking. Was infection setting in? 'I carry it everywhere. You never know when you might need it. Once, I thought someone was following me and I—'

'What *is* it, Malcolm?' Raf interrupted.

Malcolm blinked, then made eye contact, not with Raf but with Zak. 'It's a cellphone jammer,' he said. 'You see, if the guards are using short-wave radio frequencies to talk to each other, I can just set this dial and their radios won't work any more.'

'They'll get suspicious,' Gabs said immediately.

'I don't think so, Gabs,' Raf disagreed. 'Radio comms fail all the time, and for all sorts of reasons. I think it's a good idea, if Malcolm can be sure it'll work.'

'Of *course* it'll work,' Malcolm muttered. He sounded rather offended.

Gabs was looking around almost in desperation now. 'Well, I don't see how he's going to get inside. The walls are too high, the gate's guarded . . .'

'Actually, I've got an idea,' said Raf. 'Zak will be able to scale those walls in a matter of minutes. Easier and quicker than you and me, in fact, because he's lighter.'

Gabs looked from Raf, to Zak, then back to Raf again. '*Fine!*' she hissed. 'Just . . . just . . . *fine!*' She stomped off, fuming, to the edge of the jungle.

Twenty seconds passed before Raf dragged his eyes away from Gabs and turned to Zak. 'Do me a favour, mate,' he said. 'Don't get yourself caught.'

'I wasn't planning to.'

'Good. Because if you do, I'll seriously never hear the end of it.'

As they waited for nightfall, Raf kept busy.

He found two pieces of wood on the forest floor, about the right size for Zak to grip them firmly. Then he took the six-inch nails that had pinned the warning dolls to the trees. With a heavy, flat stone, he hammered one nail through each piece of wood, then bent each one down at a right angle about an inch from the point.

'Hold these,' he told Zak. 'The nails need to point out and down.'

Zak did as he was told.

'You can use these to climb the fencing,' Raf explained. 'Just use the nail to hook onto the holes in the mesh. We kept you in good shape back at the island – you should be strong enough to keep holding them.'

'What if I let go?' Zak asked.

'I wouldn't do that. This isn't really the time and place for a broken leg.'

Point taken, thought Zak.

Like the night before, night fell quickly. This time, though, they had no fire. With the camp just metres away, it would be too much of a risk. But it was far from pitch black. A glow from the camp itself gave Zak and the others just enough light to see by.

Just after midnight, Raf stood up from where they were huddled in a circle. He sniffed the air. 'We're going to get more rain,' he said. 'It'll probably send everyone inside the camp into their buildings. That would be a good time to scale the wall. Agreed?'

Zak nodded. His mouth was dry with fear and excitement. He stood up too, clutching his improvised grappling hooks.

'Remember, Zak. All you need to do is confirm that Cruz is there, then get out. Once we know his location, we can work on our next move.'

Almost instantly they heard the sound of raindrops hitting the canopy. Seconds later, the skies had opened.

It was suddenly too noisy to speak. Zak simply shook Raf's hand and gave Gabs a hug, before dumping his rucksack at her feet – it would only slow him down. She mouthed the words 'Be careful!', then hugged him again. Malcolm was sheltering under his rucksack, fiddling with his short-wave radio jammer. He was paying no attention to Zak, who now hurried through the dark, sodden rainforest towards the clearing where the camp stood.

He was able to approach it with ease, because the tall logs that formed the solid part of the perimeter wall stopped anyone looking out just as well as preventing anyone from looking in. His clothes were saturated now, and water gushed down his face and into his eyes, but he didn't let it slow him down. Clutching his grappling hooks firmly, he stretched both arms out as high as he could and hooked himself onto the mesh fencing.

He felt his biceps flex as he pulled the weight of his own body a few centimetres higher, then loosened his right grappling hook. He stretched up his right arm and hooked onto a higher mesh hole, before repeating the process for his left hand. He peered upwards, squinting against the driving rain that now streamed down his neck. He reckoned he had another five or six metres before he reached the top of the wooden logs. Then he would have about four metres of just mesh. Which meant he'd be on display. He needed to scale it before the rainstorm stopped.

He yanked himself further up. Already, his arms were burning from hauling the weight of his body. But it was a feeling he was used to from the regular, punishing fitness regimes Raf and Gabs had put him through back on St Peter's Crag. There had been times when he'd wondered why it was necessary for them to keep pushing him to the very edge of his ability. Now he understood the reason. He was totally relying on his own strength, and it gave him confidence to know that his fitness levels were high.

The rain started falling more heavily. Zak was awash. It pounded on his head and stung his face, making it difficult to breathe without snorting in water. Still he continued climbing. All his attention was on the hooks, and slotting them correctly into the mesh. A single mistake and he'd be hurtling to the ground, a jumbled mess of broken bones.

His right arm reached a level with the top of the log wall. Very carefully, very slowly, he pulled himself up so that he could peer over the top of the solid, interior part of the wall.

It was difficult to see, because the rain was so thick. But a sudden flash of lightning came to his aid. It lasted only a fraction of a second, but it was enough to tell Zak that Raf had been right. The storm had sent everyone indoors. There didn't even appear to be any guards at the gate.

Grab your chance while you have it, he told himself. *Move!*

Zak started grappling his way up even faster. The

mesh fencing wobbled and he was sure it was making a dreadful noise. He thanked God for the rain: it wasn't just masking him, it was masking any sounds he made.

He was at the top of the fence now, holding on carefully as he raised one precarious leg over the top.

He slipped.

He immediately clamped his left grappling hook against the top line of mesh. He caught himself just in time, but now he was hanging precariously by just his left hand. He gripped at the block of wood for all he was worth. He was sideways on to the mesh fencing now and suddenly the whole sky lit up with another momentary but massive flash of lightning.

He wondered if Raf and Gabs could see him silhouetted against the fence.

Then, suddenly, his heart stopped.

The scene had changed.

Six figures were facing the fence. They were arranged around him in a semicircle, each one about fifteen metres away.

Get out of here!

Zak swung his right arm around, trying to hook the fence. No luck. He was still hanging by one arm.

Another flash of lightning. The figures were still in a semicircle, only this time they were nearer. Ten metres.

They were closing in.

Panic surged through him. He made another desperate attempt to hook the fence with his right hand.

Disaster!

The grappling hook hit the fence at an awkward angle. It fell from his hand.

In what felt like slow motion, he saw it hurtle through the rain-filled air by the light of another streak of lightning. He desperately tried to catch it, and came agonizingly close – he felt the wood brush against his wet fingertips. But then time sped up again, and it tumbled to the earth.

The figures were only five metres away. And two of them had raised their weapons to point in Zak's direction.

Zak scrambled, trying to worm the fingers of his free hand into the small holes of the mesh fencing, but it was impossible. The holes were just too small.

A sudden, more brutal, lashing of rain crashed against him. He felt his left hand slipping. He knew he couldn't hold onto the remaining grappling hook for much longer. Not that it mattered, because any second he expected to hear the retort of an assault rifle firing a round into his body.

A round that would surely kill him.

He looked down. There was a two-metre drop to

the top of the log wall. In the instant before he let go of the remaining hook, he focused on it, leaning his body back towards the mesh so that, when he hit it, he had room to bend his knees and a chance of keeping his balance on the top and not falling the full ten metres to the ground.

His hand finally lost its hold and he fell. His feet slammed against the top of the wall. He was about to topple, but at the last moment steadied himself.

His back was against the mesh now. He was looking into the camp and although it was raining more heavily than ever, he could still see the figures standing in the semicircle below him. One of them stepped forward. He seemed taller than the rest and although Zak couldn't really make out his features, he recognized his gait as he walked.

And he certainly recognized his voice as he shouted above the noise of the thundering rain.

'I'm going to give you a choice, Harry,' Cruz bellowed. Harry Gold was the name he had used back on his first mission when he had infiltrated Cruz's house in Mexico – the name by which Cruz knew Zak. Zak couldn't help feeling a sense of dread when he heard it on his adversary's lips.

Cruz drew a gun.

'Go ahead and shoot me, Cruz,' Zak shouted. If this was the end, he wasn't going to face it begging for his life. 'That's what you want, isn't it?'

'Not just yet, Harry. Not just yet.' Another figure was thrown onto the ground in front of him. 'This is Latifah,' Cruz shouted. 'She's eleven. And, if you don't do as I say, she's dead. I've noticed you have a rather charming reluctance to let innocent people die, so I'm sure you wouldn't want that to happen. My men, on the other hand, would rather enjoy shooting her.'

Silence. The rain pounded down.

'What do you want me to do?' Zak shouted.

'Jump, Harry. Just jump. My men will catch you and then you and I can have a little chat. I'd say it was long overdue, wouldn't you?'

Zak's eyes were flitting left and right. His mind was turning over. What else could he do? What were his other options?

He had none.

Two of Cruz's crew were moving to the bottom of the wall. They had their arms spread out, ready to catch him.

Zak felt his jugular pulsing. Bile in his stomach and in his chest. His clothes heavy with rain, he spread out his own arms, took a deep breath and fell, face forward.

Latifah screamed.

The ground flew up to meet him.

12

DEADFALL

It wasn't a soft landing, but it was a safe one.

Cruz's boys caught Zak with strong arms. But as soon as his fall was broken, they dropped him heavily to the ground and Zak felt the air shoot out of his lungs as his abdomen hit the wet earth. Winded, he gasped for breath.

'Pick him up!' Cruz yelled through the constant noise of the heavy rainfall. 'And get the girl back to the hut.' He had a high-pitched, slightly manic edge to his voice. As though he was excited.

Zak felt a hand grab a clump of his hair and he winced in pain as he was yanked upwards. Once he was on his feet, he saw that his scar-faced assailant had an ugly grin on his face as he twisted the hair tighter and pulled his head back.

Cruz was bang in front of him, his dark

eyes glinting, water streaming down his face.

Zak opened his mouth to say something, but Cruz raised a finger to silence him. 'I want you to hear something,' he said. His voice almost hissed, like the sound of the rain sizzling against the ground all around them.

They didn't have to wait long. Five seconds. Maybe ten. Then the sound of two gunshots rang through the air in quick succession. They came from outside the camp.

From the direction where he had left Raf, Gabs and Malcolm.

Cruz's lip curled into a sneer. 'Nobody's coming to rescue you, my friend.' He bent down, and picked up one of Zak's makeshift grappling hooks from where it had fallen to the ground. 'Pathetic,' he said, before throwing it away and addressing his associates. 'Get him inside.'

Cruz marched quickly towards the largest of the camp buildings. Zak was dragged by his hair in his wake, his mind a whirlwind. He had left three companions back in the jungle. There had been two shots. The conclusion he had to reach was sickening. At least one of his Guardian Angels was dead.

If not both of them.

Zak felt his knees buckle at the thought. Cruz's guards laughed, then continued to drag him roughly into the building, where they threw him once more to the floor.

For a moment, Zak didn't move. He was stunned. Paralysed. He listened to the sound of the rain hammering against the corrugated-iron roof. After thirty seconds he rallied as best he could. Dripping wet, he pushed himself to his knees.

He was in a room about fifteen metres by fifteen. There were no windows, nor any chairs or tables. Wooden crates – perhaps twenty of them – were piled up along one side. At the far end was a bright lamp facing towards Zak. It dazzled him, but as he squinted he could just make out the silhouette of two people behind it. Zak could tell that one of them was Cruz. He was dragging the other person by one arm. As they grew nearer, the features of this second person grew clearer.

It was a woman, about the same height as Cruz, but more solidly built.

White skin. Her hair in a bob.

It was the same person Zak had glimpsed from the treetops. Her face was a picture of terror. Desperately, Zak tried once more to place her. But he simply couldn't.

'Take her outside,' Cruz instructed.

One of his boys took the woman's arms and dragged her out into the rain.

Then Cruz turned to Zak. 'I thought you'd never get here, Harry,' he said.

'What do you mean?'

Cruz barked a short, humourless laugh.

'You're so impressed with your own cleverness,' he said. 'It makes it so easy to lead you around by the nose.'

Zak peered at him. He felt faintly sick. 'What do you mean?'

'You're so *predictable*, Harry. I knew that if I showed my face you'd come sniffing after me. I must say, it was a surprise that you got caught so easily at the toy shop.' He smiled thinly. 'And I suppose you spent all your time in the jungle looking up for deadfall. So typical of you, Harry, to do that and not see what's right in front of your eyes.'

'Maybe you should keep one eye open for deadfall yourself, Cruz. When my friends come to get me, you won't know what's happening till you've been crushed.'

'I really don't think so, old friend. I'm afraid you've done your last Houdini impression. How *did* you break out of the warehouse, by the way?'

'We've all got to have some secrets, Cruz,' Zak barely whispered, unable to keep the fear from his voice. His mind was turning over, trying to get ahead of Cruz, but deep down he knew that somehow his enemy had got the better of him.

Cruz shrugged. 'If you *hadn't* got away, we wouldn't have needed to go through all this pantomime of getting you *here*. Though I must say, that would have been a *bit* of a shame.' He swung one arm around the brightly lit room. 'Do you like my little jungle hideaway? It's been in the family for some time, you know.'

Zak didn't want to reply, but he knew that the longer he could keep Cruz talking, the better. Because if he was talking, he wasn't killing.

'It's charming,' he said.

Cruz gave a bland smile. 'I'd like you to see someone,' he said. He turned to one of his guys. 'Bring him in.'

The scar-faced boy left the building. He returned moments later. This time, he had company.

It was Malcolm.

Zak's companion was also soaking wet. He was trembling. Infection, or terror? His glasses were misted up, but Zak could still make out an expression of utter fear. It wasn't clear, though, whom he was more scared of: Cruz or Zak. His gaze flitted, terrified, from one to the other.

'What the . . .' Zak whispered.

But he didn't finish his sentence. He had noticed something else. Malcolm's guard had carried in another gun. Zak recognized it immediately: Gabs's AK-47 with the Maglite still taped to the body.

He felt unsteady on his feet again. Like he was living in a horrible nightmare, and nothing around him was real.

'Did you not stop to think, Harry – or should I call you Zak? – that Malcolm managed to locate my flight just a little *too* easily?'

Zak paused. 'I know how good he is . . .' he started to say, but again the words died on his lips as he realized how badly he'd been outmanoeuvred.

Cruz gave a sarcastic sigh. 'Such loyalty! No, I'm afraid he knew my flight details all the time. I must say, though, that I wasn't quite convinced that he would be able to send us the signal that you were about to break into the camp. I mean, look at him. He's not very impressive, is he?'

Zak tried to stay calm. 'What signal?' he asked in a level voice.

Cruz pretended to look surprised. 'Jamming our radios, of course. It needed to be something that you wouldn't suspect . . .' His voice trailed off as he looked cruelly at the miserable Malcolm. If he hadn't been bubbling up with anger, Zak might have felt sorry for his former companion. Malcolm was wringing his hands and he refused to catch Zak's eye.

'Why?' Zak breathed.

No answer.

'*WHY?*' he shouted, all the anger bursting out of him.

'Shall we show him why, Malcolm?' Cruz asked.

No reply.

'I'll take that as a yes,' Cruz murmured. He looked over at one of his crew. 'Bring her in.'

Moments later, the frightened woman with the bobbed hair was dragged back into the room, soaking wet and bedraggled.

'Malcolm,' she whispered. She struggled, trying to run towards him, but was held back by her guard.

And then it all clicked in Zak's brain. He knew where he recognized her from.

The photograph in Malcolm's house in Jo'burg.

This was Malcolm's cousin. Matilda. The woman who had looked after him. Perhaps the only person in the world who Malcolm really cared about.

'This is—' Cruz started to say.

'I know who she is,' Zak interrupted him.

For a moment, Cruz looked surprised. Wrong-footed. But he quickly regained his composure. 'It took a little while to persuade Malcolm to reveal her whereabouts, didn't it, Malcolm?'

Malcolm stared, dejected, at the floor.

'But these East Side Boys can be very persuasive. Once I'd abducted her, I knew our little hacker would do whatever I wanted. By which I mean, Harry: bring you to me.'

The woman was crying. Desperate sobs. Cruz wandered up to her and put one hand lightly on her cheek. 'Don't worry,' he whispered, and Zak struggled to hear him over the noise of the thundering rain. 'It's all over now. I have what I want.' He looked over his shoulder at Malcolm. 'The other two, the man and the woman. They're dead?'

Zak felt his stomach twist again. Malcolm didn't move a muscle.

'*Are they dead?*' Cruz bellowed.

Malcolm looked up. There were tears dripping down his face. 'Yes,' he said, his voice wavering as he spoke. 'I stole their gun and shot them, like you told me to. Both of them. They're dead.'

It happened so quickly. Just as Zak felt his whole world imploding, Cruz pulled a gun from inside his clothes. Before Zak could even move, he had placed it up against the head of Malcolm's cousin.

He fired a single shot, the sound of the gunshot making Zak start violently.

The woman's head exploded in a flurry of blood, bone and brain matter.

Cruz walked out of the building, the gun still in his hand.

And Malcolm shrieked, '*NO!*'

It was a desperate, pitiful sound. Like all the pain in the world was distilled into that one, single word.

13

BURIED

The rain had stopped. It was quiet outside. But in Zak's head, it was very, very noisy.

Raf and Gabs: dead.

Malcolm's cousin Matilda: dead.

Malcolm himself was crouched in a far corner of the building, clutching his knees, his head buried in his chest. His whole body shook, as if he was crying. But there was no sound coming from him. He was a silent, quivering wreck. For a moment, Zak felt sorry for him. He had obviously thought he was saving his cousin; he had no idea just how ruthless Cruz could be.

But then Zak remembered the chilling sound of the two gunshots from the rainforest. He pictured Malcolm shooting his Guardian Angels, who had sworn to protect him, and he felt his jaw set firm.

They had bandaged Malcolm's arm and given him antibiotics. That boded well for Malcolm, kind of. It meant they wanted to keep him alive. Zak was by no means sure that the same was true for him.

Three of Cruz's scar-faced guards were loitering by the entrance to the building. The bare skin on their arms was glistening with sweat, and they all carried assault rifles. One of them had dragged Matilda's body out into the camp, and he still had her blood smeared on his hands. It didn't seem to worry him. He was laughing with his friends, and nodding gently in time to the harsh gangsta rap that had started blaring out from somewhere in the camp, even though it was still night.

Zak looked at his own hands. They were shaking. He was scared. More scared than he'd ever been.

He was angry with himself too. If only he and Raf had listened to Gabs back in Jo'burg. She hadn't wanted to take Malcolm with them. If they'd followed her advice, if Zak hadn't been so dead set on fronting up to his nemesis, he wouldn't be in this situation.

His Guardian Angels would still be alive.

His body shook with nausea at the thought. He remembered Gabs's farewell hug. The words she had mouthed: Be careful!

Zak tried to bury his fear. He strode up to

the guards. 'You speak English?' he demanded.

The guards grinned. The one with blood on his hands faced up to Zak. He raised one stained finger, and was about to smear the blood over Zak's face when Zak quickly knocked the boy's arm away. The grin instantly fell from the boy's scarred face. He stepped back and raised his weapon.

It was cocked, and Zak could see that the safety was off . . .

'Leave him alone.'

Cruz's voice came from the doorway, where he was half shrouded in darkness. Zak saw indecision in the boy's face. He was clearly feeling violent, but didn't dare disobey Cruz's order. He stepped aside.

'Harry, come with me. The rest of you, make sure that halfwit in the corner doesn't move.'

The boys were no longer grinning. Zak felt their hot eyes on him as he walked towards the exit where Cruz was waiting, leaving Malcolm to his thoughts.

'I have something to show you, Harry,' Cruz said conversationally, as if they were just two old friends chewing the fat. 'I hope I can trust that you won't try to escape. My East Side Boys – that's what they like to call themselves – are everywhere, and I've noticed that they *are* rather trigger-happy.'

'They're not the only ones,' Zak retorted.

'You mean Matilda? I confess, she was beginning

to annoy me. But she had to die anyway. Malcolm is a useful asset for a man in my position, but he is rather like a puppy. If he receives a mixture of punishments and rewards, he'll soon learn to obey his new master.'

'The Cruz I *used* to know would never have done that.'

Cruz stopped walking. He turned to look at Zak, his eyes dead and dark. 'The Cruz you *used* to know died – along with his father, at your hands.'

A pause. Cruz smiled and the darkness in his eyes was suddenly gone.

'Which reminds me,' he said. 'I don't only have something to *show* you. I have someone for you to meet. Please, follow me.'

Cruz led Zak across the dark camp. With every step, Zak's eyes were searching, looking for an escape route. But he knew there was only one: the main gate, which was heavily guarded. And if he did try to run, Cruz's East Side Boys were everywhere.

Cruz was right. There was no escape.

He led Zak to another building, just slightly smaller than the first, and politely held the door open for him. Zak entered.

There were two people in this building. One was a very young-looking East Side Boy whose facial scars looked as if they had been recently inflicted.

They glistened in the artificial light of the bare bulb hanging from the ceiling, and the skin around the cuts was all puffed up.

The second person was an older man. Black dreadlocks, flecked with grey. Zak recognized him – he had seen him through his scope from the treetop.

Zak looked at the contents of the room.

Coffins.

There were perhaps thirty of them, all empty, just piled up at one end. With the exception of one. That was in the middle of the room, and contained a body: Malcolm's cousin. The man and the boy were lifting a coffin lid, one at each end. As Zak entered, they lowered the lid onto the coffin. It landed with a dull thud.

The man handed the boy a hammer and a bag of nails. He didn't need to give any instructions – it was clear what the boy had to do. The kid looked sickened. But also terrified. Something told Zak he wasn't like the other East Side Boys he'd met.

The kid started to hammer nails into the coffin as the man stood over him.

'I believe the boy's name is Smiler,' Cruz said quietly. 'They call the man Boss. His real name is Sudiq. They say it's important for a man to know the full name of his enemy, and his is a name the world will soon know very well. Sudiq Al-Tikriti Gomez is an old friend of my family.'

But Zak didn't care about Cruz's friends. He cared about the coffins. 'What's going on here?' he breathed.

Cruz stepped further into the room. 'I'm surprised you haven't worked it out for yourself, Zak. A clever boy like you. This little camp is where my people stuff drugs into soft toys, so that they can be distributed across Africa. It's a method that served my father well for a long time. The children are cheap labour, and easy to control.' Cruz frowned. 'They do, unfortunately, have a habit of dying on us. If we buried them without coffins, the wild animals in the jungle would soon dig them up. So, unfortunately, I must go to the expense of boxing them up before we dispose of them. But – what is your English phrase? "Every cloud has a silver lining"? Come here, I want to show you something.'

Cruz walked to the far end of the room, where all the coffins were stacked. Zak followed, ignoring the way the man called Sudiq stared at him.

One coffin had no others stacked on top; its lid was resting on it at a slight angle. Cruz stood at the head end and Zak felt his enemy's eyes on him as he looked down at the lid.

A small brass plaque was screwed to the coffin.

Engraved upon it were the words 'AGENT 21'.

'I didn't want you to think,' Cruz breathed, 'that your death would go unmarked. Un*mourned*, perhaps, but not un*marked*.'

Nausea coursed through Zak. He felt dizzy. He was vaguely aware that Smiler was edging, terrified, to the side of the hut as Zak himself looked back to the door, on the verge of running towards it. But then he started as he realized that the man called Sudiq – Boss – was standing right behind him. He was broad-shouldered and sturdy. He stank of stale sweat, and Zak saw beads of perspiration on his pockmarked face.

Sudiq grabbed him.

Zak struggled, but strong as he was, he was no match for Sudiq. Cruz kicked the lid from the coffin, while Sudiq wrestled him down into it. In about thirty seconds, Zak found himself lying in the coffin, Sudiq's booted foot pressing heavily against his ribcage.

And the barrel of a handgun pointing down at him.

Helpless, Zak stopped struggling. He looked up and saw beads of sweat on Sudiq's face, and his curling sneer displaying yellow teeth. *So this is it*, he thought. *This is the moment it ends.* He closed his eyes, wondering if he would even hear the gunshot before it killed him.

'Shall I do it now?' Sudiq asked.

'You hear that, Harry?' Cruz demanded. 'He wants to be the one who kills you. I must say, there would be a certain symmetry to that.'

Zak opened his eyes. 'What do you mean?' he rasped, his voice hoarse and dry.

'I'm glad you asked,' Cruz said. 'Like I told you, Sudiq is an old friend of the family. He worked for my father. Would you like to know what one of the last jobs Sudiq did for him was?'

Zak could barely breathe from the pressure of Sudiq's foot on his chest. He gasped for air.

'It was in Nigeria. Lagos. The Intercontinental Hotel, wasn't it, Sudiq?'

Sudiq grinned.

Zak froze.

The Intercontinental Hotel was where his parents had died.

Where his parents had been murdered.

Cruz was speaking again.

'There was a man there my father needed to eliminate. It turned out to be simpler to poison everybody around him. It was Sudiq's idea, and him who carried it out. He's a genius, don't you think?'

Zak looked up, into the eyes of the man who had killed his parents. His lip curled.

He saw Sudiq's fingers twitching around the handgun.

'So?' Sudiq asked. 'Shall I kill him now?'

A moment of silence.

'No,' said Cruz. 'Not yet. A simple bullet in the head would be too easy. Too painless. I want our friend to *suffer*, Sudiq. I want him to have time to regret the moment he ever set eyes on me. To *really* regret it. For the rest of his short, pitiful life.'

Cruz looked over at the boy he'd called Smiler.

'You! Bring me the hammer and nails. Sudiq, give me your gun and replace the coffin lid.'

A nasty grin spread over Sudiq's face. He passed the gun to Cruz and removed his foot from Zak's chest. Zak breathed in deeply – it hurt – then tried to sit up in the coffin. Almost immediately he felt a brutal blow to the side of his already bruised face as Sudiq kicked him. He sunk down into the coffin again.

Seconds later he saw the lid descending onto him.

'Let me out!' he shouted. 'You don't have to do this, Cruz. *Let me out!*'

Everything was dark. The coffin lid was on top of him. He tried to push up against it, but with no success. It was a heavy weight. He imagined Sudiq sitting on top of the lid.

Zak screamed again. '*Let me out!*' He banged

furiously against the lid. It was only a couple of centimetres from his face, and there was barely any room to move his limbs. He was gripped with panic. '*Let me out! LET ME OUT!*'

Bang.

The first nail was being hammered into the lid.

Bang.

The second.

Zak was screaming insanely now. But the banging just continued. He couldn't think straight. He couldn't move. He could barely even breathe . . .

And still the banging continued.

Then, after a couple of minutes, it suddenly stopped.

He heard Cruz's voice. It sounded as though he was on his knees and speaking close to the coffin.

'My people will take you to the burial site now, Harry. There's no point shouting. The East Side Boys will ignore you, and there's nobody else out here to listen to your screams. I'll think of you, waiting for the sound of dirt to be shovelled over your tomb. I'll think of you, buried in the ground, begging for death. It might take a while before that happens. I'm closing down this camp in a few hours. When I do, Latifah and all my little workers will have outlived their usefulness, so they'll be joining you. The East Side Boys will dump the coffins into one big grave and then, my friend, they and I will move on to bigger and better things. But really, I needn't bother you with such details. You won't be alive to see them happen.'

'Don't count on it, Cruz.'

'Oh, I think that this time I *will* count on it. Goodbye, Harry. I'd say it has been a pleasure knowing you, but we both know that would be a lie.'

Silence.

'Cruz! *Cruz!*'

There was no reply. Instead, Zak felt the coffin being lifted up.

'*Let me out! Let me out of here!*'

The coffin was moving.

Zak wriggled furiously. Perhaps if he made enough movement, whoever was carrying the coffin would be forced to drop it. He kicked and punched the inside of the box as best he could. He jarred his body up and down.

But the coffin kept moving.

Zak was sweating, yet his body felt ice cold with fear. Minutes ago, he had been preparing himself for a swift death. An *easy* death. Now, he understood that Cruz had planned for him the worst death imaginable.

He wanted to scream, but there was no breath in his lungs . . .

All he could hear now were footsteps crunching on the ground outside. He couldn't tell which direction he was headed in, but after a couple of minutes he heard voices speaking an African dialect he didn't understand. There was a scraping sound, and Zak pictured the main gate of the compound opening up.

More movement. He knew he was in the forest now. It wouldn't be long.

Five minutes passed. His body was bruised and battered, his throat tight with fear.

The movement stopped.

Silence.

Suddenly he was falling. Only for a couple of seconds, but it was enough to leave his stomach behind.

Then: impact. Zak felt as if every muscle in his body took a hit. The coffin landed with its head end tilted downwards. For a split second, Zak felt his head crack against the head end of the coffin. There was a moment of sharp, all-encompassing pain. He thought he might vomit . . .

But then, before he could even cry out for a final time, the nausea increased threefold. He felt a bright, stabbing pain behind his eyes.

Then he blacked out.

14

EAVESDROPPING

02.30HRS

Latifah trembled.

She was not normally weak, like this. But when that strange boy had climbed into the camp, and terrifying Señor Martinez had threatened to shoot her, all her courage had dissolved. Now she huddled up on the floor, just by the door of the hut where the other worker-children were kept. The East Side Boys had thrown her back in here half an hour ago, and she hadn't moved since.

She was *so* hungry. They hardly fed them anything here. The last time she'd had a decent meal was the night the two East Side Boys abducted her from her village. That was, what, three months ago? In that time she'd seen seven of the other children die.

Or was it eight? She could no longer keep track.

Her limbs were so thin that it hurt to move them. But she forced herself to sit up.

Which was when she saw her captors' mistake.

The door of the hut was slightly ajar. Just a few centimetres. They'd forgotten to lock it.

Latifah knew perfectly well that none of the other children would dare to escape – they'd had all the fight beaten out of them. She wasn't even sure if any of them were awake. They lay, exhausted, on the floor, all of them keeping a good distance from the corner of the hut that they had to use as a toilet.

She quietly pushed herself up to her feet and looked around.

No movement in the hut. She didn't think anyone was watching her. She edged towards the door and peered out.

The door of the hut was about ten metres from the wall of the camp. Twenty metres away in the opposite direction was the back wall of another hut. She had peered into it once, and seen piles of wooden coffins. Ever since that day, she had avoided it. Now, though, having checked that none of the awful, scar-faced East Side Boys were around to see her, she ran towards that building and pressed her back against the wall while she caught her breath.

What was she doing? She didn't really know. Just

looking for a place to hide, she supposed. The guards never counted the prisoners, so she didn't think she'd be missed. If she could remain hidden for long enough, perhaps she'd get a chance to escape the camp.

She edged slowly round the side of this building, keeping carefully to the shadows. After a couple of minutes, she found herself by the open door. She could hear voices inside. They were speaking English, which Latifah understood.

'Listen carefully.' The voice belonged to the older man that the East Side Boys called Boss. 'You two are my most trusted lieutenants, and now I have valuable work for you to do. Señor Martinez and I have prepared everything very well, so you must do exactly what we tell you, OK?'

Latifah told herself that she should keep away. But she had always been a curious girl. Maybe if she kept on listening, she'd hear something that could help her. She edged closer to the hinged side of the door. Through the crack she could see four people. Boss was there. So were two of the more brutal East Side Boys. Latifah, in her head, had named them Puncher and Kicker, because that was what they liked to do.

And Señor Martinez. The very sight of him made Latifah feel sick, and cold.

Puncher and Kicker were murmuring their agreement, their faces filled with pride.

'Later today, someone will arrive to take away the final batch of dolls that the children have been stuffing with Señor Martinez's product. They will leave money – two million, three hundred and forty-six thousand, six hundred and twenty-five US dollars.'

Latifah's eyes widened at the sum.

'The money needs to be placed in one of these coffins. I have carved a Vodun symbol onto it. Nobody will dare to open it.'

Latifah suppressed a shiver. Vodun meant witchcraft, and she, like the rest of her village, believed that its symbols brought bad luck.

'I should warn you that if a single dollar is missing from the coffin, the person responsible will regret it. Understood?'

'Understood, Boss,' the boys replied.

'When that is done, Señor Martinez no longer has any use for this place. We will leave eight of you here. Your job will be to kill the child-workers, then bury them. Is that understood?'

Latifah gasped, then quickly put her hand over her mouth to silence the noise.

'What about the rest of us?' asked Kicker.

'The rest of you,' purred Señor Martinez, 'will come upriver with me and your boss. We are heading into The Gambia, to the capital Banjul.'

Latifah didn't know much geography, but she knew about The Gambia, of course – a small, sausage-shaped country entirely surrounded by Senegal.

'You see,' Señor Martinez explained, 'this method of getting our product into Africa is slow and in-efficient. It would be much better if my ships could simply arrive at the port of Banjul, unload there without any problems, and my people could distribute the drugs in an orderly, efficient fashion. Don't you agree?'

Puncher and Kicker agreed. But then, who would *dis*agree with a person like this?

'We have tried to bribe customs officials,' Señor Martinez continued, 'not to mention politicians, and even the president of The Gambia himself. But with no success.'

'So . . . what are you going to do?' Kicker asked tentatively.

'It is quite simple. If one president will not do as we ask, we will have to install a *new* president.'

Latifah blinked. Even inside the building there was a moment of silence.

'It sounds audacious, I know. But The Gambia is small and its armies are weak. What is more, we have a secret weapon.'

'What?'

'The boy Malcolm.'

Another silence.

'He looks like a weakling,' Puncher said.

Señor Martinez laughed. 'Don't be fooled, my friend. His body might be weak, but his mind isn't. There is a communications tower near the airport in Banjul. Malcolm has the skills to tamper with it. He can bring down all cellphones and radio communications in the city. If they are unable to *communicate*, the president's pitiful army will be next to useless. There are already a hundred East Side Boys in Banjul, preparing the ground, waiting for us to arrive. We have boats waiting on the river near here. It will take us a few hours to get there. The coup – for that is what we are planning – happens tonight.'

A pause. Latifah felt her heart beating fast. Her English was not perfect, but living in this part of the world she knew what a 'coup' was – an attempt to bring down, and replace, the government of a country. Sometimes they were non-violent. Mostly, they were *very* violent.

'I have a special job for *you*,' Señor Martinez continued. He was addressing Puncher. 'There are many tourists in The Gambia. We don't want to encourage them to keep coming. In fact, I want the rest of the world to avoid the country completely. While the coup is taking place, I want you and several others to plant bombs in a tourist hotel. I want as many casualties as possible. I want the news outlets around the world to call it an atrocity. I want them to see pictures of injured westerners. Of women and children dying. Of blood and amputated limbs. It will make people realize that Banjul is no longer a safe place to come. Can I trust you with this?'

Another pause.

And then: 'Yes, of course,' said Puncher.

'Good. I shall explain more as we travel.' He turned to Kicker. 'Your job is to stay here and eliminate the children once the final batch of dolls has been picked up and the money safely delivered. That will happen later today.' A thoughtful look crossed his face. 'We need all the weapons we can put our hands on in Banjul, so we will just leave you a couple of rifles. That will be enough for the job. The children are thin and unable to fight back.' He paused, thinking for a moment. 'I want you to make that kid called Smiler do it. He looks weak. I want him to be toughened up, and to know that I have his absolute loyalty. If he refuses, kill him and stick him in the ditch with all the others.'

'And with your friend who tried to climb over the wall?' Kicker said.

Señor Martinez's face darkened. 'Yes,' he spat. 'With him.' He paused for a moment, then snapped back to the conversation in hand. 'As soon as the children are dealt with, burn this place down and follow us up the river. Bring the coffin containing the money with you. And remember, just in case you are thinking of stealing it, know this: if even a single dollar – a single *cent* – of that money fails to reach me, I will hunt you down and cut your throat.'

Silence, as Señor Martinez allowed that to sink in.

'Explain to the rest of your friends what is happening. By nightfall, The Gambia will have a new president. I'm sure he will see fit to reward you boys handsomely for your role in his appointment.'

'You haven't told us who it's going to be,' said Puncher.

'Who do you think?' Señor Martinez said contemptuously, as though it were a very stupid comment. He held one arm out to the older man called Boss. 'Gentlemen, meet the new Gambian president. Serve him well and I imagine he'll see to it that you're well rewarded.'

There was a moment of silence. Then the two East Side Boys doubled over with laughter. With a casual, arrogant swagger, they started walking towards the door. Latifah quickly scrambled to the side of the building and stood there silently, holding her breath.

'You get the best job,' she heard Puncher say to Kicker. 'These kids get on my nerves. I'd love to watch Smiler shooting them.'

Latifah didn't get to hear whether Kicker agreed. They had walked out of earshot, leaving her – breathless and terrified – to think about what she had just heard.

She should be scared, she realized. These brutal people who were keeping her enslaved were about to kill her and all the others. Somehow, though, it just made her more determined. Braver. Because if she was going to die anyway, she had nothing to lose.

She *had* to get out of here. To find help. All she knew was this: at some point in the next couple of hours, Señor Martinez, Boss and half the East Side Boys would be leaving the camp. That meant they would have to open the gates. If she was hiding nearby, maybe she could slip out.

It wasn't much of a plan, but it was the best she had.

Breathing deeply but calmly, she edged back along the side of the building. Once she was at its corner, she had a direct line of sight to the exit. It was a hundred metres away. A direct run. To the left of the gate was a small timber shelter where the guards could protect themselves from the midday sun. But she couldn't see any guards in there now. Nor any manning the gates themselves.

Should she run? Would the darkness of the night cloak her? Would anybody see her? If they did, it would all be over.

They would probably kill her there and then.

But if she didn't, they would kill her anyway.

A flinty, determined expression crossed her face.

She ran.

Even though she was doing her best to tread lightly, her footsteps still seemed horribly loud. She winced as she crossed the ground, sure that the patter of her feet was going to rouse the whole camp. But she kept her eye on the prize: the gate, and the shelter. If she could hide behind it, maybe – just maybe – she could escape.

She stopped. Her stomach knotted in terror. One of the East Side Boys had stepped out from behind a hut. He was just fifteen metres away. And he was staring straight at her.

Like a rabbit caught in headlamps, Latifah froze.

What should she do? Turn back? Beg this boy not to hurt her?

She looked at his face. She'd never seen this one before. He was very young. His eyes, she thought, did not look unkind. Not like the other East Side

Boys. The scars on his face were very new. Very sore. They glistened slightly in the moonlight.

Slowly, Latifah raised one finger to her lips. As if to say: *Will you keep quiet?* Then she inclined her head. As if to say: *Please?*

The boy looked uncertain. His eyes darted left and right. But then they fell on Latifah again.

He nodded.

Then, with his head down, he walked back the way he had come.

Latifah breathed again. She continued running. Ten seconds later she was by the gate.

She looked over her shoulder. There was movement in the main area of the camp. Figures hurrying around. She didn't think they'd seen her so she scrambled towards the shelter. There was a small gap, no more than a metre or so deep, between the shelter itself and the perimeter wall. Latifah wormed her way into it. Then she crouched down, head low. She could see the gate, but if she wanted to remain hidden she knew that she would have to stay very, very still.

Very, very quiet.

And hope that the young East Side Boy with the fresh scars did not turn her in.

Apart from that, all she could do now was wait.

* * *

Malcolm did not know how much time had passed. It was only when he saw a watch on the wrist of one of his guards that he realized it was five in the morning. His brain, normally so focused and logical, felt like cotton wool.

He barely even knew where he was.

He felt empty.

Alone.

His mind kept replaying the moment when Cruz had murdered Matilda. The noise of the gun. The explosion of blood. The way her body had slumped to the floor.

It was the first time, he realized, that he had ever felt sadness. He couldn't understand how other people lived with it.

He looked up. The door of the hut in which he had been sitting had just opened. It was getting light outside. Cruz stepped in and walked up to him.

'You promised she would be safe if I brought Zak to you,' Malcolm croaked.

'I lied,' said Cruz. 'I do that quite a lot.' He knelt down so he was face to face with Malcolm. 'But I promise you I'm not lying now. You're coming with me. If you even *think* about not doing as I say, I'll do exactly the same thing to you as I did to your cousin.'

'I don't care,' said Malcolm. And it was true. He didn't.

Cruz's eyes narrowed. He pulled a gun and placed it to Malcolm's head.

Malcolm closed his eyes. He wondered what it would be like to die like this. Would it hurt? Would his brain stop working the moment the bullet pierced his skull? Or would there be a few seconds while the computer shut down? He knew he was smart – that his brain was different to other people's. It seemed impossible that the neurones would stop firing, the calculations he was always making grind to a halt, the facts disappear. He was proud of his mind. Proud of his ability to out-think other people.

To out-think other people.

A thought struck him. Why was he still alive? It must surely mean Cruz must *really* need him for something. Which put Malcolm at an advantage.

He could out-think this madman, surely. And if he could out-think him, maybe, he could make him pay for what he had done.

He opened his eyes.

'Please don't,' he said.

Cruz smiled and lowered the gun. 'I knew you'd come round,' he said.

'Where are we going?'

'You'll find out.'

'Where is Zak?'

'Dead. Like his stupid friends.' Cruz looked over

his shoulder at the armed guards who had been keeping an eye on Malcolm all night. 'Bring him,' he instructed. Then he turned on his heel and marched out of the door.

Before he knew what was happening, Malcolm was being lifted to his feet by two of the guards, and dragged outside.

Cruz was standing in the centre of the camp. Nine or ten of his scar-faced boys were milling around him, and so was the older man with dreadlocks. They were all armed. Many of them had bandoliers and bullet belts draped over them. They looked ready for action.

'Let's go,' Cruz shouted. 'Today's the day you rule a little bit of Africa, my friends. But you have some chaos to cause first.'

The armed boys grinned. One of them pushed Malcolm in the back and forced him to walk towards the gate, along with the others. The gates were opening now, revealing the misty jungle morning beyond. Malcolm stumbled towards them, while the boys whooped and hollered, pointing their guns up in the air. One of them even fired a shot, which echoed loudly and sent crowds of birds flying up from the trees.

None of them seemed to be paying much attention to the gates. Which was perhaps, Malcolm thought, why they didn't see what he saw. It was the slight figure of a small girl, creeping out from behind a small wooden shelter, slipping out of the gates and disappearing, cat-like, into the forest beyond.

'Move!' hissed one of Malcolm's guards, pushing him again. Malcolm joined the others, and passed through the gates. He looked round, his eyes searching. He couldn't see the child, but he knew she was there. Somewhere. Watching.

But then he felt the barrel of a gun in his back. He upped his pace and followed the others into the jungle.

Ten minutes later he was by the bank of a river. There were ten speedboats here, each one containing several jerry cans of fuel. Mist and insects were rising from the water, birds shrieking in the trees.

At a curt instruction from one of the boys, Malcolm found himself in a boat with Cruz, the older man whom the others all seemed to call Boss, and two more armed boys. One of them started the outboard motor.

'Where are we going?' Malcolm asked Cruz.

Cruz looked at him with a sinister smile. 'Banjul,' he said.

15

BREAK OUT

Latifah didn't dare move.

She was lying on her front, covered in wet vegetation. Through the foliage she could just glimpse the gates of the camp. The East Side Boys were spilling out. They were rowdy, waving their guns in the air. Señor Martinez was there too, and Boss. Her eyes picked out Puncher.

But there was another boy as well. A white boy. He wore spectacles and was obviously frightened. He looked around, as if he was searching for something. After a moment, his eyes seemed to fall on the exact place where Latifah was hiding. She gasped, and remained very still.

Then an East Side Boy prodded him in the back. The white boy moved on, along with the rest of them, the camp gate slid shut and Latifah was alone again.

Her heart was beating fast. But not as fast as her mind was working. The children inside the camp had hours to live. Unless she found help.

But where could she find help in the middle of the jungle?

She lay there, helpless and scared. Time passed. An hour, maybe two – she was too panicked to tell. The sun started to grow hot. Slowly she got to her feet. Something slithered in the undergrowth nearby, and she froze again. Then everything went silent.

Latifah thought of the boy who had tried to scale the wall last night. Who had given himself up rather than see her killed. He was dead – she had over-heard them say that he'd already been buried. She remembered the two shots that had been fired in the jungle after his capture. If he had any companions, they were surely now corpses.

She shuddered. The thought of coming across dead bodies in the jungle was not a nice one. But maybe they had weapons on them. Latifah had never held a gun before, but how else could she stand up to these awful boys who were about to kill everyone in the camp?

She moved quietly round the edge of the camp, treading as silently as she could and keeping a distance of at least twenty metres from the high wall.

Her plan was to reach the point in the wall where the boy had climbed over. She did this in about five minutes. She could tell it was the right place because the mesh squares of the fence were slightly damaged. From this point she looked into the jungle. Her keen eyes picked out a narrow path where the foliage was trampled down. She decided to follow it.

The path was straight. Easy to follow. Latifah walked along it reluctantly, scared of what it might lead to.

Forty metres from the camp wall, she tripped over a tree root and fell to the ground, grazing her knee painfully against a piece of bark. Tears welled up in her eyes. She fought them back, but her vision was misty as she looked up.

So the bodies, when she saw them perhaps fifteen metres in the distance, were slightly blurred.

They also seemed to be leaning up against a tree.

For a horrible moment, Latifah thought they had been hanged. But then she remembered the gunshots. She wiped the tears from her eyes so that she could see more clearly.

It was a man and a woman. Both had white skin and blond hair. They were tied to the tree with a length of rope, and their heads were drooping down onto their chests. There was a rucksack at their feet.

There was no blood anywhere but Latifah couldn't tell if they were dead or alive.

She stepped forward. A twig cracked underfoot.

Both figures immediately looked up.

She gasped.

Their faces were dirty, their eyes bloodshot. They scared her.

Latifah stepped back. But now she saw that both the man and the woman had gags across their mouths. The little girl swallowed hard. She had come into the jungle to look for help, but now that she'd found it, she didn't know whether she could trust these people. She continued to edge backwards.

Then she saw something in the woman's eyes. She was desperate. Latifah could see that. She understood the way the woman was looking imploringly into her eyes.

Latifah nodded faintly, licked her dry lips and moved forward to the tree. She had always been an observant girl, so she immediately noticed, when she was about five metres from the tree, that there were two bullet shells on the ground. Again, she remembered the gunshots of the previous night, and tried to work out what had happened.

Had someone fired these shots to make it *sound* like they were killing these two people?

With a trembling hand, she removed the piece of cloth gagging the blonde woman.

The woman spoke immediately. She attempted certain African dialects that Latifah couldn't understand, before saying: 'Do you speak English?'

Latifah hesitated. 'A . . . a little bit,' she stammered.

Relief crossed the woman's face. 'OK, sweetie,' she said. 'You don't need to be scared. My name's Gabs. This is Raf. Untie us. We'll make sure you're safe.' And when Latifah looked uncertain, the woman added: 'Please. We need to find our friend. He's in very great danger.'

'Do you mean the one who climbed the wall?' Latifah asked.

Gabs nodded. Her face was hungry for information.

'I'm sorry,' Latifah said, her voice breaking. 'I think . . . he's dead.'

Gabs closed her eyes. She drew a deep breath. When she spoke again, her voice had a different quality. Very quiet. Very determined. 'Untie us,' she said.

Latifah didn't dare disobey.

The knots that bound them were tight. They had cut into their skin. But neither Gabs nor the man called Raf seemed bothered by that. 'Why do you think he's dead?' Gabs demanded as soon as they were free.

'I . . . I heard Señor Martinez talking. He said they had buried him.'

'Where? Do you know?'

Latifah nodded. The East Side Boys had made the children dig the ditch on the far side of the camp, and had laughed when they explained that the children would probably end up buried here in the end.

'Show us.'

They hurried through the jungle. This strange couple didn't seem to care if they made a noise. If the rainforest got in their way, they burst through it. If they could sprint, they did. It took them no longer than ten minutes to reach the deep ditch that Latifah had hoped never to see again.

The three of them looked down into it and Latifah gagged. There was a terrible smell here. It came from the two coffins that lay in the ditch. Flies swarmed and crawled all around them and their buzzing filled her ears.

One of the coffins was unmarked. The other looked like it had been carelessly thrown in. Its head end was embedded in a puddle of water from last night's rain. On the front was a brass plaque. It said: AGENT 21.

Gabs let out a low moan. Latifah thought that the blonde woman's legs might give out. The same thought obviously occurred to the man. He grabbed hold of his friend and together they stared into the ditch.

Thirty seconds passed.

A tear rolled down Gabs's dirty face. She suddenly buried her head in Raf's shoulder. 'We should never have brought him here,' she said weakly.

Latifah cleared her throat. 'I'm sorry,' she said. 'I'm very sorry. But I need your help. Something terrible is going to—'

Knock.

Latifah stopped. All three sets of eyes were on the ditch again.

Silence.

Knock.

Latifah suppressed a shiver. The sound was coming from the coffin with the plaque. But how could it? Dead people don't . . .

Knock knock knock.

Gabs leaped down into the ditch. Dirty water splashed up around her ankles. The flies, suddenly disturbed, buzzed round her head.

'Zak!' she shouted. '*Zak!*'

Suddenly the knocking became frenzied. The

whole coffin was shaking. Latifah had heard stories of corpses that had come back from the dead, and it looked like that was happening now. She covered her eyes with her tiny hands.

Then she heard a muffled voice from inside the coffin. Latifah recognized the voice – it belonged to the boy who'd tried to get over the wall.

'Get me out of here!' he shouted. '*GABS! FOR GOD'S SAKE, GET ME OUT OF HERE!*'

16

BREAK IN

Zak's knuckles were raw with knocking. His muscles ached from lack of movement. His head throbbed. His eyes were wild from the horror of the last few hours. Every time he remembered the sensation of being in that coffin, waiting for the pitter-pattering sound of earth to fall on the lid, he shuddered. It was a relief to think of something else, even if it was only his explanation of what had happened in the camp: how Cruz had captured him, Malcolm's betrayal and the murder of his cousin; the moment he'd come face to face with the man who'd actually killed his parents.

'Malcolm said he'd killed you,' Zak said weakly when he'd finished. 'I thought you were dead.'

They were sitting, shaken, by the ditch. Zak's coffin was still down there, but Raf had prised the lid off with his knife. Zak couldn't bring himself to look at it, so he concentrated on his friends, and the strange young girl who was with them.

'We nearly were,' said Raf. 'Malcolm stole the AK-47 and crept up on us. I think he'd been working himself up to doing it, but when the time came . . .'

Zak stared at him in astonishment. '*Malcolm?*' he said. 'Overpowered *you*?'

Raf looked rather embarrassed. 'He *did* have a gun,' he said, a bit defensively.

'You know what I think?' said Gabs. 'I think Malcolm listens more than we give him credit for. You remember when we were refuelling and Raf told him off for suggesting we should have just killed those men at the petrol pump? I think he took that on board. And he was clever too. Made us tie our own feet together and rope up one wrist each, then made me tie you up first so we couldn't overpower him . . .' Her face twisted, and Zak thought she looked almost embarrassed for a moment.

'Whatever,' Raf said. 'When push came to shove, he couldn't shoot us. But he couldn't let Cruz know he'd spared us. That's why he tied us up at gunpoint – so we didn't walk in and put his cousin's life at risk. Fat lot of good *that* did.'

'We need to find him quickly,' Zak said. 'He's in a lot of danger.'

'It's too late,' the little girl, who had introduced herself as Latifah, piped up.

Zak, Raf and Gabs turned to look at her.

'Señor Martinez took him away.'

'We have to find him,' Zak breathed. 'We—'

'Please,' Latifah interrupted. '*Please*. You have to listen to me. They are going to kill all the children in the camp. We must not let them.'

Before any of them could reply, there was a new sound. It came from the sky, and was quiet at first, but grew louder. Zak knew immediately what it was. A chopper, flying in over the jungle.

'Who's that?' he shouted.

The little girl, as usual, had the answer. 'They fly in every week,' she shouted over the increasing noise. 'They pick up the dolls we have stuffed, and leave money in exchange. But this is the last time they will come. After today, Señor Martinez has no use for the camp. When the helicopter leaves, they will kill everyone. *Please*, you have to help me stop them.'

She was only small, Zak observed, but she had the heart of a lion.

Gabs obviously thought the same. She put a reassuring hand on Latifah's arm. 'Don't worry, sweetie,' she said. 'Señor Martinez has killed enough people for one day. We're not going to let anybody else get hurt.'

The helicopter appeared in the clearing above the camp. It hovered for a couple of seconds, adjusting its position. Then it lowered and went below the level of the wall.

Zak felt Latifah tugging his clothes. 'Come on! *Come on!* As soon as the helicopter goes, they will murder my friends.'

Zak looked at his Guardian Angels. 'How do we get in there?' he urged.

Gabs stood up. She looked like she meant business, and she stared meaningfully at Latifah.

'Come with me, sweetie,' she said. 'And remember to do everything exactly like I say. That's the only way we'll all stay safe . . .'

Latifah stood two metres outside the camp gate. It was closed. Inside the camp she could hear movement and voices. The helicopter had gone, only touching down for a few minutes, and the remaining East Side Boys were shouting orders at each other. Their voices sounded ugly. Brutal. They were gathering the children together. Rounding them up.

The little girl looked at her hand. It was shaking. She felt like she was in a dream. Any moment now she would wake up to find that she hadn't *really* agreed to go back into the lion's den. That she was safe with these strange white people in the jungle after all.

But that wasn't true. She *had* agreed to do this, and she knew why: without her help, there would be a massacre here very soon.

She stepped forward, raised her little fist and clenched it. Then she rapped it lightly against the gate. There was no hint of her nervousness in her bright, clear voice. She spoke just loudly enough, she hoped, that only the guards at the gate – there were normally two of them – could hear her.

'Hey, stupid boys,' she called. 'You didn't know I got away, did you?'

Latifah's eyes grew narrow as she listened for the response.

At first there was none. Just a shuffling of feet and a kind of murmur as the guards spoke together in low voices.

She wiped a trickle of sweat from her brow and called out again. 'Your friends will think you're real idiots,' she taunted. 'All those guns and you can't even keep a little girl safely locked up.'

More murmuring. Latifah stepped back from the gate until she was about ten metres away.

Any minute now, she thought to herself. *They'll*

open the gate. They'll have their guns strapped round them. They'll be pointing them at me.

Her eyes darted around. To either side of the gate was a tangled mess of vegetation, thick and knotted. Behind her, the jungle itself did not start again for another fifteen metres. All about her were patches of low scrub, but as soon as the gate slid open, the guards would see her alone and exposed.

And the gates were opening now.

Not fully. Just a metre or so – enough to allow two East Side Boys to step out. One of them wore army trousers and no top. His gun was strapped across his bare, glistening torso. The other wore a khaki sleeveless jacket, and was unarmed. They both had suspicious looks on their faces. But when they saw Latifah standing alone and vulnerable in the clearing, their lips curled into contemptuous sneers. In a single movement, the first boy raised his rifle in Latifah's direction.

Latifah froze. She knew she was supposed to run. She had practised this moment in her head. But when it came to it, she froze. The only thing she could think about was what it would feel like to be shot in the back as she ran.

It meant she saw it happen.

The East Side Boys never knew what hit them. The two knotted patches of vegetation suddenly sprang to life. The man and the woman – Raf and Gabs – emerged from their hiding places and hurled themselves at the East Side Boys. At the same time, the boy called Zak jumped up out of a low patch of greenery lying just a couple of metres to her left. He wrestled her to the ground. 'Keep low,' he hissed. 'Don't move.'

They stayed there, pressed against the earth, for what seemed like a minute but was in fact no more than a few seconds. Then they heard a whisper from the direction of the gates. '*Clear!*'

Zak released his grip and they looked towards the camp gates. Raf and Gabs had completely over-whelmed the two East Side Boys. The guards were on the ground, belly down. Each one had a booted foot on their back and Gabs had their gun. Their earpieces and boom mikes had been ripped from their heads.

Latifah quickly covered her eyes. She had seen enough violence in her short life, and could not bear to see any more. She steeled herself as she waited for the shots.

But no shots came.

When Latifah looked again, peering through a gap between her fingers, the scene had changed. Each boy had a length of rope over his mouth and tied at the back of his head. Their hands were behind their backs. Raf and Gabs were tying their wrists tightly. The two East Side Boys, who had seemed so threatening to Latifah with their guns and their cruel faces, now looked like what they were: scared kids.

Zak grabbed Latifah's wrist and pulled her to her feet. Together, they ran towards Raf and Gabs, who were forcing the trussed-up East Side Boys into a sitting position against the outside wall, just to the left of the gate. Once the boys were on the ground, Gabs turned her gun round so the butt was in front of her. She gave the two boys an appraising look, then yanked the butt sharply against each of their heads. Their eyes misted over and they slumped to the ground.

'They'll be fine,' Gabs said to nobody in particular. Latifah was a bit scared of this blonde-haired woman whose expression changed between kindness and grim ferocity. 'You did very well, sweetie,' she said, with an expression that was now somewhere between the two. Then she turned to Raf and Zak. 'I think it's time for us to head inside, don't you?' she said very quietly.

The man and the boy nodded.

'You don't have to come, Latifah,' said Gabs. 'You've done more than enough to help already.'

But Latifah felt like she was on auto-pilot now.

She shook her head. 'I'm coming,' she said, praying there would be no argument.

There was none. Zak was peering round the edge of the camp gate. He turned back to look at them.

'They've rounded up the kids,' he hissed. 'I think they're about to kill them. We have to move!'

17

KNOW YOUR ENEMY

All four of them slipped inside the camp and Zak immediately heard the sound of wailing.

There was a crowd of young people 100 metres to his twelve o'clock. They formed two distinct groups. The worker-children – there were about thirty of them – were on their knees. They were lined up with their backs against the wall of one of the huts. They were the ones wailing, of course. It was a horrible, low moan, like the hum of insects somewhere on the edge of Zak's hearing. The sound of terror.

The second group was made up of East Side Boys. Zak instinctively counted them out: it was crucial to know your enemy. There were six of them. He wondered for a moment if there were any others hidden elsewhere in the camp, but somehow he didn't think so. Latifah confirmed his suspicion. 'They said there would be eight in all,' she whispered. 'That is all of them.'

None of them had noticed the newcomers. They were not well organized and there seemed to be an argument going on. The East Side Boys, with their mismatched clothes and cruelly scarred faces, all seemed to be crowding round one of their number and a few were shouting instructions. None of them, to Zak's surprise, seemed to be armed.

'Stand back, you two,' Gabs breathed. She and Raf stepped in front of Zak and Latifah. Gabs held the weapon she had confiscated from the guards. The butt of the assault rifle was pressed into her shoulder. She didn't hold it with the arrogant swagger with which Zak had seen the East Side Boys brandish their guns. She held it like a pro.

The wailing of the children continued. Zak saw one youngster – he couldn't tell from this distance if it was a boy or a girl – with their head in their hands, crying.

Movement among the East Side Boys. They thinned out, to reveal one kid at their centre. Zak immediately recognized him – he had been in the room when Cruz and Sudiq had stuffed him into his wooden coffin. Cruz had called him Smiler.

'I know that one,' Latifah whispered. 'He . . . he let me escape . . .'

Smiler was the youngest of them by far. He looked miserable. Unlike the other East Side Boys he carried a weapon. And unlike Gabs, he *didn't* hold it like a pro. More like a live snake. But his finger was on the trigger and now he was pointing the weapon at the line of children up against the wall.

Gabs said nothing, but Zak could hear her movements fluently. She seemed quite relaxed, but had suddenly altered the direction of her gun. She was preparing to take Smiler out.

'*Wait*,' Zak hissed.

'Stay back, Zak,' Gabs breathed.

'*No!*' He stepped out in front of them. 'I've met this guy before. He won't do it. Trust me.'

'He doesn't have a choice, sweetie. I'm sorry, but neither do I . . .'

As she spoke, one of the East Side Boys barked out a warning. The others all spun round to look at them.

They were in a diamond formation now: Zak at one tip, looking back towards Raf and Gabs who kept their weapons trained on the East Side Boys. Latifah behind them.

'I can talk him out of this,' Zak said. He

remembered the sickened expression little Smiler had on his face when Sudiq was forcing him to deal with Matilda's corpse. 'I know I can. You don't have to shoot him.'

Both Raf and Gabs had flinty expressions. *Unconvinced* expressions.

'He's just a kid,' Zak breathed. 'You have to let me try.'

A pause. Then Gabs nodded.

Zak spun round, then started walking forward. He was aware of Raf and Gabs flanking him.

'Smiler!' he shouted. 'Put the gun down. We won't hurt you, but you have to put the gun down first.'

Distance between them: seventy-five metres. Zak could tell, even from here, that the boy was trembling.

'I know you don't want to do this, Smiler,' Zak called, still moving towards the younger boy. 'And you don't have to. You're not like the others. I can tell. You're not a killer. Put the gun down. Put it down and we can make all this OK again. I promise.'

Fifty metres.

Smiler's glance alternated between the group of East Side Boys who were surrounding him, and Zak. Zak saw him waver. The gun wobbled in his hands. His shoulders slumped . . .

Suddenly, another of the East Side Boys moved, very fast. From somewhere among his clothes he had pulled a handgun. He pressed the butt up against Smiler's head. An arrogant expression spread across his face.

Zak and his companions stopped. 'What's this dude's name?' Zak whispered to Latifah.

'I don't know,' Latifah replied. 'I call him Kicker, but that's just my nickname for him.'

Kicker's face threw out a challenge. *Put your guns down*, it seemed to say, *or the kid dies . . .*

Zak started walking forward again. He knew he was gambling, and he didn't like it. Surely Kicker understood that the moment he pulled that trigger, Raf and Gabs would open fire. He'd be dead before Smiler hit the ground.

Or was he not bright enough – or too arrogant – to realize that his life hung by a thread?

Gunfire.

It came from Gabs's weapon.

Several of the captive children screamed. Zak nearly jumped out of his skin. For an awful moment, he expected to see a shower of blood. But he didn't. Just a cloud of dust billowing up from the ground at Kicker's feet, where a round had landed.

All of a sudden, Kicker didn't seem so brave. He jumped back and his handgun fell to his side.

Thirty metres.

Smiler was still clutching the weapon. The other East Side Boys were edging back. Some of them looked like they would disperse at any moment. Others looked aggressive. The situation was still not defused.

Twenty metres.

The East Side Boys were looking desperate now. Their eyes flitted from left to right and many of them were flexing their fingers, ready for a fight they couldn't have, because they were held at gunpoint.

Smiler slowly turned. The gun turned with him. It was pointing in Zak's direction.

Zak's heart stopped.

But Smiler didn't stop moving. The gun didn't stop swinging round. Now it was pointing directly at the remaining East Side Boys. The closest of them was only five metres from Smiler's position.

The captive children had fallen completely silent. Now the only sound came from the East Side Boys themselves. It was a low murmur, with an undertone of fear and indecision — they didn't know what to do.

Ten metres.

Zak, Raf, Gabs and Latifah stopped. The eyes of everybody else in the camp were on them.

A moment of tense silence. A bird called

somewhere overhead. It sounded louder than it should.

'Are you going to kill them?' Latifah breathed, quietly enough that only her new friends could hear.

Another pause.

'That's not really the way we operate, sweetie,' said Gabs. 'They might be messed up, but they're still just kids.' She glanced at Raf. 'But we do need to think what to do with these guys. If we set them free, they'll only regroup and come at us again.'

Raf had steel in his eyes and Zak couldn't help thinking that he had a more terminal solution in mind.

'I've got an idea,' Zak said.

'I'm all ears, sweetie,' Gabs replied. Her mouth barely moved as she spoke.

Zak stepped over to Smiler. Now all eyes were on him alone. One of the captive kids was still sobbing, but they had mostly fallen silent. 'Give me the gun, mate,' he said. 'Then go over there and stand behind my friends. They'll make sure you stay safe.'

Smiler swallowed. He looked reluctant to let go of his gun.

'Trust me, Smiler. Look at these boys. They'll kill you if they get their hands on that weapon.'

The barrel of the rifle dropped a couple of

centimetress. Zak stretched out one hand and grabbed it.

Sudden movement from the East Side Boys. One of them – it was Kicker – was darting towards Zak and Smiler.

A massive bang as Gabs immediately let loose a round from her weapon.

Kicker hit the ground.

A groan from the East Side Boys. For a shocked instant, Zak thought Gabs had killed him. But there was no blood. Kicker was still alive. The bullet had hit the ground perfectly in front of him. He'd dropped to the dirt in surprise and terror.

Smiler let go of his rifle, leaving it in Zak's grasp. Then he scurried the ten metres back to where Latifah was standing. Like everyone else in the camp, he stared at Zak.

Holding the weapon as professionally as Gabs held hers, Zak turned to the group of East Side Boys.

'Take your clothes off,' he shouted.

Nobody moved.

Zak gave Gabs and Raf a sideways glance. Gabs had a sly smile. 'You heard him,' she called. 'Strip.'

All of a sudden, these aggressive East Side Boys looked like surly, scolded children. Half-heartedly, they each removed a single item of clothing – a bandanna, maybe, or at best a khaki jacket. They dropped the clothes on the floor in front of them, casting sidelong glances at each other. Then, chins jutted out, they looked back at Zak.

'*All* your clothes,' Zak said. He raised the rifle slightly to emphasize his point.

If the situation wasn't so serious, it would have been funny. And that's what Zak wanted; he wanted to embarrass them. The East Side Boys slowly stripped, casting mortified glances all around them as they did so. Within a minute they were standing among piles of clothes, all six of them wearing nothing but their underwear. It was amazing how, now that they were semi-naked, they looked a lot less scary. Zak even heard a giggle from one of the captive children behind him.

'What do you think, sweetie?' Gabs called. 'Do we let them keep their pants?'

Zak shook his head. He wanted them naked, because a naked kid in the jungle has more to think about than causing trouble for other people.

'I don't think so,' he said with a frown. 'Without their clothes, they're totally harmless. If you can think of a better way that doesn't involve bullets, I'm all ears.' Gabs shrugged, so he turned back to the boys. 'Lose them,' he instructed.

Steaming with embarrassment, the East Side Boys removed their underwear.

Zak looked at Kicker. 'Pick up all the clothes and put them in a pile, then step away,' he said. '*Now!*'

His eyes burning with shame, Kicker did as he was told. Moments later there was a pile of clothes on the ground. The East Side Boys, huddled in a group about ten metres away and covering themselves with their hands, couldn't take their eyes off their clothes.

Zak still had the little flask of fuel in his rucksack that they'd taken from Cruz's aircraft. He unstoppered it and sprinkled the remainder over the clothes. Then he set his lighter to the pile. It immediately whooshed up in flame. While it was burning, he looked through the shimmering haze above it, to the awkward, naked East Side Boys beyond. For a moment he felt sorry for them, but then he remembered what they'd been trying to make Smiler do.

'Get out,' he called across the fire. 'Stay away from the camp and stay away from the river. If we see any of you ever again, we won't be so lenient.'

The humiliated East Side Boys started filing towards the exit. Without their warlike clothes and their weapons, they were just skin and bones. As they got closer to the exit, they started running. They clearly wanted to be out of there.

And that suited Zak just fine.

He felt himself relaxing. Gabs had lowered her gun. She had walked over to the trembling Smiler and had one hand lightly on his shoulder as she checked he was OK. Raf was heading over to the gate to relieve the unconscious guards of their clothes too. Latifah, however, was still a picture of anxiety. She tugged on Zak's sleeve. 'We can't wait,' she said urgently. 'We have to follow Señor Martinez.'

Zak blinked. 'Why?' he asked. 'What's happening?'

Latifah's lip wobbled. She looked like she was about to cry.

Zak listened, stunned, to what she had to say next.

18

VODUN

Zak, Raf and Gabs stared at Latifah in astonishment.

'They're trying to do *what*?' Gabs exclaimed.

'I . . . I'm *sorry* I didn't tell you everything. I was just worried that you might leave the children in the camp in your hurry to go after Señor Martinez.'

'Forget about that now,' said Zak. He was standing in a group with Raf, Gabs and Latifah. Latifah seemed to be more comfortable talking with someone more her own age, so it was up to Zak to lead the conversation. 'Let me get this straight. Cruz and Sudiq have more than a hundred heavily armed East Side Boys, and they want to bring down the president of The Gambia. Then they're going to install Sudiq in his place. I mean, is that even possible?'

'It depends what sort of army he has with him,' Gabs said. 'The situation in The Gambia is fluid at the moment. It's just left the Commonwealth, and they've got a history of sudden regime change.'

'I think there are at least one hundred East Side Boys,' said Latifah. 'All armed.'

Raf looked grim. 'You can do a lot with a hundred armed thugs. There have been coups in bigger African states than The Gambia, using fewer men than that.'

'And in the meantime,' Zak continued, 'they're going to mastermind some sort of atrocity against a tourist target in Banjul, to scare westerners out of the place.'

'You forgot about Malcolm,' Raf butted in helpfully.

'Right. And they've got Malcolm, who they're going to use to disable all communications in the capital.'

Latifah nodded silently. 'Does he really know how to do that?' she asked.

'You bet he does.' Zak turned to his Guardian Angels. 'We *have* to warn someone.'

'Pass the phone,' Raf scowled. 'I'll call 999.'

They stared at each other.

'What sort of a head start does he have on us?' Gabs asked.

'Three hours,' Latifah said. 'Maybe four.'

Gabs cursed. 'We could do with that helicopter,' she muttered.

'If the East Side Boys we just scared away were going to join them, there must be more boats down by the river,' Zak said.

'If we're going to go, we need to go now,' Raf added. He looked around at the other children. '*They* can't come with us. Latifah, you need to stay here with them. We'll leave you a weapon and I'll show you how to use it. If any of those East Side Boys come back, you'll need to defend yourself. As soon as we get to Banjul, we'll get word to someone that you're here. Can you look after these children?'

Latifah nodded.

Raf looked over at Smiler, who was sitting on the ground hugging his knees. He lowered his voice. 'We should take *him* with us, though. He has the marks on his face and Cruz is expecting him. If we need to get close to Cruz, that could be useful.'

'Don't you think he's gone through enough?' Zak asked.

'It doesn't matter. This thing's bigger than any of us. We'll need to throw everything we have at it. We'll need to take the coffin full of money too. How much did you say was in there, Latifah?'

'Two million, three hundred and forty-six

thousand, six hundred and twenty-five US dollars.' Latifah recited the number like it was imprinted on her brain.

'That's a lot of dough, even for Cruz. He won't want to lose it. The money and the kid could be our ticket to get in to see him, wherever he is. But we need to get moving. Gabs, spend fifteen minutes with the kids. Calm them down. I need to show Latifah her way round this AK-47.' Raf turned to Zak. 'Speak to Smiler,' he said. 'We need him on side.'

'We're asking a lot,' Zak said.

'Then you'd better be persuasive. Let's get moving everyone. Time's running out, and Cruz sure as hell isn't going to wait for us.'

Zak's Guardian Angels strode off to attend to their business, so he hurried up to Smiler. 'You OK, mate?' he asked.

Smiler nodded, but he didn't look OK. The wounds on his cheeks were inflamed and sore, but it was the haunted look on his face that gave him such a dejected air. Zak wondered what was going through Smiler's head. Would he have shot those children if Zak hadn't stopped him? Had he been on the point of no return?

'What's your real name?' Zak asked. 'I mean, you're not really called Smiler, right?'

Smiler shrugged. 'My name is Kofi. But I prefer Smiler. It's what my parents called me.'

Zak put one hand on his shoulder. 'You did a very brave thing back there, Smiler,' he said. 'Thank you.'

Smiler didn't reply, but Zak thought he perhaps looked a little better.

Zak drew a deep breath. 'We want you to come with us,' he said. 'I can't guarantee you'll be safe, and we know we can't force you into it. We can leave you here if you want.'

Smiler glanced down at his shoes.

'The truth is,' Zak continued, 'I was hoping you could help us. Sudiq and Señor Martinez, they've got my friend. He didn't want to be involved in this any more than you do. But sometimes . . .' He gave a little shrug. 'Sometimes, you don't have the choice, right?'

Smiler raised his head and looked straight at him.

'I'm giving you the choice now, though,' Zak said quietly. 'You can stay here where it's safe – well, saf*er* – or you can help us stop them killing a *lot* of people. It's up to you.'

There was a moment of silence.

'Did Sudiq really kill your mother and father, like Señor Martinez said?' Smiler asked.

Zak nodded.

'So you have no family, like me?'

Zak thought about that for a second. 'Oh, I have family all right,' he said finally. He pointed at Raf and Gabs. 'They're right here.'

'The East Side Boys said they would be my family,' said Smiler. 'At first I thought that would be a good thing. But I've changed my mind.' A hint of steel entered his expression. 'If *you* can choose your family, so can I.' He paused. 'If I come with you, might I die?'

Zak hesitated. Then he nodded. 'It's a risk we'll all be taking.'

Smiler looked at the ground. 'It doesn't matter anyway. I don't have much to live for. I'll do whatever you ask. Sudiq and Señor Martinez are bad men. I see that now. They need to be stopped. What will I have to do?'

'I don't know yet. It depends what we find when we get to Banjul. For now, can you show me where the money is?'

Smiler nodded and got to his feet. 'Follow me.'

He led Zak to one of the iron-roofed huts. The camp looked different in the daylight, and it was only once they'd entered the hut itself that Zak realized this was where Cruz had stuffed him into his own coffin. He banished that memory with a shudder, and focused on another coffin in the middle of the room.

The lid was leaning against the box. It was carved with a horrific image: a gruesome face with eyes that wept blood. The coffin itself was stuffed with cash: thick wads of hundred-dollar bills. Zak was surprised at how little room just over two and a quarter million dollars took up. He reckoned he could fit it all into a couple of large carrier bags if he wanted to. Or, at a push, into the rucksack he had over his shoulder.

He stared at it. Then he turned to Smiler.

'Go back to the others,' he said. 'Wait for me there. If anyone asks where I am, tell them I'm sealing the coffin, then checking the other East Side Boys have dispersed before we leave.'

Smiler glanced first at the money, then back up at Zak. 'Is that *really* what you're doing?' he asked.

Zak gave him a piercing look. He didn't reply.

'Do you know what the picture on the lid means?' Smiler asked.

Zak shook his head.

'In the Vodun religion, it means death. Nobody will open that coffin, once it is sealed. People will not talk about Vodun, but they believe it.' He paused. '*I* believe it.'

'It's just a picture.'

'Maybe. Maybe not.'

Zak breathed in deeply. It had suddenly grown a little colder in the hut, and he didn't like it. 'I don't know what's going to happen in the next few hours, Smiler,' he said. 'But whatever comes, you need to trust me. Can you do that?'

Smiler nodded, and Zak felt a quiet pang of guilt. He was pulling the wool over this boy's eyes, and over the eyes of his Guardian Angels too.

But something told him he was about to make the right call.

At least, he *hoped* he was.

Their farewell to Latifah had been quick and abrupt. It needed to be. Half of Zak felt anxious leaving her in charge of those vulnerable kids. The other half told him that she'd proved herself to be pretty capable so far. Maybe they'd be OK. *Maybe.*

Having trekked through the jungle for two days, it was easy to follow the beaten path that led from the camp through the vegetation to the river. The river bank itself was covered in high mangroves, but there was a small clearing, only about ten metres deep, which formed a mini-shore where two wooden boats were beached.

They were ramshackle, to say the least, but ready to be used. Each had a ten-horsepower outboard motor and a spare jerry can of fuel. They were wooden, and had once been painted white, but now the paint was mostly peeled off. They looked watertight, though, and each was big enough for eight people – or four people and a coffin, which meant that Zak, Gabs, Raf and Smiler would only need one of them.

'I never knew two million, three hundred and forty-six thousand, six hundred and twenty-five dollars could weigh so much,' Raf said sarcastically. They were carrying the coffin awkwardly on their shoulders, like pallbearers at a funeral. Slowly, they lowered it down onto the beach. Gabs examined the two boats, before selecting the one on the left and stealing the second fuel can from its partner. Zak rubbed his painful shoulder. Then, at a nod from Raf, he took one end of the coffin and placed it lengthways inside the boat. He found himself averting his eyes from the picture on the top.

'Let's get this boat in the water,' Raf said. Zak nodded. Together, they pushed the stern of the vessel and the hull slid across the marshy bank and into the still waters of the river. Raf stood, feet immersed, holding the boat. Zak looked back at Smiler. He hadn't moved, but was staring at the boat itself with obvious anxiety.

'It's just a picture, mate,' Zak said quietly.

Smiler gave him a piercing look. 'It's not the

picture that I'm worried about,' he said. Then he pushed past Zak, jogged down the bank and scampered into the boat where Gabs was already sitting. Zak followed and climbed in after him. Still holding the hull, Raf waded out another couple of metres, then hurled himself into the boat. It rocked ominously, but stayed upright as Raf cranked up the outboard motor, then lowered it gently into the shallow water. The boat sped off from the shore. As the water became deeper, he let the motor sink to its full depth. Within a minute, they were roaring up this broad lazy river with water spraying all around them.

They travelled in silence. Raf was fully focused on steering the boat, Smiler stared nervously at the engraving on the coffin, and Gabs and Zak scanned the river and its banks. They were the only people in sight, and there wasn't much sign of wildlife either. Now and then a bird rose from the dense mangroves on either side of them. Occasionally, Zak saw something break the surface of the water ahead. A fish, or something else? Zak couldn't tell, and he wasn't sure he wanted to know.

After so long in the jungle, it felt strange to be under open skies. Zak couldn't help feeling weirdly exposed. The mangroves could hide all manner of threats – he couldn't help imagining images of naked

East Side Boys crouching in the bushes, waiting to attack him – but Zak had to remind himself that they'd have other things on their minds. Moreover, Cruz didn't *know* he was being pursued.

Cruz. He found that his lip was curling at the thought of him. There was a time when Zak had thought he could save his former friend. Turn him back into the kid he used to be. But as they sped upriver, he realized he no longer thought that. Cruz was too far gone. His actions had long been those of a mad man. And a *bad* man. It had taken a long time for Zak to accept it. Now he knew they had to do whatever it took to stop him. And to stop Sudiq.

Sudiq. The expression on Zak's face grew fiercer. He looked at the AK-47 that Gabs was still carrying. Then he looked at the coffin.

Zak had never killed a man. He'd always done whatever he could to avoid it. But if Sudiq was here, now, what would he do?

He didn't know.

PART THREE

PART THREE

19

BANJUL

The Palace Hotel, Banjul, The Gambia

Molly Middleton was enjoying her holiday, and didn't want it to be over. She knew that her mum and dad didn't have much money. She also knew that the cost of the plane tickets to The Gambia had been expensive, and so had the hotel room that she was sharing with them. She knew that it might be a long time before they went on holiday again. So she was determined to make the most of her last day.

After breakfast, the three of them had walked down to the pool. Mum had laid down on a sun bed where she was staring at the screen of her pink mobile phone. Probably playing *Angry Birds*, Molly thought. Dad had got into the water with her and played for a bit. Now he was drying off in the sun, flicking through his book on bird-watching. Dad was a keen ornithologist. That was one of the reasons they'd come here – so he could spot birds that were rare in other parts of the world. Molly stayed in the water. The pool was very crowded with lots of people splashing around and squealing. That wasn't Molly's style. She was happy just to bob around, avoiding the noisy kids, and watching what was going on around her.

There was a high stone wall surrounding the hotel, which meant you could only see the beach from the rooms on the second floor. It wasn't the kind of beach, though, where you'd want to spend much time. The sand was hard and muddy and the water had some kind of green scum floating on the surface. On her first day here, Molly had seen some fishermen pull an enormous, wriggling eel out of the water. So she and her mum and dad had been happy to stay by the hotel pool, and Molly had got to know the faces – and in some cases the names – of all the hotel staff.

Or so she thought.

Because now, as she trod water in the deep end, she saw someone in the same green jacket that all the staff wore. She knew she hadn't seen him before, because she would have remembered the lines on his face. There was a thin, pale scar on each cheek, leading from the edge of his lips up to each ear.

He was young. Fifteen, maybe, which would make him only about three years older than Molly herself. And he wore a deeply unpleasant scowl as he stood with his back up against the exterior wall. He was half hidden by a palm in a large pot, but Molly saw that he was carrying a plastic bag. As he looked around the pool area, Molly knew, with a flash of insight, that he was looking for somewhere to hide it.

Suddenly, his head turned. He was looking directly at Molly, and his eyes seemed to pierce her. Molly instantly dropped below the surface of the water. The screams of excited children became muffled. Through her half-closed eyes, the world was a blur. She stayed there until her lungs burned. When she broke the surface of the water again, she quickly wiped her eyes and looked back to where the boy had been standing.

He was gone.

She looked around, her sharp eyes scanning the pool area. He was nowhere to be seen.

Nor was the package he'd been carrying.

Molly climbed out of the pool and trotted over to the beds where her mum and dad were asleep in the sun. She wrapped herself in a towel and slipped on her crocs. She was about to go and have a look around for this strange boy and his strange package, when her mum opened her eyes.

'Put some more sunscreen on, love, if you've finished in the pool.'

Molly blinked. Sunscreen. Right. She looked around for the bottle. 'I think it's up in the room,' she said.

Her mum sat up and fumbled in the bag for her key card, which she handed over to Molly. 'Go and get it then,' she instructed.

Molly knew it was no good arguing. Her mum was *obsessed* with sunscreen. She took the card and headed away from the pool area, into the hotel and towards the lifts.

Their room was on the third floor. She pressed the 'up' button and waited for the clunky old lift to arrive.

Its doors hissed open and Molly's heart stopped. It was not the same boy from the roof who stood in the lift, looking out. But he had the same markings on his face, and he too carried a bulky plastic bag.

He stared out of the lift. Molly felt her face going red.

'I, er . . . sorry, I'll wait for the next one . . .'

But the doors were already closing. The boy disappeared and the lift went up.

When it returned two minutes later, it was empty.

Molly stepped inside and pressed the button marked '3'. The lift juddered up. A minute later she was stepping into the room she shared with her mum and dad.

It had a sea view. Molly had enjoyed watching the sun set over the horizon as the locals congregated on the beach to fish and chat. Now, as she looked around for her sunscreen, she noticed something else. A group of three boys, standing together and pointing at the hotel.

Dad's bird-watching binoculars were on a little table by the window. Molly grabbed them and put them to her eyes. Everything was blurry, so she adjusted the little knob between the lenses and the boys' faces came into sharp focus.

She couldn't help a little gasp from escaping her throat. These boys were not wearing the green uniform of the hotel. They were wearing bandannas, sleeveless jackets and army trousers. But they all had the same markings on their cheeks: the thin pale scars. They were discussing something to do with the hotel – there was no doubt about it. Molly lowered the binoculars and sat down on the edge of her bed. She told herself that she was being silly. Her mum always said she was a worrier, and she knew it was true. After all, what had she really seen? Nothing.

That was what there was to worry about: nothing.

She took a deep breath, and started to rub sunscreen into her arms. She would forget about the boys with the scarred faces, she decided, and concentrate on important things. Like sunbathing, and enjoying the last day of her holiday.

The residence of the Gambian president was larger than every other house in Banjul, and in much the nicest area. Unlike the rest of the small but sprawling town, the buildings in this quarter were not dirty, ramshackle concrete blocks with tin roofs and poor sanitation. They sat in broad, spacious streets lined with palm trees. Almost all the houses had a Mercedes parked outside. Admittedly, most of these were at least ten years old, but they were still a lot finer than most of the cars in the country, which were held together by bits of string and imaginative welding.

There were more policemen here too. Some strutted up and down the street, impressed with their own uniforms and with pistols swinging by their hips. Others sheltered from the sun in the shade of the palm trees, smoking cigarettes. Outside the president's residence itself there were three soldiers. Everybody knew that meant the president was at home. When he left, two of the soldiers would go with him, leaving only one to guard the tall iron gate.

It was an important job, guarding the president. A job only given to the most trusted members of the small army of The Gambia. More than ten years ago, the president had seized power in a coup. Nobody had died. It had been easy, but the president knew that if *he* could do it, somebody else could do it to *him*. So the soldiers were even more heavily armed than the policemen. They carried MP5 sub-machine guns and wore sturdy body armour.

The presidential guard carried their weapons like trophies. Nobody dared come near them. They were untouchable, and a little arrogant. So they barely even saw the two boys who walked, shoulder to shoulder, past the presidential residence. They certainly didn't notice the searching way both boys stared in their direction, noting how many of them there were, and where they were standing.

Nor did they notice the thin scars on each boy's face.

One of the policemen *did* notice them, however. Unlike some of his colleagues, he was not resting under a tree or trying to look cool. He was a conscientious officer, with a family to care for. Moreover, he saw the markings on these boys' faces. He had heard the rumours – that a few of the West Side Boys from Sierra Leone had formed their own splinter group. That there had been sightings of these boys all around Banjul over the past week.

That there had been unexplained deaths whenever they'd cropped up.

Which was why he was following them now, past the presidential residence that they seemed so interested in.

Past the grand houses and the Mercedes cars.

Past the other policemen who wouldn't have stopped these two boys even if they *had* been suspicious.

'Boys?' he said. They had reached the end of the street and were on the point of turning left into the broad, busy main road. Cars thundered past: white bush taxis, pick-up trucks with smoke billowing out of their exhaust pipes. '*Boys?*'

The two boys stopped and slowly turned to look at him. He had a better view of their faces now: of their thin white scars, and spiteful expressions.

'What are you doing in this part of town, boys? Let's see some identification, hey?'

They boys didn't move. They just stared at him, their cold faces unpleasantly amused.

'Come on, you heard me. Some ID.'

'Sure, boss,' said one of the boys. He wore a red and white bandana that matched his bloodshot eyes. His reached inside his baggy khaki top.

The policeman saw too late that the ID he was fetching was of the gun-metal grey kind, with a barrel and a trigger. He instantly felt for his own gun, but his fingers hadn't even reached it when he heard the shots.

The first felt like a heavy blow in his stomach. It knocked him backwards about a metre. He looked down in shock, to see blood gushing through his pale grey shirt. Then he looked up at the boy who had just shot him.

The boy fired again. The second bullet entered the policeman's body about five centimetres above the first and he collapsed to the ground unable to breathe. In a corner of his mind, he wondered if anybody would come to help. But the sound of the gunshots was drowned out by the heavy traffic and he knew nobody was coming.

He tried to speak. To tell the boys that he had a little daughter at home, who needed her dad. But he had no breath. Instead, he reached out his right arm, begging the boys to show him some mercy.

But they weren't in the mercy game. The boy with the gun bent down. The policeman's eyes were growing dim, but he could see the beads of sweat on his killer's nose.

'Congratulations,' the boy rasped. 'You're the first one to die here today.' He had a menacing glint in his eyes, and seemed to be enjoying himself. 'But don't worry,' the boy continued. 'You won't be the last.'

He fired a third shot, and the policeman's world went black.

The communications tower on the edge of Banjul airport was a tall, concrete structure. It was 750 metres from the large white terminal building where, in the summer months, tourists crowded on and off international flights.

The tower had a large, rotating radar dish on the top. At ground level was a single entrance. A flight of steps led to the control room itself. This was circular, with curved windows all around giving a 360-degree view over the airport and the sur-rounding area. During the daytime it was guarded by a middle-aged Gambian man called Robert who'd had this job for ten years. He liked it. He could sit in the sunshine all day and watch the planes landing and taking off in the distance. One day, he even hoped to get on a plane himself, but he needed to save up more money first.

Nobody ever approached the communications tower except the people who worked there, and Robert knew them all by name. There were air-traffic-control personnel, and guys from the mobile phone company. There was a government man who never told Robert his business but was friendly enough. They all had passes to enter the tower, but Robert never asked to see them. That would be ridiculous, after all these years.

He recognized their cars too: beaten-up old saloons, mostly, which they parked up within the high wire perimeter fence that surrounded the communications tower. Robert was supposed to keep the perimeter gate locked, but he almost never did. Why bother? Nobody strange ever came to the tower, and it was a hundred metres from the gate to the tower itself. A long way to walk in the sun.

Today, though, a little voice in his mind told him that perhaps he *should* have locked the gate. Because as he sat on his rickety stool at the foot of the tower, he saw three vehicles entering the perimeter, shimmering in the heat haze. He didn't recognize them – they were not the run-down old cars that Robert was used to seeing, but were big, shiny four-by-fours. Range Rovers maybe. They drove slowly in convoy and something about them made him feel uneasy.

Robert squinted in the sunlight as they approached. He didn't move. When the convoy stopped, about thirty metres from his position, he stayed sitting down. In all his ten years guarding the tower, he'd never had to draw the gun he carried by his side and he didn't intend to now. He was a peaceful man.

The side doors of the Range Rovers opened in unison. Four people emerged from the first vehicle. They were young – not much older than fifteen – and Robert's eyes were immediately drawn to their faces. Each youngster had a thin scar stretching from the corner of his mouth to his ear. Like a hideous, fixed grin. They wore a strange combination of clothes. Bandannas, army camouflage trousers, dirty T-shirts and sleeveless jackets that showed their lean, muscly arms.

And guns. They each had an assault rifle strapped across their chest. It looked to Robert like they knew how to use them.

Four more boys climbed out of the Range Rover at the back of the convoy. They also had scarred faces and weapons.

Only then did two figures emerge from the middle vehicle.

These two looked different. They were also young, but they weren't African. One was tall and thin, with a pronounced Adam's apple and a cold, cruel look in his eyes. Robert thought that perhaps he looked South American. The other had pasty white skin and thick glasses. His eyes darted in every direction, and he seemed terrified. It was the sight of that scared kid that persuaded Robert to stand up.

'Hey!' he shouted out, choosing English as his language because this was such a strange collection of people. 'What's going on?'

'Sit down, Grandad,' one of the scar-faced boys shouted back. A few others laughed. 'Maybe we let you live, hey?'

More laughter. Something snapped inside Robert. Sure, he was a peaceful man – some might even say lazy – but he had his pride. Fumbling, he felt for the old pistol by his side.

If you're going to draw a gun on an armed man, you need to do it quickly. If you're going to draw a gun on *eight* armed men, you'd better be like lightning.

Robert was neither.

His fingertips had barely touched the handle of his gun when there was a cluster of clicks as eight safety catches were released. Robert looked up to see the boys aiming their weapons directly at him.

A pause. In the distance, the roar of an aircraft taking off filled the air.

And then the tall South American boy from the second car spoke.

'Kill him,' he said.

There was no hesitation. Eight guns fired a single

round each. They all found their mark. Robert only heard the sound of the one that killed him.

Malcolm was indeed weak with terror. As he watched the man at the foot of the communications tower fall, bloodied, to the ground, he felt his own knees buckle beneath him. Cruz caught him before he collapsed, but it wasn't out of kindness. He yanked Malcolm back up to his feet again, then barked at the East Side Boys. 'Clear the tower,' he said.

Four of the boys stepped forward, past the corpse of the guard that was bleeding heavily onto the tarmac. One of them stepped in a puddle of blood, but it didn't seem to bother him. He just walked scarlet footprints up to the entrance of the communications tower as he and his three companions disappeared inside.

There was a minute's silence, followed by a sudden burst of muffled gunfire from inside the tower. It didn't last more than thirty seconds. Then it fell silent.

Cruz turned to the remaining East Side Boys. 'Guard the tower,' he instructed. 'We're going in.' He seized Malcolm roughly by his upper arm. 'When we get inside, you'll do exactly as I tell you. Understood?'

Malcolm was too scared to answer. He just swallowed nervously as Cruz dragged him away from the cars.

Inside the base of the tower there was nothing but a spiral iron staircase disappearing into a low ceiling. Cruz pushed Malcolm towards it with a single word: 'Up.'

Malcolm staggered towards the staircase and started climbing it. The iron clattered noisily as he walked up, and he counted precisely thirteen steps before he emerged into a large circular room on the first floor. Around the walls were banks of old computers and communications terminals. Curved windows looked out towards the perimeter fencing. On one side Malcolm could see the white airport terminal. On another, thick trees in the distance. The four East Side Boys had taken up position around the edge of the room, facing inwards. And on the floor were six dead bodies, bleeding as heavily as the guard downstairs.

Cruz entered the room behind Malcolm. With a sweep of his arm he gestured at the banks of computers. 'There you go, Einstein,' he said. 'Knock yourself out.'

Malcolm simply stared – not at the terminals, but at the bleeding corpses.

Cruz stepped round to face him. He grabbed

Malcolm by the scruff of the neck and looked at him like he was the lowest form of life.

'Listen carefully, you freak,' he said. 'Those idiots that you led through the jungle are dead. Your stupid cousin is dead. You've got nobody except me. I'm your best friend and your worst nightmare all in one, do you understand that? And if you don't do *exactly* what I tell you to do, I won't instruct my East Side Boys to kill you. I'll get them to hurt you so badly, you'll wish you *were* dead. I promise you, Malcolm, you'll beg me to finish you off.'

To emphasize his point, Cruz suddenly pulled a knife from under his clothes. He pressed the point against the soft skin just below Malcolm's right eye. Malcolm felt a scarlet tear drip down his cheek. Terror was not an emotion to which he was accustomed, but he felt it now: cold dread, seeping into every limb.

'What do you want me to do?' he croaked. Cruz had told him already, of course, but he wanted to make sure he had it right.

Cruz's eyes went narrow with impatience. 'I want all wireless communications in the capital disabled. Cellphones. Short-wave radios. Wi-fi. Everything. You can do that from here.'

Malcolm's eyes flickered round the tower. He shook his head. 'It's not possible,' he said weakly. 'I don't have the right equipment.'

There was a silence in the control tower. Cruz didn't take his eyes off Malcolm. There was a sense that everybody in there was holding his breath.

'Two things, freak,' Cruz said quietly. 'Number one: you're not the only brainbox in here. I was a scientist before I became a businessman. I *know* what's possible and what isn't. And number two: the only reason you're alive is to do this for me. If you really think you can't do it, say the word and my men will deal with you.'

Malcolm swallowed hard.

'I'm going to ask you this question just once.' Cruz's voice was deathly quiet. Malcolm could feel his enemy's hot breath on his face. 'Can you do it?'

Another pause. Then Malcolm nodded.

'Then do it *now*.'

Cruz stepped back and once again swept his arm towards the computer screens. Malcolm edged forward, stepping round a bleeding corpse and selecting a terminal that looked at least fifteen years old. Within a few seconds his face was bathed in a green light and his fingers were flying over the keyboard.

'How long will it take?' Cruz demanded.

'About twenty minutes,' said Malcolm.

A pause.

'You've got ten,' said Cruz.

20

THE COUP

Albert Market in Banjul had not changed for 150 years, or so all the guide books said. Stallholders – mostly women – sat cross-legged on the ground with their wares spilled out in front of them. Baskets of fruit, brightly coloured clothes, hair extensions, electrical goods, shoes and worthless trinkets to sell to tourists were all on display. A butchered cow was laid out on a wooden table, flies crawling over its dark red meat. Fishermen offered huge barracuda with rows of sharp teeth. It was noisy, hot, dirty and crowded.

So crowded that nobody would ever notice the sudden influx of fifty young teenagers with strange scars on their faces. The East Side Boys had no fixed abode. They slept wherever they lay, and stole whatever they wanted. They were used to living on the streets, and now they swaggered, as if they owned them.

They came in pairs, entering from all sides of the busy market. They carried weapons, but kept them hidden for now. Instead, they held sturdy poles, which they pretended to use as walking sticks.

They ignored the stallholders who implored them to buy their goods. They ignored the angry looks of the men and women that they shouldered past as they headed towards their positions. But finally, at 09.00hrs, they stopped.

Then they pulled their weapons.

Each of the fifty boys dotted around the market raised their guns above their heads and fired a single shot.

The noise was deafening. Like fifty bursts of thunder in quick succession. All movement and noise in the marketplace stopped.

The boys went to work. They raised their walking sticks and started swinging them around. They didn't care what or whom they hit. The more chaos and damage they caused, the better. Their sticks cracked against the cheeks of old ladies swathed in colourful cloth. They upturned trays of fruit and baskets of vegetables. They snarled at young children, who ran away with frightened tears in their eyes.

All around the marketplace, stallholders and punters hit the ground, pressing themselves onto the stone floor in the hope that it would make them less visible to these scar-faced marauders. Some of them felt heels grind their cheeks into the ground. They knew better than to complain. Nobody was dead yet. But with so many guns around, it was surely only a matter of time.

There was one stallholder, though, who was braver than the others. She was a teenage girl with intricately plaited hair, selling bracelets that she had embroidered herself. Now she crawled behind the little pile of wooden boxes on which she displayed her goods. From her pocket she pulled a chunky mobile phone. She normally kept it switched off, because the battery was old and didn't hold its charge very well. Now she pressed the button on the top with shaking hands. It seemed to take for ever to switch on. All around she heard the chaotic sounds of the boys terrorizing the marketplace, and of people screaming.

The screen on her phone lit up. She typed in her brother's number. He would know what to do. He would bring help.

She hit dial and put the phone to her ear.

Then she winced. There was no ringing tone. Just a harsh, whining, white noise.

She checked the screen again. The service bars were full. She redialled.

Same thing.

Something was wrong with her phone, she decided. But she didn't get the chance to dial for a third time. Someone kicked the boxes over to reveal her crouching down behind them. She felt a foot in her stomach. Winded, she dropped her phone.

One of the boys knelt down to look at her. He had a wild, crazy look on his scarred face.

'No good trying to use your phone,' he said with a spiteful grin. 'No good *anybody* trying to use their phones.'

As if to emphasize his point, he stood up, then stamped on the handset. It shattered. Then he booted the girl in the stomach again and turned his back on her. She was out of play now, and there were plenty of other people to terrorize.

Sudiq strode down a long street in the centre of Banjul. He was flanked by two armed East Side Boys, and he had a cruel smile on his face.

Behind him were scenes of chaos, worse even than those at the market. Three cars were burning on the side of the road. Shop windows were shattered. Stalls were overturned. Members of the public were screaming. Some of them tried to yell into their phones, but no phones were working. East Side Boys – they seemed to crawl out of every alleyway – strutted around, bullying the local populace and peppering the air with the sound of gunshot. They were doing their job very well. In a few hours, this would all be over.

There was no sound of sirens. Sudiq was pleased about that. He hadn't really trusted Cruz's plan to wipe out all communications in the capital, but it seemed to be working. The emergency services clearly had no way of coordinating their response to the sudden rioting in the city. The police and the army would be trying to respond as best they could. But if they couldn't talk to each other, they would be all over the place. They were so busy trying to communicate, they were seriously weakened.

It was a good plan. Sudiq had to give Cruz that. The thought even crossed his mind that he was smarter than his father, whom Sudiq had served for so many years.

And Cruz's plan would make what Sudiq had to do now child's play.

He picked up his pace, almost oblivious to another burning car he passed, then turned right. The road in which the presidential residence was situated was just up ahead. Sudiq's eyes flashed eagerly. He walked towards it so swiftly that his guards suddenly had to trot to keep up.

At the top of the road, he passed the body of a dead policeman. Two more East Side Boys loitered casually around it. As Sudiq strode past, they joined him. Now he had four of them walking behind him as he marched confidently down the street.

Sudiq knew which building was the presidential residence, but he would have figured it out anyway. It was the largest, broadest house, made of white stone. There were pillars at the front and a Gambian flag hanging limply from a pole at the top. Two members of the presidential guard stood at the main gate. They knew something was up – they could hear the shouts of rioting in the distance. Glancing nervously at each other, they anxiously fingered their weapons.

When they saw Sudiq and his followers approaching from thirty metres away, they backed up against the railings of the residence. They looked even more nervous now. It's easy to be confident when you're the only person with a gun. But suddenly they were outnumbered, and things didn't look so good.

The guards started to raise their weapons.

The four East Side Boys did the same.

'Don't kill them,' Sudiq said under his breath.

'We need the army on our side. Just give them a scare.'

The East Side Boys didn't need telling twice. They fired.

The sound of one assault rifle firing a burst of rounds is loud enough. Four of them pumping out bullets at the same time can be deafening. The shots thundered towards the guards, missing them but sparking violently against the railings as they ricocheted off.

Panicked, the guards hit the ground. The East Side Boys cheered. They ran towards the guards. Within seconds they had disarmed them and dragged them to their feet. Two East Side Boys held each guard, one grabbing a clump of hair, the other clutching his prisoner's throat.

Sudiq approached. He spoke slowly and very clearly. 'You will take us to the president now,' he said. 'If you shout out, or hesitate, we will kill you. If you do as we say, you'll be well rewarded. Do you understand?'

The guards nodded vigorously. Moments later, this strange group of seven boys and men had stepped through the perimeter fence and were approaching the main entrance of the presidential residence.

* * *

The president was not alone. Nor was he a fool. Word had reached him of the rioting in the street and he had heard the sound of gunfire echoing across his capital city. He knew what was coming.

He had instructed the head of the army – a broad-shouldered, flat-nosed man who now stood to his right – to surround the residence with armed troops. The army chief had tried to make the relevant calls, but the phone line out of the residence seemed to be down. His cellphone didn't work, either. Nor did the phones of anyone else in the vicinity. There was little he could do now, except pull out the pearl-handled pistol he normally only carried for show, and wait by his president's side.

The president himself had changed into an expensive suit and tie. Now he was regretting his choice of clothes as sweat poured from his body. He paced the large, marble-floored room in which he normally conducted important business. He was proud of this room. It was open on one side and looked out onto a massive courtyard, full of greenery and fountains that tinkled gently. The courtyard served two purposes: to look beautiful, but also to provide a landing pad for a helicopter in case the president needed to be evacuated.

But there were no helicopters arriving now. The president was trapped.

He occasionally gave his army chief an irritated glare. *How could you get me into this situation?* it seemed to say. The army chief could do nothing but bow his head and look miserable.

The door opened and the army chief raised his pistol. But he lowered it again as four heavily armed boys with strange scars on their faces spilled in, aiming their weapons directly at him. He muttered under his breath, with more than a hint of contempt: 'East Side Boys . . .' Behind them, two guards hovered uneasily, then they took to their heels and sprinted away down the corridor.

A figure stood in the doorway. An older man, whose hair was tied in tight dreadlocks.

'Good morning, Mr President,' he intoned slowly as he stepped inside the room. 'I won't keep you long. As you've probably discovered, we have disabled all communications within the capital.'

No reply.

The man with dreadlocks smiled. 'My name is Sudiq Al-Tikriti Gomez. My excellent East Side Boys are busy causing chaos and death on the streets, and a few of them have been dispatched to the hotel room where I understand your wife and children currently believe themselves to be beyond harm's way.'

The president opened his mouth in outrage, but

Sudiq immediately raised one hand to silence him.

'Please, *please*, they're quite safe for the moment. Whether they *remain* safe, of course, is up to you. I will offer you and your family safe passage out of The Gambia to a country of your choosing. I've no doubt you have a stash of money hidden away in a private bank account somewhere. You'll live quite comfortably, I imagine.' Sudiq smiled. 'Do I take it that you accept my offer?'

'Do I have a choice?'

Sudiq's eyes widened. 'Of *course* you have a choice, my friend. Either you do exactly as I say, or I instruct these boys to kill you now, and your family later. But I'm afraid I don't have a great deal of time on my hands, so I must insist on hearing your decision immediately.'

There was a tense silence in the room. The president locked gazes with Sudiq. But after only a few seconds he turned to look at the army chief, and nodded his head, defeated.

The army chief stepped forward. 'I am the head of the Gambian army,' he said. 'I will instruct my men to do whatever you say, Mr . . . I'm sorry, I failed to catch your name.'

Sudiq smiled. A cruel smile, filled with greed.

'Just call me "Sir",' he said. The East Side Boys started to laugh.

* * *

Malcolm looked through the window of the control tower. He could see three aircraft circling in the clear blue sky above the airport. He turned to Cruz.

'Those planes,' he said. 'If nobody can communicate with them, they'll run out of fuel and—'

'*Quiet*,' Cruz hissed, without even glancing at the circling aircraft. He looked at his watch. 'Ten thirty,' he said. 'It will be done by now.' He turned to the East Side Boys guarding the control tower. 'You and you,' he said, pointing at two of the scar-faced boys. 'Guard him. If he does anything suspicious, put a bullet in his head.'

Malcolm felt his glasses slipping down his sweaty nose. He pushed them back up with one finger and blinked heavily. He didn't like being stuck with Cruz, but being stuck without him sounded even worse. His guards were violent. And totally unpredictable. He opened his mouth to try to change Cruz's mind, but no words came out. That was what happened when he was scared.

'The communications stay down for another two hours,' Cruz said. 'I mean it, freak. And remember what I said: the only thing keeping you alive is your ability to do what I tell you.'

Cruz turned and, without uttering another word, walked out of the control tower and down the steps.

Two of the East Side Boys followed him. The two that remained leaned on either side of the door, arrogant looks on their faces. One of them was stroking the trigger of his rifle, but neither said a word.

Malcolm edged backwards towards the computer terminal he had been using. The screen was filled with the complex code he had used to disable the city's communications systems. The cursor blinked, ready to receive more. Malcolm's eyes flickered towards it and his fingers twitched as a million thoughts ran through his panicked brain, like lines of code in themselves.

He licked his lips, glanced anxiously at the computer screen and then, still standing up, allowed his fingers to fly lightly over the keyboard. More and more impenetrable code appeared. Line after line, like it was spilling directly out of Malcolm's brain and into the computer itself.

'Hey!' one of the East Side Boys said sharply. '*Hey!* What are you doing?'

Malcolm looked over his shoulder but didn't stop typing. He wasn't used to feeling scared, as he was now. He didn't think he was doing a very good job of hiding it, but he carried on anyway.

'What I was told to do,' he said, his voice wavering. 'Do you really think the communications will stay down if I don't keep on top of them?' He gave a mirthless little laugh, as if to say: How stupid are *you*?

The East Side Boy stepped forward. He crossed the control room in four large strides, then with one brutal swipe of his arm knocked Malcolm away from the terminal. Malcolm's hands shot up to stop his glasses falling off, but he managed to avoid falling.

Then he shrugged. 'Fine,' he said. 'We'll just stand around here waiting for everything to get back up and running, shall we? Then *you* can explain to Señor Martinez why everything's gone wrong.'

Suddenly the thug looked a little less sure of himself. He glanced over at his mate, then back at Malcolm.

'Get back to work,' he growled.

Malcolm inclined his head, then stepped back over to the terminal and started typing again. He saw his face – intense, tired, frightened, determined – reflected in the screen. But in his mind's eye he saw the face of someone else.

A boy his own age, with scruffy short hair that had been dyed artificially blond.

A boy whom he had last seen being nailed into a coffin, ready for death.

But whom Malcolm knew – or heavily suspected – was *not* dead.

The advantage of being in charge of a city's communications system was that, even if nobody else could access their mobile phones or email accounts, Malcolm *could*. And as he entered lines of code into the computer, the computer spat back the information he was requesting.

It was the position of the phone Zak had taken from Malcolm's apartment back in Johannesburg, and which he had left in his rucksack before entering the camp. And the sequence of figures spat out by the computer told Malcolm that the phone was not buried in the ditch somewhere deep in the Senegalese jungle. The phone's GPS chip reported that it was moving up the same river that Malcolm himself had travelled. And it was just a couple of miles from Banjul.

He looked at his two guards in the reflection of his computer screen. They were still standing by the door.

Then he looked back at his terminal. He had only one option ahead of him, he realized, both to save himself and to save the hundreds of lives that Cruz's men were about to take.

He *had* to get a message to Zak.

21

SMILER'S CHOICE

'We must be getting close!' Zak shouted over the noise of the outboard motor.

The river traffic had grown steadily busier. Zak noticed that all the ramshackle fishing boats he saw were travelling in the opposite direction – *away* from Banjul. They passed within a few metres of one of them and an old Gambian man with a deeply lined face waved his arms and shouted at them in an African dialect.

'What's he saying?' Zak asked Smiler.

'He is telling us to turn back,' Smiler said.

'Look,' said Gabs. She pointed up ahead. In the distance, rising up into the sky, was a tendril of smoke. 'Somehow I don't think that's a barbecue.'

Zak shook his head grimly. It looked like Cruz, Sudiq and their boys had been busy already.

Raf pulled out his phone. In the jungle, they hadn't expected to get any service. Here, on the outskirts of the city, it was different. Here, they *should* be able to use their phones. 'I've got service bars,' he shouted as he continued to guide the boat with one hand. 'Maybe they didn't manage to disable the comms after all.' Zak looked at his own phone – the one he'd taken from Malcolm's house back in Jo'burg – and sure enough he could see three bars of signal strength. But then Raf dialled a number and held the phone up to his ear. He shook his head. 'Nothing,' he said.

Zak wasn't surprised. He knew how good Malcolm was. If anyone could disable the city's communications systems, it was him . . .

Or maybe not. Because suddenly, as Zak held it in his right hand, his own phone pinged into life.

The others in the boat noticed it happen. They all stared first at Zak, then at the phone.

'Message, sweetie?' Gabs asked lightly.

Slightly stunned, Zak swiped the screen of his phone. He read the message on the screen quietly to himself first, then out loud to the others.

'*It's me. Malcolm. I'm at the communications tower near the airport. There are two boys here with guns. They'll probably kill me soon. I hope it doesn't hurt too much. Cruz has gone to the president's house. He says the coup is complete. Sudiq is the president now. But he hasn't finished yet. There are bombs. They are at the Palace Hotel where lots of tourists stay, and are set to go off at midday. I hope you get this message and can do something to stop it. If not, lots of people are going to die. I have to stop now. My guards are looking suspicious. Don't try to reply. It won't work. Malcolm.'*

'The Palace Hotel!' Gabs shouted. 'We need to get there. Fast!'

But as she spoke, Raf killed the engine. 'What are you doing?' Zak demanded. 'We need to—' But he was cut short by a single raised finger from Raf, who then pointed ahead.

They were approaching some sort of harbour. It was about 250 metres away. A collection of old boats bobbed around in the water, and a rickety wooden pier extended around twenty metres into the river. Three figures stood at the end of the pier. Even from this distance Zak could see the outline of the weapons slung around their necks.

'You still got that spotting scope?' Raf asked. Zak nodded, removed it from his pack and handed it over. Raf looked through it, then handed it to Gabs, who took a look and passed it back to Zak. Zak held the scope to one eye and focused in on the figures on the pier. He immediately picked out the scars on their faces.

'East Side Boys,' he muttered.

Raf twisted the outboard motor ninety degrees and slowly chugged towards the edge of the river. Reeds and mangroves sprouted from the water and Zak could see the shadows of large fish below the surface. As the boat bobbed out of sight of the pier guards, Raf turned to Smiler and rapped on the top of the coffin containing Cruz's money.

'Smiler,' he said. 'It's still possible that we'll need to use this – and you – to get access to Cruz. You need to wait here with it. Can you do that?'

Smiler gave an anxious nod.

'We're going to get to the hotel and try to stop this bomb going off. Or at the very least evacuate the place. But we'll be back as soon as we can.'

Raf was already climbing out of the boat and stepping onto the marshy bank. Gabs followed him. Zak found his eyes lingering on the coffin.

'You need this to be with Boss and Señor Martinez, don't you?' said Smiler quietly.

Zak narrowed his eyes. 'It's OK, Smiler,' he said. 'I can't ask you to do that.' He looked over at Raf and Gabs who were almost ten metres away and disappearing from the bank. 'Stay here, like Raf told you.' He started to climb out of the boat, but then he stopped. 'I know Raf said we'd be back, but if something happens . . .' He rummaged in his backpack for a piece of paper and a pencil, hurriedly scrawled a message and pressed it into Smiler's hands. Then he clasped one hand on the boy's shoulder, gave him a reassuring nod, and climbed out of the boat.

'Zak,' said Smiler. 'I know there is something you are not telling your friends. And I don't know what's really in this coffin. But if I took it to Señor Martinez, would it help you?'

'Stay here, Smiler.' Zak avoided the question. 'Do as Raf said. It's safer.'

Smiler bowed his head as Zak turned and ran after his Guardian Angels. But a few seconds later, they heard the growl of the boat's motor. Zak spun round to see Smiler moving away from the bank.

'No!' he shouted.

Too late. The boat veered ninety degrees to the left. Smiler was heading towards the pier where the other East Side Boys were waiting.

'*What's going on!*' Raf was suddenly at Zak's shoulder, watching the boat disappear.

Zak tried to keep his voice steady. 'I don't know,' he lied. His stomach was churning. He'd made a terrible mistake. Smiler was putting himself in very great danger and Zak didn't know how to make it right again.

Raf was swearing under his breath as Gabs strode up to them.

'We can't do anything about it now. We've got to get to the hotel. If Smiler wants to risk his life, that's his business. *Let's go!*'

Raf and Gabs turned and ran. Zak clenched his jaw, watched the boat drift up towards the pier, then turned and followed them.

The ground was wet and marshy underfoot, the air thick with insects. Zak and his Guardian Angels crashed through the vegetation, driven on by urgency. It was 11.30hrs. In thirty minutes precisely, a bomb – maybe more than one – would explode at the Palace Hotel. Hundreds of people could die. Their only chance was if the three agents currently fighting their way towards the city got there in time and evacuated the building.

It wasn't looking good.

The vegetation stopped abruptly and they burst out onto a roughly tarmac'd road. It was busy, but all the cars were heading in a single direction. Zak instantly realized that they were heading *away* from Banjul.

Raf stepped calmly into the line of traffic and held up one hand. Several cars screeched to a halt and honked their horns noisily at him. He ran up to the first car, waving a hundred-dollar bill at the driver.

'Take us to the Palace Hotel,' he said.

The driver shook his head fearfully. Even the promise of money was clearly not enough. He shot off along the road.

Raf flagged down a second driver. The same thing happened.

The driver of a third car, however – a beige, battered VW Polo – couldn't take his eyes off the money. He nodded when Raf explained where they wanted to go, and indicated that they should all climb into the back of the car. Raf and Gabs hurried towards the back seat.

Zak held back.

'Come *on*!' Gabs shouted at him.

Zak shook his head. 'You go,' he said. 'You don't need me to evacuate the hotel. I'm going to find Malcolm.'

Gabs shook her head. 'It's too dangerous. He'll be well guarded. Let's stop the attack, then we'll deal with him together.'

'No. If Cruz hears that you're even in the vicinity of that hotel, he'll know Malcolm tipped you off and he'll get his East Side Boys to kill him immediately.' Zak didn't mention that this was the only way he could think of to save Smiler's skin too.

Gabs hesitated, looking uselessly from side to side.

'We got him into this, Gabs,' Zak urged. 'We have to get him out.'

Without waiting for a reply, he sprinted over to the next car in line, ignoring the cacophony of car horns that blasted through the air. He dug one hand into his pocket and yanked out a fistful of notes, which he waved under the nose of the driver. 'Will you take me to the airport for this?' he shouted.

The driver's eyes bulged and he nodded vigorously. Zak jumped into the back of the car. Within seconds, the driver had done a U-turn. Zak looked out of the window and saw the battered old car carrying Raf and Gabs do the same manoeuvre. He caught a glimpse of Gabs herself, her face troubled and nervous, and suddenly felt very alone.

'Please hurry,' he said to his Gambian driver.

The man looked nervously left and right. In the rear-view mirror, Zak could see sweat on his brow. 'All the planes are cancelled anyway,' the driver said. 'They are making circles in the sky. All the phones are down. Nobody can talk to anybody else.'

'Yeah,' Zak said. 'I heard.'

'Probably it is something to do with the weather.' The man was talking fast and Zak sensed he was trying to keep his mind occupied while they headed back into the city.

'Probably,' said Zak, looking out at the piercing blue sky.

'You will not miss your flight.'

'I'm not catching a flight,' Zak mumbled.

'Then why go to the airport? You want to wait there until you can get out of Banjul? That is a good idea. There are riots in the streets today. Buildings on fire. It is not a safe place to be.'

'How long till we get there?' Zak asked.

'It is not far. Five minutes maybe.' The man fell silent as he concentrated on the road.

'I think there's something Zak's not telling us,' Gabs said.

Their driver screeched wildly up the main road. A sign told them that they were entering the town of Serrekunda, a suburb of Banjul. It appeared to be a busy, sprawling place. But a place in a state of panic. Roadside stalls had been left abandoned. Empty cars sat at the side of the road with their doors flung wide open. They drove past shacks to the left and right where whole families seemed to have congregated. Many of the men were holding phones up to the sky, clearly trying to understand why they wouldn't work.

'What do you mean up to something? Like what?' asked Raf. He glanced at his watch. 11.37hrs.

'I'm not sure. Did you see the way he looked at that coffin? Something's going on. I don't like it.'

Raf gave her a solid stare. 'I know he's like your kid brother, Gabs, but you've got to let go sometime. We've taught him all this stuff so he can act on his own. We won't always be there to help him, you know.' He sniffed. 'He was probably just spooked by that Vodun picture.'

Gabs's cheek twitched. She wiped some little beads of sweat from her nose. 'What if he comes across Sudiq on his own? The guy killed his parents. He's going to want revenge, Raf. He's just a kid. I know he's clever and brave and all that stuff, but he's never killed anyone. I just don't think he has it in him. But if he hesitates for even a moment . . .'

Raf put one hand on hers. 'I think you'll be surprised,' he said, 'what Zak has in him.'

They stared silently at each other for a long moment. Then Gabs ripped her gaze away. 'How far is the hotel?' she asked their nervous driver.

'Two minutes,' the driver said. He honked his horn and started to overtake a white bush taxi trundling up ahead.

Then he cursed.

'What is it?' Raf asked tersely.

'There is a road block,' the driver hissed. 'I'm going to turn back.'

'*No!*' Raf hissed. 'Keep going. We'll talk our way through.'

'They have guns!' the driver screeched.

'Listen to me,' Raf snapped. 'If we don't get to that hotel, people are going to die, do you understand?'

The man was hyperventilating. His eyes were as wild as his driving. The bush taxi had pulled up at the side of the road to pick up some passengers and there was now nothing but open space between the VW and the roadblock. They were fifty metres away and closing. And they could clearly see that the armed guards blocking the road had the distinctive scars on their faces that they had grown to fear. There were four of them, standing in front of a barrier with bright orange chevrons.

'Slow down,' Raf said, his voice suddenly very calm. 'When we get there, let me do the talking.'

The driver's hands were shaking even as he held the wheel. He slammed his foot on the brake and the car skidded to a halt just metres in front of the barrier.

Silence. Two East Side Boys swaggered up to the driver's window, clutching their weapons. The remaining two stood by the barrier, their eyes narrow with suspicion.

The driver lowered his window. At a command

from one of the sour-faced East Side Boys, he then opened the door and stepped outside. Suddenly he started babbling, his words tripping over each other. Neither Raf nor Gabs could understand the dialect, but they certainly understood its meaning. The driver started pointing at them, and rubbing his fingers to indicate a wad of money.

'*He's turning us in!*' Raf hissed.

In an instant, he and Gabs had opened both passenger doors and were lunging out of the car.

But too late. The East Side Boys had spotted them. They raised their weapons and started screaming: '*HANDS AGAINST THE CAR! HANDS AGAINST THE CAR!*'

Raf and Gabs looked all around, desperately trying to spot an exit strategy. But there was no cover nearby. If they ran, the East Side Boys would shoot. They had no option but to do as they were told.

As Raf put his palms against the burning metal of the beige VW, he glanced at his watch.

11.47hrs. Thirteen minutes to go.

They were never going to get to the hotel.

It was going to be a bloodbath.

22

SPITFIRE

The road to Banjul Airport was in the opposite direction to the city itself. It did not pass through the town of Serrekunda. But it did pass some tiny, poor-looking shanties on either side. Zak observed families milling nervously around huts with corrugated-iron roofs. Occasionally he caught sight of frightened children crying.

Cruz might have disabled the communications systems for the entire area, but it was clear that word was travelling the old-fashioned way that all was not well in Banjul. He gritted his teeth and looked straight ahead.

As they approached the airport, Zak saw several military trucks. They were parked up by the side of the road and their occupants stood next to them, arguing. They clearly had no idea quite what was going on, or what to do.

He looked at his watch. 11.48hrs. Twelve minutes to go. An icy feeling trickled down his spine. 'Can you go any faster?' he asked the driver.

The driver gave him a dark look in the rear-view mirror, but Zak felt a lurch and saw their speed edge up from fifty kilometres per hour to sixty.

The car itself was disgusting. Empty drinks cans were littered all over the place, and the driver had left various musty-smelling items of clothing in the back seat. Zak was sure he felt something scurrying around his feet – cockroaches, maybe. He tried to put his mind off it by peering through the front window. He saw four planes spiralling above the airport and he had a sudden flashback: Raf's Cessna spluttering above the jungle, and the dreadful noise it made as it crash-landed. These spiralling aircraft had limited fuel. They couldn't spiral for ever. And if they came crashing down to earth, they'd make a much bigger noise than the Cessna had.

And cause a lot more death and devastation.

'There!' he said out loud. From his left-hand window he could see, about 500 metres away, a concrete tower. It had a cluster of radar dishes and aerials sprouting from the top and was surrounded by a wire perimeter fence. The entrance gate in the fence was 100 metres to his ten o'clock. 'Drop me here,' he said.

The driver screeched to a halt and looked over his shoulder at Zak. 'What? Why? The airport terminal is this way, crazy English boy.'

Zak ignored him. He looked round the back seat and picked up a brightly embroidered but rather dirty hooded top. 'I'll buy this,' he said. Without waiting for an answer, he added another hundred-dollar bill to the wad he already had in his fist and thrust it at the driver. The driver accepted the money with a look on his face that clearly said: *this kid is mad.*

Zak pulled on the hooded top. It stank of stale sweat, but he ignored that and pulled the hood over his head, nodded at the driver, and left the car. He didn't watch the driver zoom off – just heard the screech of his tyres as he put some distance between himself and the crazy English boy.

Zak didn't hesitate. With his head down and his face concealed by the hood, he strode towards the perimeter fence.

He glanced at his watch. 11.51hrs.

Nine minutes to go.

With his hands up against the car, Raf felt the barrel of a gun at the back of his head.

'What's the hurry, my friend?' said the rasping voice of the gunman.

'Lunch date,' Raf said from between clenched teeth. 'Old friend. You know how it is.'

'*Raf!*' Gabs hissed quietly. She was standing immediately next to him on the right, but none of the other gunmen seemed to think she was a threat, so she wasn't at gunpoint. 'Don't antagonize him.'

But the gunman didn't sound antagonized. He laughed a mirthless laugh and jabbed the gun harder into the back of Raf's head.

'Oh, for goodness' sake,' Gabs sighed.

She moved so fast that even Raf was surprised. Her left hand shot out and grabbed the barrel of the boy's gun, yanking it upwards so that now it pointed above Raf's head.

A shot rang out. The bullet fired harmlessly into the sky and Gabs yanked her arm round, twisting the gun so that now it was positioned across the East Side Boy's body. She thrust it upwards with colossal force and there was a massive crack as it hit the underside of the gunman's chin. The boy's eyes glazed over. As he slumped into Gabs's arms, she spun him ninety degrees and took charge of the weapon that was still slung round his neck. She fired a burst of rounds at the feet of the remaining East Side Boys. They shouted in alarm as the bullets thundered into the road surface, throwing chunks of stone up into the air.

Then they ran.

The driver had watched all this happening with bulging eyes. He staggered backwards. Then, at a fierce look from Raf, he turned and ran too. He didn't get far. Raf ran after him and grabbed him by the arm. 'You're coming with us,' he said. 'We need directions.' He dragged the man over to the waiting car and bundled him into the back, before taking his place behind the wheel.

Gabs let the gunman slump to the ground. She helped herself to his gun. Then, following Raf's lead, she jumped into the back of the car. Raf pressed his foot down on the accelerator and the car screeched forward.

'This way?' she asked the terrified man cowering next to her.

He nodded violently, unable to take his eyes off the weapon.

'What time is it?' Raf shouted at Gabs.

She checked her watch. '11.54 hours,' she said. A pause. 'The bombs go off in six minutes. We're not going to make it, are we?'

Raf stared straight ahead. 'Maybe we can help with the wounded,' he growled.

'If there are any,' said Gabs quietly.

Zak sweated heavily under the thick hood. He kept

his head down but his eyes up as he approached the concrete communications tower.

There was a black Range Rover parked ten metres from the foot of the tower. To its right there was a dead body lying on the ground. But the area was otherwise deserted. He knew from Malcolm's message that he was being held at gunpoint by two armed guards. But Zak himself was unarmed. He couldn't just walk in there. He needed to draw the East Side Boys out.

He headed straight for the Range Rover. The keys were still hanging in the ignition. He silently thanked his Guardian Angels for all the driving instruction they'd given him back on the island, then jumped behind the wheel and turned the engine over. Before knocking it into gear, he revved the accelerator several times. The engine screamed loudly – loud enough, he reckoned, for it to be heard inside the tower. Then, with one eye in the rear-view mirror, he started to drive off.

He took it slowly at first. He didn't think it would take long for the East Side Boys to come running out of the tower to confront the hooded figure who had just stolen their vehicle.

He was right.

Zak was barely twenty metres away from the tower when they appeared. They both burst out of the door and although he couldn't hear them, he could see that they were shouting.

He could also see that they were raising their guns.

In a flash, he leaned over so his head was almost lying in the passenger seat. Just in time. Two shots rang out, and there was a sudden, splintering sound as the rear windscreen shattered violently. Unable to see where he was going, Zak yanked the steering wheel down sharply to one side and pressed hard on the accelerator. The vehicle spun round, its engine screaming because he was still in a low gear. He heard two more shots, but there was no impact: the East Side Boys had missed the Range Rover this time.

A voice entered his head. It belonged to Michael, his handler. Zak remembered word for word what Michael had said to him in the Cessna as they were flying towards Senegal.

If a Spitfire pilot got hit by an enemy plane – a Messerschmitt or similar – his best bet was always to fly directly at the oncoming aircraft. That way, the enemy craft would be too busy trying to avoid a collision to spend time aiming accurately at the Spitfire.

Zak sat up straight again. He knocked the car into a higher gear, but kept the turning circle tight. Now he was pointing directly at the tower. He could see the two gunmen clearly. They stood about three metres apart on either side of the door. Although their guns were raised, they looked uncertain, and glanced anxiously at each other.

Zak continued to accelerate. He was no more than fifty metres from the tower now, and was heading directly at the entrance.

One of the boys fired a shot. It pinged off the chassis of the Range Rover. Zak kept his trajectory straight.

Thirty metres.

Twenty.

He could see the boys' faces clearly now, could pick out the alarm in their expressions. They lowered their weapons and got ready to run. But at the last moment, one of them got brave. He raised his gun again and fired out a single shot. The front windscreen of the Range Rover splintered into a spider web of cracks so that Zak could barely see out of it. He was only just aware of two forms sprinting out of the way as, with another solid yank, he twisted the steering wheel down and to the right, slamming his foot on the brake pedal and pulling up the handbrake as he did so. The Range Rover spun ninety degrees clockwise, its tyres screeching against the tarmac. Zak's nostrils filled with the acrid smell of burning rubber. Then, with a sudden, brutal crunch, the side of the Range Rover slammed against the entrance to the tower.

Zak's whole body jolted painfully. He looked to his left. The crunched-up driver's door was right against the open entrance to the tower.

He didn't allow himself time to recover. The bullets would start flying at any moment. It was impossible to open the door – he was too close to the tower. Instead, he slammed his elbow sharply into the passenger window. It shattered and Zak clambered quickly out of it, and into the tower.

More bullets: thunderous bursts of rounds now, and shouting from the East Side Boys. Zak grabbed hold of the door to the tower. It was made of heavy iron, covered with painted rivets. There was a solid iron bar on the inside which he could lower across the door to lock himself in. He slammed the door shut, plunging himself into darkness, then lowered the bar.

Gunshot.

A round pierced the iron door. A narrow beam of bright sunlight shot in from outside. It lit up a staircase leading to the top of the tower. Zak sprinted towards it as a second round pierced the door, forcing a second laser-like shard of light to illuminate his way. He thundered up the stairs and emerged, blinking and sweating into the control tower.

It was littered with blood and dead bodies. They were already starting to smell in the heat.

Malcolm was there. He was crouched on the ground, hugging his knees and rocking to and fro, utterly terrified. There was no time for small talk. Zak strode towards him and pulled him to his feet.

He checked his watch.

11.57hrs.

Three minutes to go.

'We've got work to do,' he said.

11.58HRS

The tyres of the car Raf and Gabs had commandeered screeched as they hurtled down a broad road in the opposite direction to almost every other car. They could see more plumes of smoke on the horizon now – sure signs that the city was being plunged into chaos.

'*How far?*' Gabs shouted at the sweating owner of the car she was holding at gunpoint.

'Two minutes,' he jabbered. 'Perhaps three.'

Raf and Gabs both glanced at their watches. They said nothing as they continued to burn towards the hotel.

For a moment, Malcolm didn't speak. He looked like he *couldn't* speak. Like he was in a daze. Zak raised one hand, ready to slap him across the face and bring him back to his senses. But suddenly Malcolm caught Zak's wrist. His eyes flashed. 'Don't you dare,' he said.

'Get the cellphones up and running again,' Zak instructed. '*Quickly!*'

Malcolm nodded. He turned to his computer terminal, and the tower was filled with the clackety-clack of his fingers on the keyboard. Lines of code appeared on the screen. Zak found himself holding his breath.

He checked the time. 11.58hrs. Malcolm stopped typing and turned to look at him.

'Is it done?'

Malcolm nodded.

Zak waved one arm vaguely at the roof of the tower to indicate the satellite dishes and aerials above them. 'Can you reverse engineer these things?' he asked.

Malcolm blinked.

'We haven't got time to waste, Malcolm!' Zak hissed. 'I need you to send a text message to every mobile phone in the vicinity. Is that possible?'

Malcolm pressed his glasses further up his nose. He nodded. Then he jumped as a burst of gunfire rattled into the door downstairs, before stepping towards his computer terminal.

'Wait,' Zak said, grabbing him by the arm. 'Do you have mobile numbers for Cruz and Sudiq? Can you block their phones – stop the message getting through to them, and them only?'

Malcolm nodded again.

'*Then let's do it!*' Zak shouted. '*NOW!*'

Molly Middleton had covered herself with her beach towel to protect her legs from the midday sun. She was lying on her sun bed with her mum's pink mobile, trying to beat the high score on *Angry Birds* that her mum had managed that morning. She'd thought it might take her mind off the strange boys with the scarred faces she'd seen earlier, but somehow it didn't. Normally she was brilliant at this game, but today she couldn't get her eye in.

Which was hardly surprising. Something was wrong.

The guests in the hotel had heard shouting from outside the hotel's boundaries. The noise of traffic on the road outside was much louder than usual. And the grown-ups – most of them, at least – were huddled in little groups, talking in low, urgent voices. It was obvious that they didn't want the kids to hear what they were saying. Many of the little ones were still splashing around in the pool.

But Molly was a bit smarter than most kids. And

a bit better at eavesdropping. She'd caught snatches of their conversation. *Unrest in the city . . . gunshot . . . a coup . . . no mobile phone service . . . not safe on the streets . . . better to stay in the hotel . . .*

She lowered the phone and looked around. No sign of the scar-faced boys. She told herself to calm down. To forget about them. It was nothing. She was inventing problems that didn't exist.

All of a sudden the phone vibrated. But it wasn't just *her* phone. All around the swimming pool, within a window of about five seconds, thirty or forty other phones vibrated and jingled. Single tones to indicate that a text message had just arrived.

The buzz of conversation among the little groups of anxious grown-ups died away. The hotel guests looked perplexed. Then, as one, they reached for their phones.

Molly felt like she was in a dream as she looked at the screen of her mum's pink mobile. Sure enough, there was a message.

A bomb will explode at the Palace Hotel at 12.00hrs. Evacuate immediately. EVACUATE IMMEDIATELY.

There was, for a few seconds, a strange silence.

Then the air was filled with screams.

Molly jumped up from her sun bed, her eyes desperately searching for her mum and dad. She saw them running towards her, Mum's sarong flapping, Dad barefoot and still in his trunks. He grabbed her hand, and together the little family of three sprinted towards the hotel's exit along with crowds of other holidaymakers and hotel staff.

Molly's ears were full of the sound of screaming. Of panic. She stumbled with her mum and dad out of the swimming pool area and into the atrium with its tiled floors and fake palm trees. The wide glass doors of the hotel were twenty metres ahead of her.

They stopped suddenly and a cold sickness twisted round in Molly's stomach.

The exit was blocked. Four of the scar-faced boys stood there, with wicked leers on their faces. They stood several paces back from the hotel entrance but they were holding guns, which they aimed directly at the hotel doors.

Molly screamed, just as her dad stepped directly in front of her and her mum to protect them.

And then she screamed again at the thunderous sound of gunfire from outside.

The glass doors shattered. Molly felt her knees go beneath her. But as she sank to the ground in terror, she peered round her dad. The bullets had not been fired by the scar-faced boys guarding the hotel. They looked as surprised as anybody. They turned and looked outwards. Then there was another burst of fire. Bullets sparked around the feet of the young gunmen, and they shouted out in alarm. Another burst of fire.

More shouts.

Then, as one, they dispersed.

There was a shocked silence inside the atrium. A couple of seconds later it was replaced by a murmur from all the guests who were trying to escape.

And then, two figures burst into the hotel: a man and woman, both with blond hair, the woman with an evil-looking rifle strapped round her neck.

'*GET OUT OF HERE!*' the woman shouted. '*THERE'S A BOMB! YOU'VE ONLY GOT SECONDS!*'

And when nobody seemed to move, the man added his voice to hers.

'*GET OUT OF HERE!*' he bellowed. '*NOW!*'

Gabs stood at the glass-fronted entrance to the hotel while crowds of people swarmed out. Men and women in their bathing costumes, hotel staff in dapper uniforms. They crowded round the door and squeezed themselves through. Along with Raf, she was grabbing them as they emerged, then urging them to get as far away from the hotel as they could.

She checked her watch. Thirty seconds till midday.

Twenty-five seconds.

Screaming. A woman's voice. More terrified and panicked than any of the other voices she could hear. 'Molly! *MOLLY!*'

A man: 'Oh my God, I thought she was *with* us . . .'

Gabs looked to her left. A woman in a sarong and a man in his swimming trunks had their faces up against the glass. They were looking into the hotel atrium where a young girl wrapped in a swimming towel was standing stock-still. She looked terrified. Unable to move. Like a rabbit caught in headlights.

Her parents continued to scream at her but the girl didn't move. Everyone else was too busy trying to squeeze out of the hotel to notice a single, scared child.

Twenty seconds.

Gabs marched up to the parents, still firmly gripping her assault rifle.

'Stand back,' she said.

'But our daughter! She's—'

'*STAND BACK!*'

Maybe it was the fierceness in her eyes, or maybe it was just the weapon she was clutching. Whatever. The girl's parents stepped back. Gabs stood five metres from the glass frontage of the hotel and aimed her weapon directly at the lower part of the window. Then she fired a burst of rounds. The screaming from all the escapees became louder, but it was suddenly drowned out by the crashing noise of shattering glass as the whole frontage of the hotel cracked and then collapsed in a rainfall of shards.

Gabs barely waited for the shards to finish falling. The glass crunched under her feet as she ran through the destroyed window into the atrium.

Ten seconds.

'Come with me, Molly,' she whispered urgently. When the terrified girl still didn't move, she simply lifted her over one shoulder. Then she turned and sped back towards the open window.

The crowd had left the atrium now. They were all sprinting away from the hotel. All except Molly's mum and dad, who stood agape, watching what Gabs was doing and ignoring Raf's shouts at them to get away.

'*Run*,' Gabs bellowed as she burst out of the atrium with Molly over her shoulder. '*RUN!*'

They ran.

And not a moment too soon.

Raf, Gabs, Molly and her parents were barely fifteen metres from the hotel when the explosions began. There was clearly more than one bomb – Gabs counted five explosions in quick succession, each of them a deafening crack that seemed to split the air – and the force of the first blast threw all of them several metres forward and knocked them to the ground. They hit the tarmac with a heavy thump. Gabs couldn't be sure if Molly had screamed, because the remaining blasts were exploding behind her. But she knew that at any moment, the shrapnel would start falling, and that could kill them just as surely as the bomb blast itself. Aware that Raf was already hauling Molly's mum and dad to their feet, Gabs lifted Molly and started running again.

Within seconds, she heard debris falling behind her. Something caught her right shoulder, and she shouted out in pain. But she kept running, clutching the young girl firmly, and clearing the blast site in about ten seconds.

Only then did she stop and look back.

The Palace Hotel was an inferno. Huge plumes of thick, black, choking smoke billowed up into the sky. Somewhere at its heart, violent orange flames licked up into the air. The front was nothing but debris, and as she looked Gabs heard a great crash as some other part of the building collapsed. All around her, the sound of sobbing came from the escaped guests as they watched the devastation that would have killed them if they'd left the hotel only seconds later.

She laid Molly out on the ground. The young girl's face was black with grime, and there was a small cut on her left cheek that oozed deep scarlet blood. But she was alive and whole, and she even managed a small smile as Gabs wiped away a strand of hair clinging to her forehead.

Gabs stood up. A woman next to her was wearing nothing but a bright pink bikini. Her skin was filthy from the blast. Tear tracks ran down her dirty face and her eyes were red.

'How did you know to evacuate the hotel?' Gabs demanded urgently.

The woman was clutching a mobile phone. With a trembling hand she held it up. 'A . . . a text message,' she stuttered. 'Someone warned us.'

Gabs looked to her right. Raf was there, a deep frown on his craggy, sooty face.

'Zak?' he said inquiringly.

Gabs nodded uneasily. Their protégé had done it again. No doubt about it.

He'd foiled Cruz Martinez's atrocity. But Cruz was unstable and murderous. It meant Zak was in even greater danger than ever.

'We need to find him,' she breathed. 'Now.'

23

$2,346,625

'*Get down!*'

Malcolm, still standing by his computer terminal, turned to Zak and blinked. He clearly hadn't noticed that one of the East Side Boys had run twenty metres from the tower and was now raising his rifle to aim at the curved window that surrounded the circular control room.

Zak threw himself at his companion, tussling him to the ground even as a burst of rounds slammed into the glass. Three panes cracked like ice under a hammer. A fourth shattered completely.

'Whatever you do,' Zak hissed, 'don't stand up.'

Malcolm was shaking. 'But . . . but how . . .'

'Did you get the message out?'

Malcolm nodded.

Zak closed his eyes. Maybe – just maybe – it had been enough to divert the atrocity.

His eyes strayed up; the planes in the sky needed to land urgently. 'You've got to get the airport comms back up and running,' he whispered to Malcolm.

Malcolm nodded, but gestured towards the computers. 'I'll need them then,' he said, his face tight with fear.

More gunfire. Bullets burst through the broken window and ricocheted off the far side of the control room and Malcolm gasped. Zak remained perfectly still, sitting with his back up against the bank of computer terminals. His eyes were closed, his forehead screwed up in a frown.

He felt like he was playing a game of chess. Checkmate was just round the corner, but so many things had to happen first.

He had to reverse a coup. He had to make sure Smiler was safe. And was it bad that the thing at the very front of his mind was revenge: on Sudiq, the man who had killed his parents?

He opened his eyes suddenly and turned to Malcolm. 'I need you to do some things,' he said. 'Get those planes down, quickly. Then we've got work to do, and we haven't got much time.'

Malcolm nodded again, and Zak was relieved

that he didn't argue. The last few days had changed him.

'Cruz is at the president's residence, right?'

Another nod.

'Can you get me a video link with him?'

'We can just use our phones.'

Zak nodded with satisfaction. 'Just one more thing,' he said. 'Please answer me honestly, Malcolm. When you were in Jo'burg, you had plenty of money. You were just hacking into other people's bank accounts and twiddling the figures, right?'

Malcolm's eyes fell. Once more he nodded his head.

'Can you do it again? Now? From here?'

'It's a piece of cake,' Malcolm said quietly.

'OK.' Zak looked up. They were sitting right below the computer terminal Malcolm had been using. 'Remember . . . stay down,' he instructed. Then, as quickly as he could, he jumped to his feet.

The gunshots started again as soon as Zak became visible through the windows of the control tower. Both of the East Side Boys were firing now, aiming through the broken window, and Zak felt a rush of displaced air as the bullets pinged above him and to his side. But he remained on his feet as he grabbed the screen and the keyboard of the terminal and yanked them off their bench. Seconds later, he was on the floor again, surrounded by a mess of wires that spilled from the computer equipment, nervous sweat pouring off him. He checked the screen: its cursor was flashing, waiting for someone to start inputting data.

He looked at Malcolm. 'OK,' he said. 'Planes first, and then listen carefully. This is what we need to do.'

Smiler's hands were shaking. How had he got himself into this position? Why was he here?

The two East Side Boys he had approached at the pier had clearly been expecting Smiler – or someone like him – to approach with a coffin full of money. And they'd swallowed his story that the boys he'd left behind in the jungle had tried to steal the money for themselves rather than bring it to the boss in Banjul. They'd given him a friendly slap on the back, then lifted the coffin out of the boat and carried it into a waiting truck. Then they'd driven Smiler and the coffin straight into the city centre.

Which was how he found himself, now, in a great white house with pillars at the front, far bigger and more grand than any other dwelling he'd ever seen, let alone set foot in. He had his back against the wall, trying to make himself as small and inconspicuous as possible as he watched the scene that unfolded.

There were ten other people in the room. One of them was Boss – or Sudiq, as Smiler now knew his real name to be. He was strutting round the room like a proud cockerel. At one point he ruffled Smiler's hair, like a fond uncle congratulating his favourite nephew.

Near him was the young man Cruz Martinez, who frightened Smiler far more than Sudiq ever could. His eyes had dark rings around them. They were cold and harsh.

Two men had their hands tied behind their backs. One wore a suit, the other a military uniform covered with decorations. From their conversation, Smiler had worked out this was the president of The Gambia and his military chief. Or rather, the *ex*-president of The Gambia, and his *ex*-military chief. They scowled with anger and humiliation, but were mostly ignored by the other six people in the room: swaggering East Side Boys. Their scarred faces were twisted into looks of supreme arrogance, and they strutted around like Sudiq, brandishing their firearms proudly.

In the centre of the room sat the coffin full of money.

'Silence!' Cruz shouted suddenly. Everyone

stopped moving. 'Ten seconds,' Cruz announced.

It felt for a moment like everyone was holding their breath. The seconds ticked down. Then, in the distance, they heard five low booms. Explosions.

A look of triumph crossed Cruz's face. 'It's done!' he shouted. 'Scores of tourists have now died on Gambian soil. Soon it will no longer be a holiday resort, but a rogue state that exists to serve *our* purposes.' He strode up to Sudiq and clasped his hand – Smiler saw an expression of the utmost greed pass between them. Then Cruz turned to address the president and his military chief and glanced at the coffin. 'In ten minutes' time,' he said, 'a stealth helicopter will arrive to airlift me' – he smiled – 'and my money, of course, out of here. You'll be coming. Say goodbye to your country, gentlemen. You won't be seeing it again—'

His speech was suddenly interrupted by the ringing of a cellphone. It came from Cruz's pocket, and echoed around the suddenly silent room. Everyone stared at him, and Smiler knew why. The phones weren't supposed to be working. So why was this one ringing?

Slowly, Cruz removed his phone, his eyes suddenly very dangerous. He stared at the screen for a moment, while the phone continued to buzz in his hand. Then he slowly pressed one finger to the screen and the ringing stopped.

A pause. Cruz stared at the screen.

'Malcolm,' Cruz breathed. 'What the—?'

Then he fell silent again.

A voice emerged from the loudspeaker of the phone. 'Hello, Cruz.'

Smiler recognized it immediately.

It was Zak.

Still crouching on the floor of the control tower, Zak stared at the screen of his phone. It was, he had to admit, satisfying to see the look of shock and confusion on Cruz's face.

'You're dead,' Cruz hissed.

Zak raised an eyebrow. 'Dead? I don't think so, mate. You haven't got quite the body count you wanted today, I'm afraid. I've managed to warn the tourists you were trying to butcher at the Palace Hotel, by the way. I'm pretty sure they'll have had enough time to evacuate. And the planes round the airport are down – no casualties there either.'

Cruz's eyes grew narrow. 'You're lying,' he whispered.

Zak shrugged. 'You can think that if it makes you feel better,' he said. 'Or, of course, you can look around you. You know, for deadfall.' He put on a patronizing voice, like he was talking to a kid. It was childish, he knew, but Zak had his reasons. He wanted to goad Cruz, to anger him.

To stop him thinking straight.

And by the look on Cruz's face, it appeared to be working.

'Anyway, mate,' Zak continued conversationally, 'it's been lovely to catch up, but this isn't just a social call. There's something I thought you might like to see.'

Zak glanced over at Malcolm, who was crouched next to him at his computer terminal, and nodded. Malcolm started typing furiously. 'It's gone,' he whispered after a few seconds.

Zak heard Cruz's phone pinging at the other end. 'I've just sent you a document,' he said. 'Have a look. I think you might find it interesting.'

Zak's screen was filled with the image of Cruz's fingertip tapping his own phone. He looked anxiously at Malcolm, who in turn was staring anxiously at his computer terminal.

They waited.

Smiler wanted to run, but his legs wouldn't move. In the distance – maybe hovering somewhere close to the open courtyard but not quite loud enough to drown out the tinkling sounds – he heard the beating of a helicopter. But he only paid it scant attention. Like everyone else in the room, his eyes were fixed on Cruz.

Cruz stared at the screen of his phone for what seemed like an age. Then he turned to Sudiq. If the look in his eyes had been dangerous before, now it was positively deadly.

'Tell me, old friend,' he whispered in the unfriendliest voice imaginable. 'Do you have a Swiss bank account in the name of Sudiq Al-Tikriti Gomez?'

Sudiq's eyes widened in surprise. But he didn't deny it. 'Yes.'

A moment of stark, uncomfortable silence.

'Then perhaps you'd like to explain to me why it is that the sum of two million, three hundred and forty-six thousand, six hundred and twenty-five US dollars has been paid into that account in the past twenty-four hours.'

Silence.

'A very precise amount, wouldn't you say?' Cruz added dangerously.

Sudiq blinked at him. 'Don't be stupid, Cruz.' Cruz's eyes flashed at the word. 'That money's there, in the coffin. You know it is.'

Smiler felt his mouth go dry. All of a sudden, he understood. He knew what Zak had done back at the camp . . .

'Show me,' said Cruz. Nobody in the room moved.

'What is this?' Sudiq said. He looked genuinely

baffled. 'Cruz, your helicopter will be here any moment. You need to leave, get back to Mexico . . .'

'*SHOW ME!*'

Sudiq flinched.

Cruz stormed up to one of the East Side Boys. '*Open it!*' he hissed. The boys stepped towards the coffin.

The lid was firmly nailed down. One of the boys pulled out a sturdy, broad-bladed knife and yanked it in just underneath the lid. He started levering it up. There was a cracking, splintering sound as the lid separated from the base. It gave enough of a gap for the East Side Boys to worm their fingers in. There was another great cracking sound as they forcibly ripped the lid from the coffin. It was like jaws opening. The nails protruded like teeth.

The coffin was open. The East Side Boys stood back as Cruz approached. He stood over it, staring into the box for several seconds. From where he was standing, Smiler couldn't see the contents. But then Cruz bent over and picked something out of it.

A rock, about the size of a human head. And then another. No wonder the coffin had been so heavy.

'Would you care to explain this, Sudiq?' ·Cruz whispered.

Sudiq staggered back. 'I . . . I . . . I *can't* explain it. It . . . it must be a trick.'

Cruz let the rock fall back into the coffin with a clatter. Then he started walking slowly towards Sudiq. 'What did you think I would do when I found out, Sudiq?' Cruz asked. His voice was calm, but his eyes were wild and Smiler noticed that his hands were shaking. 'Laugh it off? *Forgive* you?' He said the word 'forgive' with an unpleasant curl of his lip.

'Cruz, please, I would never—'

'*QUIET!*' Cruz pulled a handgun from inside his jacket.

'Señor Martinez, I served your father well for many years—'

'And now,' Cruz raged, 'because I am not him, you think you can pull the wool over my eyes? You think you can steal money from me? You think you can make me a fool? Well, think again!'

Gunshot. So sudden and violent that Smiler felt his whole body jolt. It easily drowned the noise of the helicopter, which was getting much louder now.

Smiler's eyes clamped shut of their own accord, then he slowly opened them.

He wished he hadn't.

Zak flinched at the sound of the gunfire too. It sounded tinny and distorted through the speaker on his phone, but he knew what it meant. He continued to watch the scene with cold eyes.

He sensed that Cruz was very deliberately show-ing him the image of Sudiq's murdered body. Cruz was holding his camera phone about a metre away from the dead man's butchered head and Zak could see through the blasted skull – the mashed-up brain matter was oozing like a yolk from an egg, covered with strands of matted, bloodied hair.

Zak stared, strangely unemotional, at the hideous corpse of the man who had killed his parents.

But only for a few seconds. Because then Cruz was there again, his face filling Zak's screen.

'That will be you, Harry,' Cruz said without emotion. 'Next time we meet.'

Zak said nothing. The temptation to tell him that he'd been duped – that Zak had tricked Cruz into killing his own accomplice, and Zak's mortal enemy – was strong. He had to fight the urge to gloat, to tell him that Sudiq had never stolen so much as a dollar. That it had been Zak himself who had switched the money for a pile of useless rocks.

But some things were best left unsaid.

'I think you've got a helicopter to catch, Cruz,' he said finally. 'I'd hop aboard now, before the Gambian military catch up with you. I doubt they'll take too kindly to what you've just done. And I don't think you can rely on the East Side Boys to protect you, now you've just killed their boss. Do you?'

Cruz stared at the phone for a full ten seconds. Then, almost like a wild animal, he roared in frustration.

Zak couldn't be sure, but he sensed that his enemy had just thrown his mobile onto the ground. Maybe even stamped on it. There was a clattering, crunching sound through the loud-speaker.

Then the screen started to flicker.

Smiler didn't know where to look. At Cruz Martinez, blood-spattered and angry, standing over Sudiq's dead body, his crushed phone lying at his feet? At the president and his army chief, who shrank back from Cruz's sudden burst of fury with horrified faces? At the East Side Boys, who just looked like they wanted to run?

Or at the helicopter, whose underbelly he could now see hovering over the open courtyard adjoining this room that had just become a bloodbath?

In the end, his gaze flickered between Cruz and the helicopter. The young man had so much hate in his eyes that it chilled Smiler to watch him. Cruz stared at the other occupants of the room in turn. Nobody spoke. His dead eyes fell on Smiler, and for a moment Smiler thought he was going to raise his weapon against him. He bowed his head and prepared to die.

But no shot came over the sound of the helicopter setting down outside. Smiler felt the breeze of its downdraught blowing against his skin and he looked up again to see Cruz striding across the room and out into the courtyard. The drug cartel leader's shoulders were slumped. Defeated. Although he carried his pistol by his side, he showed no sign of raising it.

The helicopter touched down. The side door opened and Smiler saw a glimpse of two men dressed in black. One of them stretched out an arm to help Cruz into the aircraft but Cruz knocked it away impatiently, stepped in through the side door and disappeared.

The helicopter rose from the ground before the door was even shut. The downdraught increased. The engines roared and the aircraft continued to rise, like a great black insect, into the sky.

From the corner of his eye, Smiler saw the East Side Boys scrambling out of the room. They clearly did not want to be left alone with the president and his military chief now they no longer had the protection of Sudiq and Cruz.

Which left Smiler, alone, with only the politician and the soldier, whose hands were still tied behind their backs.

Could he ever explain to them that he was no longer on Cruz's side? If he told them the truth, would they believe a word of it? Or would the scars on his face instantly condemn him?

He should get out of here. He knew that. But something stopped him – the sight of the damaged mobile phone lying on the marble floor ten metres away.

Smiler scurried towards the phone and looked at the cracked screen. It flickered on and off, but he could just make out – blurred and indistinct – Zak's face.

'Smiler!' Zak's voice was crackly. 'Can you run?'

Smiler looked round the room. Then back at the screen. He nodded.

'Then *run*!' Zak hissed. 'You know what to do. *Go!*'

The screen went dead and Smiler dropped the phone.

Seconds later, he found himself sprinting out of the presidential residence, out onto the streets of Banjul. Looking up, he could see Cruz's helicopter vanishing into the distance. All around him, he could see East Side Boys, scattering and disappearing.

$2,346,625

He put his hands into his pocket. There he felt the slip of paper that, just a couple of hours ago, the strange English boy had given him. He clutched it tightly.

Then he put his head down, and sprinted away from the scene of the crime.

24

EXIT

'Stay down! *Stay down!*' Zak hissed again.

A round pinged through one of the control tower's smashed windows. It ricocheted off the metal door frame with a flash of sparks, then hit the floor just a couple of metres from where he and Malcolm were still crouching.

The screen on Zak's phone was blank. Grimy sweat dripped into his eyes. He glanced over at his companion. Malcolm was looking at Zak with a kind of awe.

'That was clever,' he said breathlessly.

'Couldn't have done it without you, mate,' Zak panted back. He gave Malcolm a serious kind of look. 'We make a good team.'

'Not for much longer,' said Malcolm. He frowned. 'They'll kill us as soon as we stand up, won't they?'

'I guess the solution,' Zak said with a rueful grimace, 'is not to stand up.'

Another round pinged over their heads. This time, it smashed into one of the far windows, which immediately shattered in a shower of tinkling glass. Malcolm clenched his eyes shut.

'I'm sorry I betrayed you,' he said.

Malcolm's plaintive apology was enough for Zak. Cruz was in the business of ruining lives, and he'd just ruined Malcolm's. He felt bad that he hadn't forgiven Malcolm before. 'Forget about it,' he said. 'You didn't have any choice. Cruz had Matilda.'

An expression of unbearable sadness crossed Malcolm's face. 'If we get out of here, I'll kill him for that,' he said, quite matter-of-factly. 'And I don't care who catches me.'

Zak was about to speak. To tell Malcolm that the last thing his Matilda would want was for him to risk his life chasing after a lunatic like Cruz Martinez. That killing people wasn't the answer.

Then he thought of Sudiq. Dead. Cold satisfaction seeped through him. Zak hadn't killed him, precisely. He hadn't been the one to pull the trigger. But he'd been the one to force Cruz's hand. He was beginning to understand that he lived in a murky world. In a sudden flash of insight, he realized that for people like him, the usual rules didn't apply.

Maybe the same was true, now, for Malcolm.

His thoughts were interrupted by a new sound: the scream of a car engine, the screeching of tyres.

He cursed under his breath. Did the East Side Boys have backup? How long would it take them to break into the tower? He heard two rounds being fired, and winced, ready to see the rounds ricocheting inside the control tower. But suddenly he realized that the bullets were not being fired towards them.

'Keep your head down,' he told Malcolm, even as he pushed himself up from his crouching position.

'But—'

'*Keep your head down!*'

Zak crawled over to the edge of the control tower. The car engine was getting louder now, and Zak heard three more gunshots. Gingerly, he pushed himself up to his feet and peered over the bank of computers and out of one of the shattered windows – ready to pull himself back down again if he saw anyone targeting him.

The two East Side Boys were there, but they were no longer facing the control tower. Instead, they had turned 180 degrees and were aiming their fire at a beat-up, beige VW Polo. It was swerving violently as it approached the tower, to make it more difficult for the East Side Boys to hit. And sure enough, their bullets flew harmlessly through empty air.

Zak recognized the vehicle. It was the same one his Guardian Angels had commandeered to get to the hotel in. He pumped his fist in relief. 'Get ready to go,' he hissed at Malcolm.

At the same moment, he saw Gabs. She had leaned out of the open passenger window, clutching an assault rifle. Even from a distance, Zak could see the look of sharp determination in her face. She wasn't going to miss. Not a chance. Zak almost averted his eyes, to avoid the sight of her bullets ripping into the East Side Boys.

She fired, but not directly at the boys. Her bullets sparked at their feet. They shouted out in alarm, and jumped a couple of metres backwards. They made a half-hearted attempt to fire back, but had barely raised their own weapons when another burst of fire landed in front of them.

That was enough. They turned and ran, scurrying like frightened animals towards the perimeter fence.

The VW screeched to a halt at the foot of the tower. Its engine continued to turn over as Gabs opened her door and crouched behind it as a shield, with her weapon through the open window covering the retreating East Side Boys. Raf emerged from the car, his face grim and purposeful.

'We're here!' Zak yelled. 'We're coming down!'

Raf looked up and nodded once. His expression seemed to say: *hurry!*

Zak turned to pull Malcolm to his feet, but he was already standing. They ran to the door and thundered down the stairs. Zak raised the locking bar on the door and yanked it open. They both clambered over shattered glass through the cab of the Range Rover and tumbled out the other side. Together, they sprinted round the front of the tower towards the VW. Gabs was still in position behind the passenger door. Raf was back behind the wheel, but leaning out of his window and looking back.

'Get in!' he bellowed.

Zak and Malcolm didn't need telling twice. They jumped into the back of the VW, where they sat, breathless and sweating, while Gabs lowered her weapon, took her seat again and slammed the door shut. A millisecond later, Raf had slammed his foot on the accelerator and they were speeding towards the exit.

'The hotel?' Zak demanded. 'The bomb?'

'Evacuated a few seconds before detonation,' Raf said. 'No casualties. I take it that text message was your idea.'

Zak nodded.

'You might have told us in advance, sweetie,'

Gabs chided as they flew past the wire perimeter fence.

'I was sort of making it up as I went along,' Zak admitted. He paused. 'Sudiq's dead,' he said. 'Cruz got away. But I think the president's safe.'

At the words 'Sudiq's dead', Raf and Gabs had glanced at each other. 'Want to tell us how it happened, guys?' Gabs asked.

Malcolm was just opening his mouth when Zak gave him a warning nudge. 'It's . . . it's kind of complicated,' he said.

Gabs looked over her shoulder and gave him a piercing look. 'Why am I not surprised?'

'If Sudiq's dead,' Raf interrupted, his eyes back on the road, 'his East Side Boys will disperse. It's time for us to get the hell out of Dodge. We've done everything we can, and Michael won't thank us for being picked up by the Gambian authorities. We'll get away from Banjul and try to make contact. I'm sure he'll arrange a pick-up for us in the next day or so – if we're lucky.' He glanced at Malcolm in the rear-view mirror. 'I think you'll be coming with us too, young man. You've proved your worth in the last couple of days. Maybe we'll find some more work for you in the future. If you want it, that is.'

Malcolm said nothing, but Zak couldn't help

noticing that a flicker of a smile crossed his friend's face.

'Wait,' Gabs said suddenly. Her voice was quiet. Scared. 'I can't believe we forgot . . .'

'What?' Raf asked sharply.

Gabs blinked. 'Smiler,' she said. 'We promised him he'd be safe. We have to find him, Raf. We *have* to.'

Now it was Zak's turn to smile. 'Don't worry, Gabs,' he said. 'Smiler got away. He's fine.'

In fact, he thought to himself, *he's more than fine*.

'How do you know?' Gabs demanded. 'Damn it, Zak, stop being so secretive. *How do you know?*'

Silence fell in the car once again. Zak looked out of his window. The hot afternoon sun beat down on the African soil. He heard a siren and a police car zoomed past in the opposite direction. By the side of the road he saw a military truck parked up outside some ramshackle houses. Soldiers spilled out of the vehicle and started reassuring a group of nervous locals.

There was not an East Side Boy in sight.

Zak continued to stare out of the window.

'Call it a hunch,' he said.

EPILOGUE

Twenty-four hours later

It had been easy for Smiler to steal a boat. Easy for him to navigate upriver. Easy for him to find the encampment again.

It had been a lot harder to persuade the children who had barricaded themselves inside that high-walled camp to let him in. He had the mark of the East Side Boys on his face. It would be with him for ever now, and these children had every reason to distrust anyone who wore those gruesome scars. But he had called for Latifah, who spoke to him through the gate and recognized his voice. She had emerged from the camp – carrying a rifle that was almost as big as her – and hugged him, like a mother would hug her child.

And then, together, they had looked at the piece of paper Smiler had in his pocket.

There were three lines, written hurriedly in capital letters:

GO TO THE COFFINS WITH LATIFAH.
FIND AGENT 21.
USE IT WELL.

'We should go now,' Smiler said. 'Before anyone else . . .'

Latifah nodded. She turned to the other children who still did not dare set foot outside the camp. 'I'll be back soon,' she said. 'Don't let anybody else in.'

Moments later, they were picking their way through the jungle towards the burial site.

'If it hadn't been for Zak and his friends,' said Latifah as the huge hole in the ground came into view, 'we would all be buried here now. But I still don't really know who he was.'

'Nor do I,' said Smiler. 'But it's not just us that he has saved.'

They stood at the edge of the hole. There were several coffins here. Smiler knew that at least one of them contained a dead body, and even from up here, he could smell the stench of the rotting corpse. He put his arms up against his nose, however, and let his eyes pick out the box he was looking for.

It was set slightly apart from the others. The plaque on the front was plainly visible. It said: AGENT 21.

Smiler and Latifah exchanged a nervous look.

'Shall we open it?' Latifah asked.

Smiler nodded. Together they climbed down into the pit.

The smell was even worse down here. Insects buzzed manically around, drawn to the stench, and Smiler felt them banging against his skin and his face, but he ignored them as he and Latifah edged towards the coffin.

They were standing above it now. Smiler's hand shook. He looked at Latifah again, and could tell that she was nervous too.

They bent down and together put their hands on the coffin lid. It shifted slightly at their touch. It was not nailed down.

'After three,' said Smiler. 'One, two . . .'

A bird called in the trees above them.

'*Three.*'

They pushed the coffin lid away and it clattered to one side.

Latifah gasped. The coffin was full of bank notes. American dollars.

They stared for a moment, speechless.

'How much . . . ?' Latifah breathed.

But Smiler interrupted her. 'Two million, three hundred and forty-six thousand, six hundred and twenty-five,' he said.

He thought of the children back at the camp. They had nothing. They were lucky to be alive.

Then he looked back at the piece of paper that he was still clutching. His eyes fell on the last line of writing. *Use it well.*

'We will,' Smiler whispered to himself. 'We will.'